"Thank you for saving my life."

A shadow flickered across his face, but he immediately schooled his features and forced a grin. "That again? You really are easily impressed. At least it got me a date with you."

Riley winked, but Ginny detected an unease behind his flirtation. "You should feel proud of it. Saving any life is major. Big-time huge."

He shook his head. "Look, I'm glad you're okay. As for my part in it, I'm a firefighter, and I was just doing my job."

She scowled playfully. "Okay, I'll let your mysterious reasons for your modesty slide...this time. But next time…"

He caught the finger she wagged at him and lowered it to the bed. The warmth of his hand curled intimately around hers knocked the teasing grin from her lips and stole her breath….

Dear Reader,

Be sure to add Silhouette Romantic Suspense's July offerings to your summer reading. Especially since *New York Times* bestselling author Rachel Lee is back in the line! And she's continuing her wildly popular CONARD COUNTY miniseries with *A Soldier's Homecoming* (#1519). Here, a hunky hero searches for his long-lost father and unexpectedly falls in love with a single mom whose past comes back to haunt her. You'll need to fan the flames for Sheri WhiteFeather's sexy romance, *Killer Passion* (#1520), the second book of a thrilling trilogy, SEDUCTION SUMMER. In this series, a serial killer is murdering amorous couples on the beach and no lover is safe. Don't miss this sizzling roller coaster ride! Stay tuned in August for Cindy Dees's heart-thumping contribution, *Killer Affair*.

A snowstorm, a handsome bodyguard, an adorable baby and a woman on the run. You'll find these page-turning ingredients in Carla Cassidy's *Snowbound with the Bodyguard* (#1521); the next book in her WILD WEST BODYGUARDS miniseries. In Beth Cornelison's *Duty To Protect* (#1522), a firefighter comes to the rescue of a caring crisis counselor as she wards off a dangerous threat. Their chemistry makes for an unforgettable story.

This month is all about finding love against the odds and those adventures lurking around every corner. So as you lounge on the beach or in your favorite chair, lose yourself in one of these gems from Silhouette Romantic Suspense!

Sincerely,

Patience Smith
Senior Editor

Duty TO PROTECT

Beth Cornelison

Silhouette®
Romantic
SUSPENSE

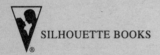 SILHOUETTE BOOKS

ISBN-13: 978-0-373-27592-2
ISBN-10:   0-373-27592-7

DUTY TO PROTECT

Visit Silhouette Books at www.eHarlequin.com

Printed in U.S.A.

BETH CORNELISON

started writing stories as a child when she penned a tale about the adventures of her cat, Ajax. A Georgia native, she received her bachelor's degree in Public Relations from the University of Georgia. After working in public relations for a little more than a year, she moved with her husband to Louisiana, where she decided to pursue her love of writing fiction.

Since that first time, Beth has written many more stories of adventure and romantic suspense and has won numerous honors for her work, including the coveted Golden Heart award for romantic suspense from Romance Writers of America. She is active on the board of directors for the North Louisiana Storytellers and Authors of Romance (NOLA STARS) and loves reading, traveling, Peanuts' Snoopy and spending downtime with her family.

She writes from her home in Louisiana, where she lives with her husband, one son and two cats who think they are people. Beth loves to hear from her readers. You can write to her at P.O. Box 52505, Shreveport, LA 71135-2505 or visit her Web site at www.bethcornelison.com.

To my sisters, Martha and Lenna, for all the years of love, laughter and support. You two are the best! Thanks to my brother-in-law, Kyle Beeson, corporal with the Athens/Clarke County, Georgia Fire Department, for his continued assistance with questions about firefighting and rescue procedures. Any errors in this regard are due to my own misunderstanding or stretching the truth for storytelling purposes. Our nation's firefighters are real heroes! Thanks for all you do!

Chapter 1

"He said he'd kill me if I left him. And he meant it."

Her client's assertion sent a prickle of ill ease skittering down Ginny West's nape. Even hearing such statements on a disturbingly regular basis didn't lessen the gut-twisting impact the words had on Ginny. The threat of such extreme violence had to be taken seriously, had to be dealt with quickly. Domestic violence by its nature was volatile and dangerous, and Annie Compton's situation had just reached critical mass.

Ginny looked up from her notepad and leveled a firm but sympathetic gaze on the battered wife sitting across from her at the Lagniappe Women's Center. Annie's freckled face sported a fresh set of cuts and contusions courtesy of her jealous and controlling husband and his nasty temper.

Ginny cleared the tension from her throat. "You need to get out of that house, Annie. Take these threats seriously, and get yourself and your kids out of harm's way."

Annie shook her head, tears welling in her dark eyes.

"Didn't you hear what I just said? If I leave him, he'll kill me! He'll find me, and he'll kill me. I know he will." She swiped at her damp cheeks with the sleeve of her oversized sweater. "You shoulda seen him last night. He was so mad. And he hadn't even been drinking. I told him what you said about him needing counseling, anger management."

"You told him you talked to me?"

Annie nodded. "He's always asking where I am and who I'm with. I had to tell him the truth. He checks up on me, and if I lie, it just makes him more jealous. Anyway, he said I had no business talking to you about private family business and that you should butt out. That's when he swore he'd kill me dead if I tried to leave." Annie closed her eyes and sighed. Her slumped shoulders were the image of defeat. "I just don't know what to do."

"You're going to get free of him and his violence and make a fresh start. And I'm going to help you. I know it's hard. But you are strong, Annie, and you can do this. You need to get yourself and your kids out of that house."

"I can't. I have nowhere to go. He'll find me and—"

"Then you'll go to the women's shelter." The springs in her wear-worn office couch creaked as Ginny leaned forward and laid her hand on Annie's arm. "He won't find you there. The location of our shelter is kept secret so that abusive husbands like Walt can't find you. You'll be safe, and you won't be alone. We have people in place there to help you get a fresh start. I'll check in on you, too. We can start working on getting a restraining order against Walt right now. Just say the word, and I can put things in motion."

Ginny met Annie's watery eyes and gave her an encouraging smile. "We're going to get you through this, honey. I promise."

"I'm scared," Annie squeaked through her tears.

"I know. I understand." Ginny's heart squeezed. The pain in Annie's eyes sliced her to the core. "What I'm asking you to do is scary. Change can be scary. But I'll be here for you the whole way. I won't let you go through this alone."

No matter how many times Ginny guided a client through this process, the emotional toll never got easier. And she knew what she felt was a mere fraction of what the frightened women she helped were experiencing.

Ginny took Annie's hands in hers. She rubbed the young woman's icy, trembling fingers, hoping to infuse her with warmth and courage. "Should I call the shelter and tell them to expect you?"

Annie hesitated, then gave a small nod.

"And the restraining order?"

"No piece of paper will stop Walt."

"But it *is* a legal tool for the police if he tries to bother you. It gives them grounds to arrest him and keep him away from you. Shall I get the paperwork started?"

Annie drew a shaky breath. "Okay."

Ginny smiled and pulled Annie into her arms for a bear hug. "Good. I have a few calls to make. You can stay here if you want, or you can go across the hall to the playroom to sit with your children if you'd rather. I'll let you know when the arrangements are finished."

"I'll go to the playroom. I need to be with my kids." Annie backed out of the hug, and Ginny walked her to the door of her office.

After alerting the playroom attendant of the arrangements being made for Annie and her family, Ginny headed down the hall to the break room. Her stomach growled, reminding her she'd worked through lunch again. But until she knew Annie and her two young children were safe at the women's shelter and the legalities of a restraining order put into motion, she wouldn't stop for more than a cup of coffee. Stepping into the break room, she took her New Orleans Saints mug from the dish rack by the sink and gave the hours-old sludge in the coffeepot a considering glance.

Yuck.

With a grunt of disgust, she turned off the pot and returned her mug to the dish rack. Once Annie was safe, Ginny decided, she'd stop at her favorite deli on the way home for some real coffee and a hot muffuletta. Just the thought of one of the spicy, New Orleans-style deli sandwiches made Ginny's mouth water.

After reclaiming her chair behind her utilitarian, charity-issue desk, she phoned the women's shelter, informing them of Annie's imminent arrival. Next she called her court liaison to start the ball rolling on the restraining order against Annie's husband. When she was put on hold, Ginny picked up a pen and began doodling on her notepad. Rather than a distraction, doodling helped her focus, think. Some of her toughest problems had been analyzed and worked through while she scratched out hearts, flowers and strange geometric shapes.

After several minutes on hold, Ginny stood up to pace, the cordless phone tucked between her ear and shoulder. She opened her office door and peeked into the room across the hall, where Annie sat on the floor with her young daughter, building a block tower. Dust motes danced in the November sunlight that streamed through the front window, bathing the woman and little girl in a golden glow. The warm hominess of the picture they made stood in stark contrast to the purple bruises shading Annie's jaw. The evidence of Walt Compton's cruelty stirred a deep ache in Ginny's bones. Annie had a hard road ahead of her, but at least she was on the right path now.

A click preceded the buzz of a dial tone in her ear, and Ginny sighed. Her connection had been cut. Shifting the phone to her hand, she punched Redial and tried again to get through to the court liaison.

Dropping into her desk chair, she glanced at her notepad and smiled when she saw what she'd unconsciously doodled: *4A.*

As in apartment 4A.

Which was where her new neighbor, Mr. Tall, Blond and Oh-So-Handsome, lived.

Since she'd moved into the complex three weeks ago, Ginny hadn't met many of her neighbors. But Mr. 4A she'd noticed. Along with his sunny smile and bare ring finger. He seemed to arrive home about the same time she left for work most mornings, and she'd finally asked him about his odd schedule a few days ago as they checked their respective mailboxes in the lobby.

"Must've been some party if you're only getting home now." She gave him a teasing grin and keyed open the tiny metal door to retrieve her daily junk mail.

Mr. 4A flashed his white grin and shook his head. "I wish I had a party to thank. Naw, I'm just getting off work."

"Graveyard shift, huh?" Ginny pulled her crumpled electric bill from the cramped mailbox and cast a sideways glance at her gorgeous neighbor.

"Wrong again. I'm a firefighter. We work twenty-four on, forty-eight off. Shifts begin and end at 7:00 a.m."

"Ah. A fireman. Gotcha." Ginny watched as he flipped through his stack of mail. Last week, when she'd started this flirtation, she'd been sure to scrutinize his mailbox for clues about her neighbor. She hadn't put her name on her box for safety reasons but hoped his mailbox would tell her something about 4A. Like a name. Or a telltale "Mr. and Mrs." that would effectively put an end to their morning flirting.

But all his mailbox said was 4A.

She'd had plenty of opportunities to ask him his name and introduce herself, but she hadn't. For now, she like the mystery and fun of knowing each other only by their respective apartment numbers.

"See ya 'round then," he said with a friendly nod and smile as he walked away.

But that morning, Ginny wasn't ready to let him get away quite so quickly.

"So tell me, 4A…"

He stopped, turned and cocked his handsome-as-sin blond head after she spoke.

She met his light gray eyes, and their piercing color and clarity stirred a flutter in her stomach. "How does one get the maintenance supervisor for our building to handle repairs? I've read over all the paperwork they gave me when I moved in, and I can't find any number to call to reach the super. I've got a list of repairs my place needs that is growing daily."

"One…" Grinning, he paused long enough to draw attention to his reciprocal use of her formal and generic pronoun. "…usually doesn't get the super to do much of anything. The guy's a bum. But he's also the owner's brother-in-law or something, so he's got job security. It can take weeks to get something fixed. I usually do my own repairs."

"Oh." Ginny scowled. "Great. So I get to keep hand washing my dishes and bailing out my bathtub for a few more weeks, huh?" She huffed pale blond bangs from her eyes.

"I'll tell you what, 3C."

Hearing him address her by her apartment number and knowing he'd taken an equal interest in where she lived sent a giddy thrill spiraling through her, spiking her pulse.

4A took a step closer and propped a muscled shoulder on the lobby wall. "I'd be happy to stop by sometime and see what I can do to help. Plumbing isn't my specialty, but I'll give it a shot, if you want."

She nodded slowly, flashing him a no-holds-barred, seductive grin. "Oh, yeah. I want…" *You* went unspoken, but not missed.

She watched his pupils dilate as desire darkened his eyes to the color of smoke. His kiss-me lips curved in a tantalizing grin. Pushing away from the wall, he backed down the corridor slowly. "All right then." His voice was deeper, huskier now. Sexy. "I'll catch up with you later, 3C."

"Bye. And thanks," she called, lingering to admire his

broad shoulders and drool-worthy, jeans-clad butt as he strolled toward apartment 4A.

Now, sitting at her desk, still on hold with the courthouse while canned music droned through the phone, Ginny smiled again as she traced the doodle on her pad with her fingertip.

4A. Even thinking about him made her pulse go a little haywire. The man was gorgeous from the light brown stubble on his square jaw to his long, muscled legs. And every taut and toned inch in between.

Mm-mm-mmm.

The slam of a car door and a shout from outside her window pulled Ginny from her erotic daydreams. Her attention shifted to the street in front of the women's center. An old model sedan was parked at the front curb, and a red-haired man in a business suit stood by the driver's door yelling obscenities toward the entrance of the center. His dress shirt was half untucked, and his tie had been tugged loose and was askew at his throat.

The mere presence of the hostile man at the women's center was enough to raise concern for Ginny. A chill of apprehension pricked at her spine. Cradling the phone on her shoulder, she opened her window a crack in order to hear all that the man was shouting and to better assess the threat he posed. The typically mild November air already carried the nip of coolness as evening approached and the sun began to sink.

The man leaned into the sedan and pulled out a six-pack of beer bottles in a cardboard carrier.

Great, the guy's drinking.

Inebriated people were all the more unpredictable and rash. Ginny had seen enough. Rather than let the situation escalate and get out of hand, she mashed the switch hook—she'd try to reach the court liaison later—and dialed 911. While she talked to the emergency operator, explaining the situation and her concerns, she watched the man shred a T-shirt and poke a strip of cloth into the end of one of the beer bottles.

Puzzled, Ginny squinted for a better look at his odd behavior, just as the man flicked a lighter and lit the cloth on fire. Alarm bells clanged in her mind. Something was very wrong with this picture.

"He's burning the strips of shirt, like they were a…"

Fuse.

The word filtered through her mind as, numbly, she watched the man hurl the bottle at the front window of the women's center. She heard the crash of shattering glass.

Screams.

Boom.

The concussion of the firebomb wasn't loud or especially powerful, but the horror of what was happening was enough to render her legs useless for a moment.

Knees wobbling, she gasped for a breath and panted into the phone, "Not beer! Gasoline. He has gas in the bottles! He's throwing Molotov cocktails at us! Our building's on fire!"

"Stay calm—"

The man took aim at Ginny's office.

Quickly, she ducked and rolled under her desk, covering her head. The top pane of her window shattered, the beer bottle crashing against the opposite wall. A small fireball blasted her office. Heat seared Ginny's arms and cheeks, but her desk protected her from the worst of the fire. The acrid scent of gasoline and smoke filled her lungs.

Covering her mouth and nose with the neckline of her blouse, Ginny scrambled out from under her desk. She assessed the damage, searched for an escape route.

Flames licked her office door, spread across the floor as the gasoline-soaked carpet was gobbled up by the fire.

She turned to the window. Shoving it open wider, Ginny gasped for fresh air. With her office door blocked by flames, she'd have to remove the screen that covered the lower half of the window, and climb out.

She glanced across the front lawn of the women's center

to the sedan. The crazy man, who had apparently launched all of his homemade firebombs, was climbing into his car.

Keeping a wary eye on the vehicle, Ginny fumbled with the latch on the screen. The rusty lever wouldn't budge.

Her eyes watered from the heat and smoke. Her lungs seized, and she coughed. Gagged. Wheezed.

Still the latch stuck. Taking a step back, she kicked with all her strength.

The screen popped loose and hung drunkenly by one corner. Gripping it with both hands, she yanked the mesh out of her way.

As she scrambled to hoist herself up to the window ledge, a woman's shout snagged Ginny's attention.

Annie Compton ran out onto the lawn with her smallest child in her arms. Members of the center's staff had also congregated on the front lawn, safe from the fire. Before Ginny could sigh in relief that the staff and her client seemed to be safe, Annie separated herself from the group and charged toward the departing sedan.

"How could you do this, Walt? You're insane!"

"No, no!" Ginny whispered under her breath. "Don't provoke him. Don't—"

The sedan's tires squealed as it whipped a U-turn, fishtailed, then roared back toward the women's center.

"Annie!" Ginny screamed, her heart in her throat.

Walt Compton punched the gas and sped straight for his wife, who held their baby in her arms.

Ginny's breath stuck in her throat. Time seemed to stretch, events passing in slow motion.

Walt drove over the curb, across the lawn.

Annie screamed. Jumped out of the car's path. Almost.

The front fender clipped her, and she spun. Stumbled. Fell.

The momentum of Walt's sedan kept the mammoth car rocketing forward. Toward the women's center. Toward Ginny's office window.

Panicked, Ginny reeled backward, tripping over her metal trash can. Staggering. Clambering to get out of the sedan's path.

Walt's car plowed through the front wall with an earsplitting crash. Wood splintered and metal tore with a screech. Broken glass sprayed the room.

The front wall of the women's center caved inward under the vehicle's assault. Tumbling drywall and splintered siding showered down on Ginny in a perilous, painful barrage. A tall filing cabinet tipped toward her. Amid the fallen rubble, she tried desperately to crab-crawl out of the way.

But couldn't.

The heavy cabinet toppled onto her, crushing her arm.

Blinding pain streaked from her arm and radiated through her entire body. When she tried to suck in enough breath to cry for help, smoke clogged her lungs and made her cough.

She was pinned down. Bleeding. Terrified.

And trapped in the burning office.

Adrenaline kicking, Riley Sinclair pulled his face shield into place as he jumped from the pumper and wove through the chaos at the Lagniappe Women's Center.

His buddy and fellow firefighter, Cal Walters, trotted up behind him. "Is that a *car* in the front wall?"

"Looks like. Dispatch said a guy was tossing Molotov cocktails through the windows. A pissed-off husband or something. I'd lay bets that's his car, his coup de grâce."

"Which means he could still be trapped in the car."

"Exactly."

"I'm on it." Cal jogged toward the imbedded car. "We may have a man inside down here!" he shouted toward the guys on the line. "Give me a blanket of water!"

Riley headed over to where his captain stood talking to a frantic dark-haired woman.

"—is still inside!" Riley heard her shout as he approached. His gut tightened. "Captain?"

Captain Shaw turned a grave expression toward Riley. "She says they haven't found one of the counselors yet. She may still be inside."

"That's her office! Where the car hit!" The woman gestured wildly toward the wrecked sedan.

Despite the adrenaline charging through his blood, Riley's heart slowed. His breath stalled in his lungs. He jerked his gaze toward the crumbled front wall.

Flames engulfed that section of the women's center, fueled by the oxygen pouring through the car-created hole in the siding.

Chances were slim anyone could still be alive in that office.

But for Riley, a slim chance was good enough. His heart kicked, and his pulse thrummed.

He spun toward the frantic woman. "What's her name?"

"Ginny. Ginny West. Oh, please, help her!"

Riley shoved his breathing apparatus over his nose.

Captain Shaw caught his arm, growling, "Sinclair, the building's too involved. I can't order anyone to go in."

Riley nailed his boss with a stubborn glare. "Then I'm volunteering."

The captain scowled. Sighed. Nodded.

Gritting his teeth, Riley hurried across the lawn, already adjusting the valve to start his flow of oxygen.

As he approached the smashed sedan, Cal was coming out, shaking his head. Cal turned toward Riley as he raced up. "There's no one anywhere in or around the car. Whoever was driving is gone, vanished. He—"

"There's still a woman inside!" Riley interrupted. "Get the imager. I'm going in."

Cal muttered a curse as he charged toward the fire truck.

"I need a hose down here! Cover me!" Riley shouted to the men on the nozzle.

They aimed the hose's spray toward the gaping hole in the wall. Riley picked his way over the pile of rubble and followed the veil of water inside. Dropping to his knees, he scanned the interior of the office, but thick black smoke obscured his view. "Ginny!" he shouted. "Ginny West!"

He listened for a reply, a groan, a whimper. Anything.

Only the roar and crackle of flames answered him.

Riley crawled forward, feeling his way, peering intently into the dense smoke. Only murky forms took shape.

Where the hell was Cal with that imaging camera?

"Ginny West!"

He found a desk and felt under it. Beside it. Nothing.

Shoving a toppled chair aside, Riley crawled deeper into the room. Flames danced around him, pushing him back. Only a tiny corner of the office hadn't yet been swallowed by fire. A large rectangular object—a filing cabinet, perhaps—seemed all that blocked the inferno's path.

"See her anywhere?" Cal called from behind him.

"Not yet." Riley grabbed the thermal imaging camera Cal shoved toward him and scanned the unburned corner of the room. Designed to detect a person's body heat when smoke was too thick for firefighters to see, the apparatus was often the only way to find persons trapped in a fire.

Riley studied the screen as he aimed the camera in methodical sweeps over the floor.

"Ginny West!" he shouted again. "Ginny, can you hear me?"

A blob of yellow and orange appeared on the screen. His adrenaline spiked. "I've got something!"

Cal crawled up beside him. "Is that a foot?"

Heart pumping, Riley nodded toward the downed file cabinet. "Someone's behind there."

Across the room a support beam collapsed from the ceiling amid a shower of sparks and flying embers.

"It's getting hot in here." Cal snatched the camera back. "Haul ass, partner."

As Cal shouted for more water support to cover them, Riley scrambled ahead. He plowed his way over the crumbled debris toward the file cabinet where the camera had detected a source of heat. Body heat.

A shower of sooty water sprayed down around him, partially clearing the smoke, clearing his vision.

He circled the fallen cabinet, his heart in his throat.

Please God, don't let me be too late.

Not again.

His young sister's ashen face flashed in his mind, and bile surged up his throat. More snapshot memories followed, clicking in his brain like a slideshow. Children he'd been too late to help, old men who'd suffocated in their beds…and Erin, who'd survived, but not thanks to him.

Shoving the haunting images out of his mind, he felt along the floor to the edge of the cabinet.

And found a woman.

Chapter 2

Another curtain of water doused Riley. For a few seconds, the smoke cleared enough for him to assess the situation.

The woman's arm was pinned by the file cabinet. And she wasn't moving.

His gut tightened.

"Ginny? Ginny West?"

No response.

He pressed his hand to her throat, feeling her carotid artery for a pulse. A gentle throbbing met his fingers, and relief swelled in his chest.

"Cal, she's alive, but she's pinned down!" He shoved his shoulder into the file cabinet. It rocked—but not enough.

"Walters!"

Cal appeared through the smoke. "Right here."

Another fire-weakened beam collapsed near them. Riley averted his face from the blast of heat and sparks. Glancing up, he found the beams overhead equally eaten by the fire.

They could come down any second. He and Cal were working on borrowed time.

"She's under here!" Riley plowed his shoulder into the cabinet again, and Cal pulled from the other side. This time the heavy unit toppled aside.

The woman's arm, free now of the cabinet, was bent at an unnatural angle. Riley's gut pitched.

"Help me get her up. Watch that arm!"

He climbed over her still form while Cal positioned himself to help lift her carefully over Riley's shoulder.

After draping her limp form into place, being as gentle with the woman's injured arm as time would allow, Riley headed out. "Let's go!"

As they picked their way through the rubble, a loud creak rent the air above them.

"It's coming down! Go! Go! Go!" Cal shouted.

Riley staggered out of the building, the woman over his shoulder and his partner on his heels, just before the roof collapsed. Flames ravaged the corner by the fallen cabinet.

Captain Shaw rushed toward them. "That was a little too close for comfort, Sinclair."

Riley didn't spare him so much as a glance. "But we got her out."

Now a safe distance from the fire, he eased the woman onto the grassy lawn, protecting her head as he laid her down.

Dusk cast the outdoors in long purple shadows, and billowing smoke contributed to the dark haze.

Kneeling beside the woman, Riley ripped off his oxygen mask and helmet.

"I need help over here!" He waved toward the EMTs hovering by a waiting ambulance.

He confirmed she still had a thready pulse, then gently brushed the tangle of pale blond hair from her cheeks. Riley's heart lurched.

He knew this pretty face.

The woman he'd just pulled from the fire was 3C.

And she wasn't breathing.

Riley's chest seized.

He battled down haunting images of his sister's lifeless body, her bloodless lips and pale face. His nightmare had started with Jodi.

You failed her.

Grief and guilt tangled with an iron determination not to let 3C die on his watch. He'd been too late for so many others, but he'd be damned if he'd give up on 3C….

Tipping her head back, he pinched her nose closed and sealed his mouth over hers. He blew his breath into her lungs, willing her to take in air on her own.

Nothing.

Another puff of air.

He tasted the smoke that seeped up from her throat. And strawberry. She wore strawberry lip balm. The sweet fruity flavor stood in stark contrast to the dark, life-stealing smoke and the bitter taste of desperation that rose in his throat. A fresh twist of pain wrenched his chest.

He remembered her lips curved in an enticing smile as she flirted with him in the apartment lobby. Vibrant, alluring, *alive.*

He forcefully swallowed the bile, the fear rising inside him as he leaned his ear near her mouth, listening, feeling, watching for signs of life.

"C'mon, 3C. C'mon! Breathe, damn it!" he muttered through clenched teeth.

An EMT arrived and tried to shoulder him out of the way. "I'll take over."

Riley refused to budge. Instead, he bent to give her another puff of air. And another. He counted the interval between breaths with his heartbeat thudding in his ears. In his head, Riley knew only a few seconds had passed without 3C breathing on her own, but those seconds felt more like hours, years…sixteen years.

Sixteen years had passed since Jodi died.

Finally, 3C coughed, wheezed. Black smoke curled from her mouth before she dragged in a ragged breath on her own.

The relief that spun through Riley brought moisture to his eyes and left his hands shaking.

3C's blue eyes fluttered open as she gasped for more air. Her gaze darted from one face hovering over her to another. Until it landed on Riley's.

Her eyes zeroed in on his. Widened. Brightened.

Across from him, an EMT had an oxygen mask ready and slipped it into place over her nose and mouth.

But her gaze clung to Riley's, recognition softening the panic and pain in her expression as she fought for each breath.

Again an EMT tried to shoulder Riley out of the way. He moved, letting the medic work, but he didn't leave 3C's side. He couldn't. Something in her steady blue eyes reached out to him and held him fast.

When he stroked her sooty cheek, she lifted her uninjured arm and linked her trembling fingers with his. As with her gaze, he sensed in her touch a connection that went beyond the mere joining of hands.

Tears puddled in her eyes, kicking him in the gut and yanking a tighter knot in his chest.

He may have failed Jodi, failed Erin, failed nameless others, but he wouldn't, *couldn't* let this woman down.

Leaning closer, he whispered, "You're going to be okay now, 3C. I'm gonna take care of you."

The EMTs finished their preliminary exam, scooted a backboard under her and loaded her onto a stretcher. Through it all, Riley stayed beside her, squeezing her hand gently and giving her encouraging smiles.

As they rolled her toward the waiting ambulance, he trotted beside the gurney. He released her hand only when the medics slid her into the ambulance and her fingers slipped out of reach.

An EMT climbed inside and closed the back of the ambulance with a thud that reverberated in Riley's heart, in his memory.

He closed his eyes and saw the door close on the coroner's wagon that had carried Jodi away to the morgue.

And then it was he who couldn't breathe for several moments. Raw emotions, unearthed by the near tragedy today, scraped through him, setting every nerve ending on fire.

"Hey, Sinclair," Cal said, clapping a hand on his shoulder. "You okay, buddy?"

Riley gathered himself quickly, shoving down the emotions that left him so exposed and vulnerable. Buried them again.

"Yeah," he rasped, then cleared his throat before continuing. "I'm fine. It's just…I know her, and—" He blew out a deep breath. "That was too close. We almost lost her."

Cal slapped him on the back. "Key word there is *almost*. You really came through for her, buddy. Good work."

Riley acknowledged his friend with a nod, then headed toward the place on the lawn where he'd discarded his helmet.

He may have saved 3C today, but it wasn't enough.

It was never enough. He had too many marks in his loss column.

Nothing would change the mistakes he'd made with Erin.

And, more importantly, he could never make up for having failed Jodi.

"The police said when they arrived at the scene yesterday, the man driving the car had already disappeared." Ginny's mother, Hannah West, sat forward in the hospital chair and stroked Ginny's uninjured left arm. "They've been looking for him all day today, but no luck so far."

Hannah had touched Ginny frequently throughout the day, as if repeatedly reassuring herself that her oldest of three children and only daughter was, in fact, alive, safe, healing.

"This Walt Compton fellow the newspaper mentions…if he *was* hurt when he crashed through the wall, his injuries apparently weren't enough to keep him from running off before the cops arrived," Megan Calhoun, Ginny's best friend, said from a chair opposite Hannah.

So much for her client's confidentiality. Thanks to the newspaper reporting the actions of Annie's husband and mentioning the police's top suspect by name, her mother and best friend already knew enough to fill in the blanks about the woman whose identity Ginny was duty-bound to keep confidential.

"Also says here that Walt Compton was dishonorably discharged from the service for assaulting an officer." Megan glanced from the newspaper to Ginny. "History of letting his temper get the best of him."

Ginny frowned but didn't answer. Smoke inhalation left her throat painfully raw, her voice almost gone. But her throat and voice would heal, as would her broken right arm.

Right now, her main concern was for Annie. Twenty-four hours after the fire, Annie's husband was still out there, still a threat, enraged enough to try to kill her and anyone else in his path.

"Is his wife…at…shelter?" Ginny whispered, despite the ache in her throat. She had to know her client was safe before she could rest and concentrate on her own recovery.

Hannah and Megan exchanged a glance.

"I don't know. We were so worried about you that we didn't ask," her mother said.

Ginny sent Megan a querying glance that needed no verbalization.

Megan, who volunteered at the women's shelter and knew the staff well, nodded. "I'll find out and let you know. If she's not, I'll make sure someone from your office knows to get her there."

Ginny released a sigh of relief and smiled her thanks.

Megan had recently been through an ordeal of her own, facing down a second attack by the man who'd raped her years before. Fortunately, Megan had stopped her attacker and gained a boatload of confidence and perspective in the process. She was well on her way to a new life, making a fresh start with her new husband, Jack, and Jack's darling daughter.

Ginny's thoughts turned to her own dependent—the furry kind—and caught her mother's gaze. "Zach?"

Her mom nodded. "Don't worry, hon. I'll stop by your place on the way home to feed him."

"Shot, too."

"And I'll give him his insulin. Your cat is in good hands. You just concentrate on healing," Hannah said.

A soft knock sounded on the hospital room door, and Ginny looked up.

"I hope I'm not intruding," said the gorgeous blond man standing outside in the hall. "I just wanted to check on you. Make sure you were doing all right."

Ginny's heart lifted, her pulse stumbling to a racing beat. *4A.*

A wide smile tugged the corners of her mouth, and she waved him in. *Hi,* she mouthed.

From the corner of her eye, she caught her mother's and Megan's curious glances, but her gaze stayed locked on her handsome firefighter neighbor.

He stepped into the room, gave the other women a polite smile and set a small vase of flowers on the tray at the foot of her bed.

"I'm Riley Sinclair," he said, shaking Megan's hand then Hannah's and nodding when they each introduced themselves.

Riley Sinclair. Ginny let the name roll through her mind, testing the feel of it. She smiled to herself, amused that *this* was how she'd finally learned his name—when he introduced himself to her *mother.*

"Riley's the man…who saved my life," Ginny rasped.

All eyes swung to her, then her mother and Megan both turned back to gawk again at Riley.

Hannah rose from her chair and pulled him into a bear hug.

"Oh, Riley, thank you! Thank you for giving my baby girl back to me!"

He smiled awkwardly, appearing decidedly uncomfortable with the attention and accolades.

Megan caught Ginny's eye and arched a brow. While Riley dealt with Hannah's motherly gratitude, she mouthed, *He's hot!*

Ginny nodded and grinned. Cutting a glance to her mom, she signaled for Megan to take Hannah and give her and Riley some privacy. With a thumbs-up, her friend grasped the older woman's arm and headed for the door. "Mrs. West, why don't we go see what we can find out about Annie for Gin? Maybe grab a bite at the snack bar?"

"Oh, sure… We'll be back later, darling!" Hannah called as Megan tugged her out the door.

Ginny gave her mom a wave, then turned to 4A.

Riley.

His silver eyes were focused on her, and his mouth curled up in a sexy grin. "Hey, 3C. How're you feeling?"

"Alive. Thanks to you."

He ducked his head and shrugged. "Just doing my job."

"Not from what…I hear." She paused to swallow and take a breath. "You went beyond the call I hear. You resuscitated me."

He shrugged this off as well, as if saving her life was a walk in the park. "Had to. I couldn't very well ask you out to dinner if you died on me." He flashed a devilish smile and moved to the chair Megan had vacated.

Ginny grinned. "If that's an invitation, I accept…*Riley.*"

"Yeah, I guess it was. So…great. Once you spring this joint, we'll compare calendars…Ginny."

Her smile brightened. "You know my name."

"Mm-hmm. Folks at the fire scene told me."

An awkward silence fell between them, and Riley steepled his fingers, fidgeting. "So…you look good."

Ginny sputtered a laugh. She touched the plastic tubing feeding oxygen into her nose. "Oh, sure. A nasal cannula…is so attractive."

Riley leaned forward and wrapped his hand around her good one. His silver eyes held hers with a piercing intensity. "It is to me."

Everything inside Ginny went still. Something in his expression spoke of a deeper concern than the relative attractiveness of hospital equipment. A memory teased the edges of her thoughts.

She recalled seeing that same piecing intensity when she'd come to at the fire yesterday. When she'd met his gaze, his pale gray eyes had brimmed with tears and swirled with emotion.

And something deeper.

Something that spoke to her soul.

In that instant, she'd known a spiritual connection with him. She'd known in a way she couldn't explain that he was the one who'd saved her life, breathed life back into her lungs.

"Thank you," she whispered.

The corner of his mouth twitched. "Just my humble opinion. Of course, it could be *you* making it look so sexy."

She hitched up a corner of her mouth, acknowledging his compliment, but pushed on. "No. I mean…thank you for saving my life."

A shadow flickered across his face, but he immediately schooled his features and forced a grin. "That again? You really are easily impressed. At least it got me a date with you, huh?" He winked, but she detected an unease behind his flirtation.

Ginny furrowed her brow. "Why does talking about it make you…uncomfortable?"

Riley blinked and sat back a bit, clearly caught off-guard by her question. He shrugged again. "I don't know. It's just not that big of a deal."

Ginny scoffed in disagreement. "You saved a life! That's huge!" She paused long enough to swallow and soothe the fire in her throat. "And not because…it was me. Saving any life is major. Big-time huge."

She stopped only long enough to pull another breath into her aching lungs, then plowed on. The passion she felt for her argument overrode the effort it took to rasp it out. "You should be proud of it. Feel good about it. Hell, you're even…allowed to gloat a little." Ginny quirked a little smile. "Just don't be obnoxious about it, you know?"

Riley shook his head, dismissal and disbelief etched in his expression. "Look, I'm glad you're okay. That I feel good about. As for me, my part in it, I'm a firefighter, and I was just doing my job."

Ginny opened her mouth to press the issue but snapped it closed again. This was her first opportunity to really *talk* to Riley. She didn't want to spend the time arguing the merit of his heroics or making him feel uncomfortable. Although as a counselor, she found his reluctance to accept praise and thanks for his good deed intriguing.

She pointed at him with her left hand, narrowed her eyes and scowled playfully. "Okay, I'll let your mysterious reasons for your modesty slide…this time. But next time…"

He caught the finger she wagged at him and lowered it to the bed. The warmth of his hand curled intimately around hers, knocked the teasing grin from her lips and stole her breath.

His work-roughened palm abraded her hand, made tender from heat damage equivalent to a sunburn. But she didn't give her sore skin a second thought. Having Riley hold her hand felt ridiculously good. Such a simple thing, that touch. Yet a crackling energy and awareness snapped along her nerve endings.

He arched an eyebrow. "Next time? Let's hope there is no next time. One near-death experience for you is enough!"

"Touché," she croaked, glad the crack in her voice could be excused as the result of smoke inhalation.

"So…have the doctors said when you can go home?"

"Tomorrow, if my vitals remain good." She noted that, although the topic had changed, he still held her hand. Warmth blossomed in her chest, put a grin on her lips.

Maybe, like her mom's constant touching, Riley's grip on her hand was a hint that he wasn't as unaffected by her close call or his part in saving her life as he wanted her to think. Ginny knew through her training, her experience with counseling, that body language spoke volumes.

"I'll be off tomorrow. I can come get you. Drive you home."

Ginny tightened her grip on his hand. "It's nice of you to offer, but…not necessary. My mom or Megan can—"

"I don't mind. I want to help." Riley's eyes held the same bright intensity she'd noticed earlier. His silver gaze held her transfixed for a moment before he seemed to realize how serious he'd become and laughed it off with a shrug. "Besides, you live in my building, so it's hardly out of the way. What are neighbors for?"

"Okay. Tell you what…you can be my buffer."

"Buffer?"

"Yeah. My mom is going to want to be here regardless, 'cause she lives to dote on her kids. Borderline smothering. I love Mom, but…hate the smothering. You can be my buffer, run interference."

Riley turned one palm up. "If that's what you need, I aim to please." He gave her fingers another gentle squeeze before he pulled away and rose from the chair. "I think I should let you rest. I'm glad you're okay, Ginny."

"And I'm glad you were on duty last night. Getting mouth-to-mouth from anyone else…" She gave him a sultry smile. "…just wouldn't have been half as much fun."

A smoldering heat flared in Riley's gaze. He hesitated a moment, as if deciding whether to match her flirtation with a suggestive comment of his own.

"Go ahead. Say it," she prompted.

He looked a bit surprised that she'd read his intent so easily, then grinned more broadly. "I think I'd rather show you." He tapped her nose with his finger. "But later. You get well, and then we'll have some *real* fun."

With a small wave, he sauntered out to the corridor, leaving Ginny with another breathtaking view of his jeans-clad backside and ample fodder for her imagination.

Compunction twisted in her chest, and she sighed. Had she gone too far? Had she misled Riley about her intentions? Maybe.

She'd mastered the art of flirtation over the years. But though she'd like to believe someday she and Riley might follow up on their banter, in truth, she was a long way from having an intimate relationship with him. Intimacy took time, took trust, took a whole lot of work. This time she *had* to look before she leaped. She had to be sure.

The real question was, was she ready to put in the work for a shot at something deeper with Riley Sinclair?

And was he ready to put in the effort to have a relationship with her?

His body thrumming, Riley strode toward the hospital elevator and indulged in a mental picture of himself having a steamy variety of *fun* with his seductress neighbor.

Get a grip. Save the X-rated fantasies for a while. The woman just had a brush with death.

A brush with death.

A chill skimmed down Riley's spine as he jabbed the elevator button. He hadn't realized until he saw Ginny again today how deeply her near miss still affected him. If he'd thought he'd put the surge of memories and emotion to bed yesterday at the fire scene, he'd been wrong. What's worse, his emotions were so close to the surface that Ginny had picked up on his edginess.

And why wouldn't she? She was a counselor. Her job was all about reading people and dealing with emotions.

The knot in Riley's gut cinched a bit tighter. Before he came back tomorrow to take Ginny home from the hospital, he definitely had to get some perspective, lock those memories of his failure with Jodi away where they'd be safe.

But he also couldn't repeat the mistakes he'd made with Erin.

He pinched the bridge of his nose as the internal push-pull of responsibilities battled inside him.

He stepped on the elevator and drew a deep breath. Reining in his emotions should be easy enough. The crisis had passed. And he felt better about Ginny after seeing her.

She had color back in her cheeks. The soot and grime had been washed from her pale blond hair, and the spark of humor and vitality had returned to her sky-blue eyes.

He'd meant it when he said she looked good. Except for a few scratches and the cast on her arm, she looked every bit the sultry siren who'd spent the last several weeks tempting him with come-hither glances and witty flirtation.

Which brought him back to the X-rated fantasy images....
Whew!

Riley dragged a hand over his jaw. He figured he and 3C could have a whole lot of steamy fun together...if he could keep the raw memories of Jodi's death in the back recesses of his mind where they belonged. Where he could manage them. Where Ginny couldn't find them.

After Riley left, Ginny closed her eyes and snuggled deeper into her pillow with a satisfied sigh. Though his surprise visit had lifted her spirits, all her talking and the effort to hide her physical discomfort left her exhausted.

In her mind, she replayed their conversation, every glance and each touch. She analyzed the visit with fresh perspective, looking for red flags she may have missed. This time she wouldn't be fooled, wouldn't be so blind. A dull pang settled in her chest for her previous naïveté with men.

She must have dozed off shortly after that, because the next time she opened her eyes, her room was much darker, the sky outside her window was tinged with the shadows of twilight.

The scuff of feet beside her bed alerted her to someone's presence.

She turned her head, expecting to find her mother.

Instead, a hand clamped tightly over her nose and mouth. Panic surged up in her throat.

She blinked hard, trying to focus in the darkness on her attacker.

Red hair. Pale face. Dark eyes.

Walt Compton.

"Where is she?" he growled. The sour scent of liquor tainted his breath.

Ginny clawed with her left hand at Walt's fingers. Even if he hadn't had his palm clamped over her mouth, her voice was too hoarse to scream for help.

"You told her to leave me. I know it was you! Now where did you hide her?" His fingers dug deeper into her cheeks.

Ginny gave up trying to pry Walt's iron grip from her mouth and fumbled in the covers for the nurse call button. But her frantic groping sent the cord slithering to the floor. Ginny's heart sank.

With her emergency call button out of reach and her voice too weak to yell for help…

"Annie would have never left me if not for you! Now tell me where she is, or I'll—"

"Time to check your blood pressure, Ms. W—"

As the nurse breezed into the room, Annie's husband whirled around, releasing Ginny. He shoved the nurse out of his way as he raced out the doorway and down the hospital corridor.

"What the—? Who was that?" The stunned woman caught her balance and pressed a hand to her chest.

Ginny gasped for air, despite the oxygen tubes at her nose. Fear compressed her lungs. Chills skittered over her skin. "Call security! Stop him!"

The nurse darted out, yelling to someone in the hall. "Get security! Which way did he go?"

Ginny sucked in a few more calming breaths. The scent of stale liquor hung in the air. Annie had said her husband became more violent when he drank. A common enough problem in the troublesome world of domestic disputes.

Ginny shuddered and sent up a prayer, hoping that Annie and her children were safe at the women's shelter. She realized, too, that she'd never gotten in touch with the court liaison to get a restraining order arranged for Annie against her husband.

She groped left-handed for the bedside phone and used her thumb to dial the courthouse. As she waited for someone to answer, she mentally replayed the desperate husband's attack, a fresh jolt of adrenaline sending shock waves through her.

The man was dangerous, desperate, unpredictable. And if he'd come after her once, he could easily do so again.

Ginny swallowed the dark taste of dread.

The man had tried to kill her, had tried to kill Annie, and had torched the women's center. The police were already looking for Walt Compton. They had plenty of reason to arrest and hold him when he was found. A restraining order was a moot point.

Ginny pressed the hook and put the phone down.

The best thing she could do until Walt was captured was protect her client, protect herself. And pray the authorities found Annie's husband. Soon.

Chapter 3

"Mom, I'll be fine. Stop worrying!" Riley heard Ginny say just as he reached her hospital room the next morning.

He stopped at the door, surveyed the scene and was immediately reminded of the role she had asked him to play today. Buffer.

Ginny sat in a wheelchair, dressed in street clothes, ready to go home, while her mother literally hovered over her. Hannah draped a thin blanket around Ginny's shoulders, which Ginny quickly shrugged off.

"Mom, it's seventy-five degrees outside. I don't need to be swaddled up like a newborn." Ginny had recovered most of her voice, but it still held a faint rasp.

Hannah sighed. "It's a mother's job to worry. And I'd just feel better if you had another layer of protection from this guy. Can't the police station a guard at your door or something?"

Ginny groaned. "I don't need a guard. I—"

Riley rapped lightly on the door.

When Ginny spotted him standing at the door, a smile lit her face. Then, as if inspiration had just struck, she turned to her mother and waved a hand toward him. "I…have Riley just down the hall. If there's trouble, I can call him. Right, Riley?"

Was it wrong that he found the smoke-induced huskiness of her voice sexy as hell? Probably. But when he got around 3C, she scrambled his thoughts and turned everything topsy-turvy for him.

Riley shoved his hands in the back pockets of his jeans and sucked in a deep breath to tamp down his runaway libido. He'd learned yesterday how easily Ginny could pick up on his moods and read his thoughts. He had to do a better job of staying in control of his reactions when he was around her.

"Riley?" Ginny prompted when he didn't answer her after several seconds.

"Um…sure. Whatever you need." He wasn't certain what sort of conversation he'd interrupted, but he could answer Ginny's question easily enough. He'd do anything humanly possible to make sure she was safe.

His answer put a smug, case-closed grin on Ginny's face. Mrs. West seemed somewhat mollified, if not entirely convinced. "I just don't think you should be alone until that man is caught. If you won't let me stay with you, what about Megan?"

"I don't need a babysitter, Mom."

"I know that. But after what happened last night…" Hannah's hand fluttered to her lips as she paused, inhaling sharply. "I'm just scared he might try to hurt you again."

Riley jerked his eyebrows together, frowning. "Whoa. Back up. What happened last night?"

Hannah and Ginny spoke at the same time.

"Nothing."

"That man—"

Ginny cut a sharp silencing glance at her mother, but Hannah persisted. "The man who drove his car into Ginny's office…the husband of her client…he showed up here last night. He tried to kill Ginny!"

Riley tensed, a punch of horror slamming into his gut. Icy chills prickled his skin. "He came here?" *After he'd left. He'd left Ginny alone and—*

"Mom…"

"Yes," Hannah declared. "And if the night duty nurse hadn't come in when she did—"

"Mom! I'm fine. The police are looking for him. The officer said they've got an APB out for him, and they promised to keep a watch on my apartment complex. A private guard is overkill."

Riley wiped his suddenly sweaty palms on his jeans. "Who is this guy, and why is he trying to hurt you?"

God, he hoped Ginny didn't hear the anxiety he heard in his own voice.

"His name is Walt Compton. His wife came to our office because he'd been abusing her and had threatened to kill her."

Riley clenched his teeth. A domestic dispute. He'd been called to the scene of enough domestic disputes to know how volatile those situations could be.

"We've given his wife and kids refuge at the women's shelter. She'd told him I was her counselor, so Walt came after me to find out where she was. He blames me for convincing her to leave the brutality of their marriage."

Riley balled his hands into fists, wishing he could ram his knuckles down Walt Compton's throat. The guy was scum. Being a wife beater was bad enough. But this guy had threatened Ginny, and that made it feel personal to Riley. He didn't stop to analyze why he felt so protective of his neighbor. Not while her sky-blue eyes were watching him as closely as they were now.

"I have to say…" He paused and cleared his throat. "I'm with your mom on this. The cops should post someone in the lobby of our apartment building. And until he's found, you should have someone stay with you."

Ginny's eyes widened, betrayal and disbelief flashing across her face. "Not you, too!"

Riley sighed. "If this guy is half as unstable as I think—and the fact that he drove his car through the wall of your office suggests he is—you shouldn't be alone. He's dangerous."

Ginny pressed her hands together in her lap and schooled her features. In a calm, let's-be-reasonable voice, she said, "This is a work issue. It's my job to handle it. I've alerted the authorities, and they are doing everything they can to find him. They offered to post a guard outside our building, and I turned them down."

Ginny's mother huffed in disbelief. "Why?"

"I'd much rather they use their resources protecting Annie and the other ladies at the women's shel—" Ginny gasped, winced, then shook her head. "Whoops. Well, now you know her name. Not that you couldn't figure it out if you'd wanted to, thanks to the paper reporting her husband's name." She rubbed her forehead. "Anyway...the police can monitor the apartments well enough from the parking lot or street. I'm sure the police will have Walt in custody shortly."

"And if they don't?" Hannah asked, tipping her head.

Ginny sighed and sent Riley a you-were-supposed-to-be-on-my-side scowl.

"Mom, I—"

Buffer.

"What if," he interrupted, "I volunteered to stay with you." Hannah arched an eyebrow in disapproval.

"On the couch," he added quickly, to appease her.

Again Ginny and her mother spoke over each other.

"You don't have to—"

"On the couch," Hannah reiterated, then turned from Riley to address her daughter. "I like that idea. It's a good compromise."

"That's no compromise. I'm being railroaded! I never agreed to having anyone—"

Hannah headed for the door and touched Riley's arm as she left. "Talk to her. I'll go see what's keeping the doctor with those discharge papers."

Ginny waved a hand toward the door where her mother had breezed out. "Do you see why I need a buffer? She'd run my life completely if I let her."

Riley gave her a lopsided grin. "She means well."

"And you!" Ginny aimed a finger at him, her expression in what-were-you-thinking mode. "You were supposed to be helping me, not taking her side!"

He raised both hands in surrender. "In my defense, I did manage to get her to back off the idea of camping out at your place. That would kinda have put a damper on my plans for a quiet dinner for two tonight."

Ginny cocked her head and curled her lips in the sultry smile that always made his blood flash hot. "Dinner for two? Intriguing. Do tell."

He ran a hand over his short-cropped hair. "Well, Ming Wa delivers, if you like Chinese. I could bring wine, and we could finally get a chance to get to know each other. You know, talk or watch a movie…whatever."

"And then *you* would camp out on my couch." Ginny lifted one eyebrow in a way that mirrored her mother.

He stepped over to the wheelchair and crouched, putting himself at eye level with her. Close enough to smell the hint of baby powder he'd come to recognize as her scent. Only 3C could make baby powder a turn-on for him.

"Yeah. I kinda promised your mother. And I do think you need someone staying with you. At least for a while."

At least until he was sure she was safe. He refused to repeat his mistakes with Erin. His gut cramped, remembering.

Ginny rolled her eyes.

"But…I don't have to stay on the couch alone." He gave her a devilish grin and waggled his eyebrow. "I didn't promise your mom anything in that regard."

Ginny chuckled. "A master of semantics. That skill can come in handy with my family." Heat darkened her eyes. "And this whole camping out thing is sounding better all the time. I'm not so much against you staying over as I am opposed to having my life dictated to me."

Riley put on an innocent face. "I would never presume to dictate."

Hannah bustled back into the room with a nurse on her heels. "Here we go."

"Just sign these release forms, and you are free to go." The nurse handed Ginny a clipboard with several papers attached.

After she awkwardly scratched her name on the forms with her left hand and handed them back to the nurse, Ginny gave the wheelchair a one-handed slap. "All righty then. Let's bust this joint."

Riley fell in behind her and steered the wheelchair toward the elevator. As he reached past her to mash the down button, he leaned into the sweet, baby powder scent at her neck and murmured, "As a bonus, while I'm at your place tonight, I could work on fixing your plumbing problems if you want."

Ginny tilted her head to glance at him, putting her tempting mouth a breath away from his. "Would this be babysitting cleverly disguised as maintenance assistance?"

He smiled. "Not at all. I'm totally clear on your feelings regarding babysitting. This is seduction disguised as maintenance assistance, pure and simple."

Her face lit with a humored grin for a moment, but then her eyebrows tugged together, and her smile faltered. "I hope you don't think I'm the kind of girl who'll sleep with a guy just because he fixed my dishwasher. I'm not that easy."

He grunted, twisting his lips in a wry grin. "Believe me, with you, *easy* never crossed my mind."

Ginny's eyes twinkled. "Then by all means, grab your tools and come on over."

* * *

Before Riley could make it around to the passenger side of his truck, Ginny had popped the door open and was struggling to climb out. She slid down from the high seat to the asphalt of the apartment's parking lot, and her knees buckled weakly.

"Hey, take it easy." He was there in a flash, his arm around her, supporting her. He narrowed his gray eyes on her, an adorable wrinkle of worry creasing the bridge of his nose. "There's a reason the hospital discharges patients in a wheelchair, Ginny. Your body's still healing. Go slow. Lean on me."

As she opened her mouth to protest, he hooked her left arm around his neck, pulled her up against his taut, muscled frame and anchored his arm at her waist. All thoughts of arguing fled.

Riley, under normal circumstances, could make Ginny's breath catch, her body hum. Riley, up close and personal, sent her body into overdrive. Her heart thrummed. Her head swam. Her skin tingled.

Being cautious about moving the relationship too fast didn't mean she was immune to Riley's…er, *charms*. Even if she could have walked in by herself, she would have faked an injury at that moment just to be held so close to his solid strength. She inhaled the spice of his aftershave, and a heady thrill swirled from her nape to her toes.

But even as she savored the sweet sensations Riley inspired, her head told her to go slow with him. His heroism on her behalf could easily be clouding her painkiller-muddled perception.

And, Lord knew, her history of misjudging men spoke for itself. Painfully so. Her own dating track record aside, she could never forget the heartache her poor judgment with men had caused her college roommate, Donna. A deep ache sliced through Ginny, lessening the headiness she felt from Riley's proximity.

Thoughts of Donna nagging her, Ginny studied Riley's rough-hewn features again. Sure, he was handsome as sin, thoughtful, brave….

But other men she'd dated had been handsome, polite, and had seemed charming—until she discovered there was a wife waiting at home or that the charm was an act to get her into bed.

Not that *in bed* wasn't where she hoped to end up with Riley…eventually. But first, she had to be sure he was as good as his first impression purported. She had a heck of a lot still to learn about this man before she'd let herself believe he was all he seemed.

The expression "too good to be true" rang in her head. What was the *real* Riley like?

"Ginny? You okay?"

She realized she was staring at him like a schoolgirl and shook herself. "Yeah. Thanks. Thought I could do it alone, but my knees thought otherwise."

"Listen, soon enough things will be back to the status quo. For now, you need to listen to your body. Don't tax yourself, okay?"

As Riley guided her, taking baby steps toward the door, she itched to move at a faster pace, take the lead and steer him along a different course. Perhaps a route that afforded her a few extra minutes of snuggling close to his sturdy body?

Instead she gave him an apologetic grin. "Sorry, I don't do pampering well. My mom says my favorite phrase from the time I could talk was 'Do it myself!' That's never changed. I need my independence."

"Nothing wrong with that…as long as it's practical. Besides, every now and then everyone deserves a little TLC." Riley slowed further as they reached a short flight of steps leading to the apartment entrance. "Consider this your turn."

"I really don't need help. Dealing with this—" She held up her casted right arm. "—will be tricky at first, but I'm up to the challenge."

To prove her point, she pulled away from his grasp and trudged up the steps at a quicker pace. The show of defiance left her a tad winded and more than a little dizzy. Apparently yesterday's brief oxygen deprivation had taken a bigger toll on her than she'd thought.

When she hesitated at the top of the steps, Riley stepped back into place beside her. She covered her effort to regain her equilibrium with a bright smile and by sliding an arm around his waist as if giving him a flirtatious hug.

The lift of his blond eyebrow said he wasn't fooled.

He braced a hand under her left elbow and drew her up against him again. "Need a minute to catch your breath?"

She tilted her head back to meet his gaze. "Maybe. But your holding me like this is not going to help. Being this close to you seems to leave me breathless."

He hitched up the corner of his mouth in a provocative grin. "The feeling is mutual, gorgeous."

Ginny shook herself from her starry-eyed daze and leaned more weight against the railing.

Slow down!

"You know, as a counselor, I spend a lot of time talking with clients, helping them decide a plan of action, ways to change their life. But all our talk is no good if they don't suit words to action, if they don't follow through."

"The whole 'actions speak louder than words' thing?"

She shrugged. "Something like that. So it's a matter of professional pride that I do things for myself. I have an example to set, you know?"

With a steadying breath, she pulled away from him again to head for the door.

"An example. Right." But he sounded unconvinced as he drew her back up against him. "Speaking of actions, I've been bummed about something since yesterday, when I visited you in the hospital."

Her brow knitted in confusion. "Bummed?"

"Yeah, bummed! When I revived you, you missed the whole your-lips-on-mine thing. I figure all this flirting is really just going over points we've already established. We know there's a definite sizzle between us."

She gave him a suspicious nod. "Yeah?"

"And rather than keep wondering what a real kiss would be like…"

Ginny saw his intent in his smoky gaze, and her breath caught. "Riley, maybe we should wait until—"

She never got the chance to finish her thought.

He swooped in and captured her lips. With gentle pressure, he molded her mouth to his, then swept his tongue inside to tangle with hers. He tasted like cinnamon, hot and sweet, and when her head swam dizzily this time, she knew it had nothing to do with the lingering effects of oxygen deprivation.

Riley cradled the back of her head with one large hand and pulled her hips closer to his with his other. The intimate contact of their bodies made her womb tighten and weep with longing.

Ginny savored the ebb and flow of his kiss, giving back every bit of the passion and heat he showed her, even as her brain screamed for her to take it slow. She had a lot to learn about Riley before she could risk getting more involved with him.

With a soft brush of his thumb along her cheek, he pulled away and grinned unrepentantly. "*That* is called follow through."

Ginny sighed contentedly. "I do love a man of action."

As Riley swept a flyaway wisp of her hair back from her eyes, a flash of color and movement snagged Ginny's attention.

She cut her gaze toward the distraction. A police car cruised slowly through the parking lot. The cop's presence reminded her why Riley was with her, why the extra patrols were needed.

She'd been attacked last night. She could have died.

A shudder shimmied through her, and she backed away from Riley's arms.

"Ginny?" He narrowed a concerned gaze on her.

She nodded toward the parking lot. "We have company."

"What?" Riley turned and looked out over the cars. When he spotted the cruiser, he gave the officer a little wave. "Why don't we get you inside now, where we can have a little privacy?"

"Privacy? You forget...my mom is on her way. She has to see for herself that I've gotten home safely and have locked my door."

"You're lucky to have a mother who cares so much." A spark lit Riley's gray eyes as he tucked her into his embrace.

"I guess. So does your mom make a big fuss over you, too, worrying and nagging?"

The light in Riley's eyes faded as he helped her up the steps to her third floor apartment. Though he forced a grin, Ginny noticed the change in his demeanor, felt his muscles tense.

"Yeah, my mom worries...but I...don't see her much."

"Why not?"

He hesitated. "She lives out by Lagniappe Lake."

"The lake is only about thirty minutes outside town." At her door, Ginny fumbled in her purse with her left hand, searching for her keys.

He shrugged and shifted his weight. "We, uh...just get busy. Time passes. I'll see her at Thanksgiving." He extended a hand toward Ginny's purse. "Need help?"

She sent him a pointed look and smiled. "No, thank you. I've got it." She dangled the keys from her left hand to prove her point, then jabbed at the keyhole.

And missed. But her poor aim was more a factor of the scrapes and small gouges beside her doorknob than left-handed awkwardness. The damage to her door was new. And distinctive.

Someone had been trying to break into her apartment. And she'd bet a week's pay that *someone* had red hair and a history of spousal abuse. Walt Compton had been here. Could still be here.

Which begged the question, what if Riley hadn't been with her?

Ginny shuddered. Maybe having him stay in her apartment was a good idea after all....

Chapter 4

While Riley returned to the parking lot to report her damaged door to the policeman on guard duty, Ginny started putting away the few toiletries she'd brought home from the hospital. Having her right arm in a cast was going to be a royal pain, especially if she wanted to prove to others she didn't need a babysitter. She'd managed alone for too long to start depending on anyone else now.

Her orange and white, diabetic tabby, Zachary, hopped up on the bathroom counter and rubbed against her arm in greeting. "Hey, fella. How's my boy? Did anyone remember to feed you and give you a shot this morning?"

Zach meowed and pawed at the faucet. When Ginny turned on the cool water, the cat ducked his head and started lapping at the trickle.

"Spoiled." Smiling, Ginny stroked her cat's back, but despite the familiar routine, her heart still raced from the shock of finding someone had tampered with her door. She took a few deep breaths and mentally reviewed the advice she gave her clients.

Fear is a tool used to control you. Take back control of your situation. Stay calm so you can think clearly.

Ginny blew her bangs out of her eyes. She had a new appreciation for the stress her clients dealt with.

Time to practice what she preached.

Your strength and healing will come from within yourself, not by looking to others.

A sharp rap sounded on her front door, and Ginny's adrenaline spiked. Clapping a hand over her scampering heart, she hurried to the living room. "Riley?"

"Yeah, it's me."

Ginny unhooked the chain guard and dead bolt, then looked through the peephole, just in case, before she opened her door.

"So what did the officer say?" she asked him as he strode into her living room, his rough-hewn masculinity in stark contrast to the feminine decor of her apartment.

"He's calling it in, getting a crime scene team to come out. He's checking the grounds now, but he'll be here in a minute to take your statement."

"Another statement." She sighed and dropped onto her gingham-covered couch. "I don't know what else I could possibly tell them. My shoe size, maybe?"

Riley gave her a sympathetic grin and shrugged.

She took a cleansing breath. "Look, I was just about to fix some lunch," she lied. The idea of food turned her stomach, but making lunch would give her something to do, might serve as a distraction from her fruitless worrying. "Do you want a sandwich?"

He nodded. "Sure. I'll help."

But as she headed toward her kitchen, her doorbell heralded the arrival of the officer from the parking lot and the crime scene crew. For the next ninety minutes, she was busy repeating everything that had happened over the past thirty-six hours. She cringed as the technicians dusted for prints, and a fine coating of the powder settled on her carpet, her furniture. She'd be forever cleaning the reminder of the would-be intruder out of her apartment.

Through it all, she was hyperaware of Riley's presence. He stood back, giving the investigators room to work, but his imposing height and wide shoulders were always in the periphery of her vision, in her thoughts. His presence filled her with a reassurance she couldn't explain. Maybe because he'd already saved her life once.

As the officer finished his questions, Riley sat next to Ginny on the couch and took her left hand in his, squeezing her fingers gently. "You doin' okay?"

"Yeah, just tired." She lifted her eyes to meet his, and a corner of his sexy mouth tipped up.

When I revived you, you missed the whole your-lips-on-mine thing.

Two hours earlier, she'd kissed those lips, been swept away by their hypnotic lure. The memory sent a renewed shimmy of heat curling through her veins, chasing out a fraction of the chill that lingered, given that Walt Compton was most likely the person who'd tried to break into her apartment.

But physical chemistry was no substitute for knowing what made a man tick, knowing who he was beneath the stunning smile and wide chest. Although having Riley near was comforting, Ginny reminded herself that his presence was temporary, and she needed to rely on her own strengths and coping mechanisms after today. She had to get back to her normal routine, back to work. People were counting on her.

"I need to check on Annie," she thought aloud. "If Walt has been this determined to come after me, what has he done about finding her? She's in more danger than I am."

"You just got home from the hospital." Riley frowned. "You've had problems of your own to deal with. I'm sure the other ladies that work at the women's center have taken good care of Annie. Right now, you need to rest."

"The other women from the center have their hands full relocating our offices after the fire and dealing with their own clients' needs." Ginny pushed herself off the sofa and scanned the living room, looking for her cordless phone. "Annie is my responsibility, no matter who picked up my slack after the fire. I won't be able to rest until I know she and her kids are safe."

Spotting the receiver on the side table by her reading chair, Ginny stepped over Riley's long legs to get the phone. While she talked to one of the women from her office, confirming that Annie and her kids were doing well at the shelter, she overheard Riley thanking the policemen for their help and reminding them to keep a vigilant watch on the apartment.

Ginny would much rather the police focused their efforts on watching the women's shelter and tracking down Walt than on guarding her door.

By the time she got off the phone, Riley had made them each a sandwich and had brought hers out to the coffee table on a paper plate. Motioning her back to the couch, he said, "Get off your feet. You need to rest."

When another knock reverberated through the room, she headed for her door, only to be sidetracked by Riley.

"I'll get it. You sit. Eat something."

She lifted an eyebrow. "You're starting to sound like my mother."

Riley opened the door and sent Ginny a wry grin. *Speaking of whom...* he mouthed.

"Why are there so many police cars outside? What happened?" Hannah rushed into the living room, and Ginny suppressed a sigh.

"Standard procedure and basic questions, Mom. Nothing to worry about."

Riley stepped forward and motioned to Hannah. "Actually, Mrs. West, Ginny was just about to take a nap. Why don't we leave her alone to rest? If you want to assist me, I was just about to help Ginny with some maintenance repairs."

Her mother divided a glance between Ginny and Riley. "You're sure you're all right? Can I do anything for you?"

Ginny smiled. "Go home, and quit worrying. I'll call if I need you."

"Promise?"

"Mom—"

Hannah raised her hands. "Okay. I can take a hint." She walked back to the door and aimed a finger at Riley. "Take care of my girl."

He nodded. "You bet."

With her home now emptied of policemen and overprotective parents, Ginny felt the tension seep from her. She wilted like a deflated balloon against the sofa cushions.

"You got a wrench?" Riley asked.

She blinked at him. "Excuse me?"

"While you unwind a little, I thought I'd tinker with your sink…or was it your dishwasher that was on the fritz?"

She lifted the corner of her mouth in a weary grin. "The dishwasher doesn't drain. Floods the floor when I run it." She closed her eyes, feeling the weight of the past two days' events crushing down on her. "If I have a wrench, it'll be in the utility closet at the end of the hall."

Flopping over on her side, she tucked a throw pillow under her cheek and worked to find a comfortable position for her injured arm.

"Holler if you need anything." Riley leaned in and pressed a gentle kiss to her temple.

Ginny was too worn out to respond, too tired to question why Riley's chaste kiss caused a knee-jerk, uneasy stir in her gut. She'd analyze that incongruity later.

Riley found and cleared the clog in Ginny's dishwasher without much trouble. Putting the contraption back together and getting it operational again was another matter. A little over an hour after he started the repair, he was washing up and returning the tools he'd found in her closet to their rightful place.

He'd heard suspiciously little from the living room since he left Ginny on the sofa to rest, and when he rounded the couch looking for her, he learned why. She was sacked out. Completely dead to the world.

Dead.

Bad analogy, Riley thought as a little shudder crept up his spine. He still had an all too clear mental image of her limp and nearly lifeless body lying in the burning office.

Even now the blue-black shadows that marred her pale skin served as a jarring reminder of her ordeal. The thick cast on her arm stood in stark contrast to Ginny's petite frame. Her fat, orange and white cat had curled up beside her and slept nestled against her chest much like a child's teddy bear.

Vulnerable came to mind as he studied her sleeping. She'd hate to be called that. That much he already knew about his seductive neighbor. She had spirit and determination and attitude in spades. And though she seemed hell-bent on doing everything for herself, never letting anyone see a hint of weakness, he still sensed something when he was around her that made him long to shield and protect her.

Or maybe it was his own ghosts rattling their chains that made him so desperate to keep Ginny safe.

He sat down on the edge of the coffee table and indulged in a closer inspection of her delicate features. Freckles paraded across her pert nose, and she'd long ago nibbled the lipstick off her full rose lips. An errant wisp of her white-blond hair tumbled across her sculpted cheek.

As he watched her, a tiny pucker formed on her brow, and she shivered, goose bumps forming on her bare arms.

Riley reached for the afghan on the back of the couch and stood to shake it out. Carefully, he draped the cover over Ginny. But the afghan had barely touched her before her eyes flew open and she bolted upright with a gasp. Her arms came up in a defensive move.

The startled cat jumped down from the sofa and trotted off in a huff.

"Easy there. It's just me." Riley sat back down on the coffee table and sent her an apologetic grin. "I didn't mean to wake you. I just thought you might be cold."

Ginny released a deep breath and, squeezing her eyes shut, dragged her fingers through her tousled hair. "I guess I'm a little jumpy."

"You think?"

She shot him a look that said *smart aleck,* but tempered it with a sleepy smile.

"Hey, you have every right to be jumpy. Your life's been threatened twice in the last forty-eight hours. That's enough to spook anyone."

"True. But I'm not usually so high-strung. I need to get a grip." She lay back down and stretched her good arm over her head, yawning. "How long was I asleep?"

"'Bout an hour and a half."

"Mmm." Her eyes drifted closed again. "How goes the battle with the dishwasher?"

"I think I subdued the monster. You had a clogged drain, but all seems to be well now."

She blinked. "You fixed it? Really?"

"Really."

Her face lit with wonder and admiration. She clapped her hand over her heart and sighed airily. "My hero!"

Though he forced his lips to match her playful grin, a biting cold balled in his gut. Her lighthearted adoration prodded his internal demons from shadowed corners of his memory. His failures from the past loomed large and dark in his mind's eye. He had to swallow the knot of bitter defeat in his throat before he could speak. "You're too easily impressed."

She shook her head. "Don't be modest. You've saved me from tedious hours of dishwashing at a time when I don't have a spare hand to do it." She held up her cast-covered arm. "That's no small thing. What do I owe you for your services?"

He scowled and waved her off. "Nothing. Glad to help."

"Dinner at least. My treat." She took the phone from the coffee table near his hip and waggled it. "You pick the takeout. Suddenly I'm famished."

The flirtatious spark returned to her eyes, the come-hither invitation that always succeeded in revving his engine. Despite the thrum of desire that swept over him, he couldn't shake the nip of apprehension that nagged him.

My hero.

If Ginny had any delusions of him being heroic or worthy of her admiration, he was doomed to disappoint her.

Just as he'd let Erin down.

Just as he'd failed his sister.

The last thing he wanted was to hurt Ginny, but the gratitude in her eyes gave him pause. He'd had all the misplaced hero-worship and high expectations he could handle. If he hadn't promised her mother to stay and keep an eye on her, he'd have made an excuse to leave, to go back to his apartment and forget his overwhelming attraction to Ginny.

Yet his own sense of duty, his deep-seated need to protect her compelled him to stay. His chest tightened with the same tug-of-war that had plagued him since he left her at the hospital the night before.

He wanted to keep her safe, but doing so risked his own peace of mind, risked exposing truths he couldn't face. Their relationship had to meet his terms, or Ginny could get hurt.

Ginny could be plenty stubborn when she wanted.

She sawed clumsily on her pizza with the edge of her fork, determined not to give up. She'd quickly found holding a gooey slice of pizza with her nondominant hand both messy and awkward. She'd resorted to using a fork, lest she end up with a lapful of pepperoni and cheese, but the fork was proving an equal challenge. Especially since Zachary kept trying to share her food.

She nudged her cat away from her plate again with a chuckle. "Vamoose, chubs. This is my dinner."

Riley reached over from his end of the couch and lifted Zach to the floor. "Scat, cat." Moving his empty paper plate to the coffee table, he scooted closer to Ginny. "Can I help? You're gonna starve before you get that fork to cooperate."

"No, thanks. I gotta figure this out for myself. I've got five weeks of eating left-handed ahead of me and I—"

"Here." Riley plucked a slice of pepperoni from her pizza and held it up to her mouth.

She cocked her head and sighed her exasperation. "I said I didn't—"

With a devilish gleam in his eyes, he poked the spicy meat between her lips.

Ginny arched an eyebrow. Two could play this game.

She caught his wrist, and as he withdrew his hand, she sucked the sauce from his finger. "Mmm."

Riley's pupils dilated, and she heard his breath catch.

She gave him a sassy grin as she chewed, then washed the bite down with a sip of red wine. "You're right. Forks are overrated."

He leaned closer. "There's more where that came from."

She met him halfway and raised her face. He molded her lips with his, then teased her mouth with his tongue. His kiss tasted like wine and heat and sweet seduction. Ginny's head swam, and she angled her head to draw him even closer.

She reveled in his kiss, sure she'd found nirvana. Riley Sinclair was too good to be true, she thought again.

Too good.

An odd flutter of uneasiness stirred in her chest, and she sat back to collect herself. Things were going too fast. Too well.

Riley was gorgeous and brave and thoughtful and sweet. But what did she *really* know about him?

Too many of her clients had used similar words to describe the men they thought they'd known before those same men had turned on them and shown a darker side. Her own history with men proved she was too easily swayed by first impressions.

The extreme events of the past few days and the intense chemistry that crackled between her and Riley had fast-forwarded their relationship. She of all people should know better than to race blindly into a situation without some level of precaution. Common sense reared its head and cooled the fire licking her veins.

She had to peel away Riley's layers and get at the heart of this man. She need assurance that he was the kind of guy she could trust. She wanted proof that his character, his soul was as golden as he seemed at face value.

Clearing her throat, Ginny set her plate aside and gave him a measuring glance. "So, fireman, I know you kiss like a pro. I know you're handy with home repairs and are skilled in CPR. But I want to know more. What's the scoop?"

Clearly not the response to their mind-numbing kiss he'd expected. Riley wrinkled his brow and eased back against the couch. "The scoop?" .

"Yeah. For instance, you've met my mom already, and I think I told you I'm the oldest of three kids. I have two brothers, the youngest being a high school senior, and the middle one is in school at LSU."

Riley got a wary look on his face. "And your dad is a CPA with his own firm."

Ginny nodded. "Right. So it's your turn. How long has your mom lived on Lagniappe Lake?"

He furrowed his brow and rubbed a hand along his jaw. "Long time. That's the house I grew up in."

Ginny smiled. "That had to have been fun. Growing up by the lake—swimming, fishing, skiing. So why don't you see more of your mom? If I had access to a lake property, I'd spend as much time as I could there. Especially in the summer."

The crease in his brow deepened, and he shrugged. "What can I say? I'm a bad son."

His assessment puzzled Ginny. The sadness in his tone touched a nerve and triggered her counselor instincts. "Bad how?"

"Usual stuff. I don't call as often as I should. I don't make time to go home and see her between holiday visits." A muscle in his jaw ticked, and he lifted his wine for another large sip.

"And your dad? Where is he?"

"He's dead." Riley looked away. He stared across her living room at nothing in particular.

She knew the evasion tactic well. Clearly, his family history was a sore subject.

"I'm sorry. Were you and your dad close?"

He hesitated a beat, then shrugged one shoulder. When he turned his gaze back to her, storm clouds filled his gray eyes. "Let's talk about something else."

Ginny's pulse tripped. The pain etched in his face raked through her with sharp tines. "Okay. What do you want to talk about?"

He stood and paced to the far side of the room, wiping his hands on the seat of his jeans. "When will you go back to work?"

"I don't know." Ginny studied him as she considered his question. "As soon as they find a place for us to set up shop while the women's center is rebuilt. Karen, the center's director, is working on it. She's supposed to call Sunday evening and let me know where to report to work."

Riley met her gaze briefly and nodded.

At the hospital, his reluctance to accept accolades for his heroism had intrigued her. Now his discomfort talking about his family and his dim view of missed calls to his mother cast a new mystery around him.

The unknowns bothered Ginny and created an obstacle

they had to get past. Both personal experience and professional training told her she needed to resolve the questions she had about Riley before she could justify letting him any closer.

Riley took the remote from the shelf by the television and turned on the TV. "I think *True Grit* is supposed to be on tonight. You a John Wayne fan?"

"I grew up in a house full of testosterone, remember? John Wayne was a staple."

"I'll take that as a yes." He crossed the floor and sat next to her, his thigh pressed intimately against hers. Wrapping a muscled arm around her shoulders, he lifted a corner of his mouth in a sexy grin.

As quickly as the tension had washed over him, it was gone again. The charming, easygoing Riley was back, his sex appeal set to stun.

A heady rush spun through Ginny as she settled against his chest to watch the movie. But beneath the intoxicating hum of pleasure warming her, the wings of doubt and caution fluttered again.

She had to find a way to tame her wild attraction to Riley until she knew what made him tick, knew for certain what kind of man lay beneath the too-good-to-be-true facade. She could too easily fall for his good looks and thrilling kisses, and neglect the voice of reason that warned her to look before she leaped.

After all, Jim Prather had seemed too good to be true when she'd introduced her handsome lab partner to her roommate in college. Soon enough, Donna had discovered Jim wasn't all he appeared—and she still had the scars to prove it.

After finding Donna bleeding and bruised in their dorm room, Ginny had sworn never to take a man at face value again. Guilt and anger over Jim's abuse of her roommate had driven Ginny to change her major, to dedicate her life to championing women and fighting all forms of abuse.

The endless pain she saw through her job only firmed her

resolve and made her more cautious, yet—somehow—*not* perceptive enough to have spotted the last several losers she'd dated. Evidence enough that her poor instincts concerning men hadn't changed—which was why all the good vibes she felt around Riley concerned her, confused her. What was she missing? Why did the idea of rushing forward in their relationship feel so right—and so wrong—at the same time?

His reluctance to discuss his family plucked at her, stirred a queasy feeling deep inside. She knew she'd stumbled across something important, something that had changed his life, his attitude, his character.

Before she could trust her heart to this man, he had to open up to her. She had to find out what that something was. And how it shaped the man Riley had become.

Chapter 5

As the credits rolled at the end of the John Wayne movie, Riley glanced over at Ginny, who'd been asleep for the last twenty minutes. She'd snuggled down in the throw pillows and stretched her legs across his lap.

He shook his head at the contradiction that was Ginny. She might look fragile and vulnerable in sleep, but he was quickly learning how tough, how perceptive and hard-hitting she could be when awake.

Her questions about his family had been normal fare for a new relationship. But she hadn't been satisfied with his dodgeball answers the way other women had. He might have changed the subject tonight, but she wouldn't let the issue rest for long. He'd seen that much in her keen gaze.

She'd caught him off-guard. One minute they'd been sharing a kiss that had rocked him to his core, and the next she'd zapped him with questions on his least favorite subject. His defenses had been down, his reactions unguarded—a critical mistake he should never have let happen. He knew she'd seen straight through his paper-thin answers.

He closed his own eyes and leaned his head back against the couch. If he were smart, he'd get up now and walk out. Leave her apartment, leave the relationship, leave the risk of having his shameful history uprooted and dissected.

But one glance at Ginny changed his mind. He was mesmerized by her delicate face, and duty-bound to protect her from the madman who had tried twice to kill her. Leaving Erin alone, when he knew she could be at risk, had proved a tragic error. A mistake he'd be damned if he'd repeat with Ginny.

But unlike with Erin, Riley felt inexorably drawn to Ginny by a magnetic attraction that tugged him from deep in his soul. He could no more walk away from her than he could walk away from his past. Which meant he had a precarious balancing act to perform. Protect Ginny and also protect the truth about his family history, his failures. Keep Ginny safe but also keep his heart safe. A difficult task, considering the spunky, gorgeous woman had already gotten under his skin.

Riley shook Ginny's shoulder lightly. "Hey, sleeping beauty, movie's over."

She roused a bit and peeked up at him through half-lidded eyes. "Sorry. I didn't mean to doze off on you."

"No problem." He stoked her cheek with his fingers. "Maybe you should go on to bed."

"You comin' with me?" She gave him a drowsy grin that was pure seduction. Her voice still held a hint of the enticing smoke-induced rasp that tickled his spine and made his every nerve ending spark.

"You want me to?"

She stretched like a cat, pulling her T-shirt taut across her feminine curves. "Oh, yeah. I want you to."

Heat slammed him in the belly and spread through his body like a backdraft. He arched one eyebrow.

"But…" she added "…not tonight. Not yet. I barely know

you. And like I told you earlier, I'm not the kind of girl who'll sleep with a guy just because he fixed my dishwasher."

Riley released the breath that had snagged in his lungs when she'd stretched her lithe body. "I totally respect that."

But his body still hummed and sang.

Not yet.

But one day. The electricity that crackled between them was too strong to be denied for long. Anticipation danced through his veins.

"In that case, you're on my bed." He scooped her legs off his lap, and in one smooth motion, he stood and slid his other arm behind her back. She gasped and clutched his shirt as he lifted her into his arms.

"My arm is broken, not my legs. I can walk to my bedroom."

He landed a resounding kiss on her lips. "Humor me."

She opened her mouth again, as if to protest, but reconsidered. She twisted her lips in a moue of resignation.

He carried her down the short hall to her bedroom and laid her down on the flowery comforter. Her walls were a pastel shade of purple, and everything from the curtains to the dried flower wreath over her bed incorporated tones of violet and cream and dark green. The room was a seamless blend of femininity and bold strength, just like the woman who slept in it.

As she pulled back the covers and cuddled down for the night, he sat on the edge of the bed.

"I have to work tomorrow. I need to be at the fire station by seven, but I promised your mom I'd stay here tonight. So if you need anything before six in the morning, I'll be on the couch."

She sighed. "And thus commences the babysitting portion of the evening."

He shrugged. "Call it what you want. But I promised your mom I'd stay, and I'm a man of my word."

"Heroic *and* dependable. Your résumé is growing." Ginny sat up and met his gaze evenly, tenderness softening her face.

As before, the respect and admiration warming her eyes made tension zing through his muscles and triggered the doubt demons inside him. He worked to keep his expression neutral, to reveal nothing of the warring emotions that clawed at his gut in the wake of her misplaced hero-worship. What would she think if she knew the truth about him and his past failures? He hoped he never found out.

When he didn't respond for several seconds, she tipped her head, and an inquisitive pucker wrinkled her brow. "Riley, did I say something wrong?"

He forced a laugh. "No. I just find it ironic that while you're praising me for being so noble and admirable, I'm sitting here fighting the urge to ravish you."

She gave him a crooked smile and slid her good arm around his neck. "But you are fighting the urge, so once again, you've shown you are noble."

Her baby powder scent teased his nose, and the press of her soft body against his chest tested his willpower.

"Noble shmoble," he growled, a wicked grin tugging his mouth. He ducked his head to capture her lips and sank his fingers into the silky hair at her nape. Holding her close, he showed her with his kiss just how easily he could toss aside polite chivalry when he wanted.

She resisted for a moment then, with a contented sigh, responded with the same fervor and recklessness. Teeth clicked and tongues dueled. He drank in all she offered and still needed more.

He fell back with her onto her bed, cautious only with her casted arm. She wiggled beneath him, encouraging him with her mewls of pleasure. The seductive sound of her sighs fueled the flames scorching his body. Only when he was breathless did he break the kiss to gasp for air.

Her own panting breaths fanned his skin as he gazed at her from scant inches above. Hunger and heat filled her cerulean eyes, inviting him to take more.

Resting his forehead against hers, he closed his eyes and sighed. "Not yet."

After a moment, he felt her nod. "Not yet."

He raised his head, slid off her. "But soon."

She smiled and drew a deep breath. "Yeah, soon."

When he shoved himself to his feet, her gaze darted to the telltale ridge at his fly. Her lopsided grin returned. "Definitely noble."

He grunted and finger-combed his mussed hair. His powerful desire for her was a dangerous thing. When he held Ginny, when he kissed her, he lost a little piece of himself to her.

As his connection to her grew stronger, protecting his heart, protecting his past got harder. And protecting Ginny became more urgent. Not just from Walt Compton, but from himself. Their relationship, for all its heat and magnetism, could so easily end badly. Already he heard doubt and caution telling him to get out while he could.

Spare her feelings and save yourself the pain of another failure, the voice inside him screamed.

"Goodnight, 4A," Ginny murmured huskily.

As his internal battle raged in his head, he gave her a quick smile, turned off the lamp by her bed and backed out of the room. "G'night, 3C."

A low whisper roused Ginny the next morning before the sun was up. She opened her eyes a crack to find the source of the voice waking her.

Riley smiled down at her. "I'm leaving. I'll call you later, okay?"

She nodded, then peeked over at her bedside clock. Six-fifteen.

"Go back to sleep." He stroked her cheek and pressed a kiss to her forehead.

A sleepy, contented smile stole across her face. "Bye."

As she drifted back to sleep, though, the pleasant warmth

of Riley's morning kiss took a dark edge. Ginny's sleep-hazed brain began playing games with her emotions.

Riley had left. She was alone now. Her heart pattered a bit faster, and she scrunched deeper into the sheets.

Had he locked the door?

Biting her lip, she tossed back the covers and stumbled to the living room.

Yes, the door was locked. She wondered in passing how he'd managed to lock the dead bolt from the outside, but only shook her head and put on the chain guard before shuffling back to bed.

Nestled under the sheets, she dozed off once more. But her dreams of cuddling on the couch with Riley transformed to nightmares of him lashing out angrily. He shouted obscenities at her and backhanded her across the cheek.

She woke with a jolt to find her phone trilling harshly.

Ginny gulped a deep breath to squash the hurt and resentment her dream left bubbling inside her. She checked the caller ID, then, reluctantly, answered the phone. "I'm fine, Mom."

"Good morning to you, too. How are you feeling?"

"Groggy. You woke me up. It *is* the weekend, you know."

"Oh. Sorry, hon. Did Riley stay like he promised?"

"Yes, Mom."

"On the couch?"

Ginny rolled her eyes. "Actually, no. He slept with me, and we had wild monkey sex all night. That's why I'm so tired." There was a pause, and Ginny could picture her mother trying to decide if her daughter was being sarcastic or not. She couldn't resist adding one last shot. "Oh, and we used up all the condoms I had on hand, so if you're coming over later, will you buy me a new box? Economy-size pack."

Her mother huffed. "Point taken. You don't need to be a smart aleck. I only ask because…well, he promised to stay on your couch, and he seems like the kind of man who keeps his promises and…I guess I just wanted to confirm my feeling that your Riley is as nice a man as he appeared. Reliable, you know."

A strange swirling started in Ginny's stomach as her bad dream rushed back to her.

"He's not *my* Riley. And appearances can be deceiving, Mom. Lots of people can make a good first impression, then—"

"What did he do?" her mother asked, her voice an octave higher.

Ginny sat up and raked the hair out of her eyes. "Nothing, Mom. I didn't mean Riley. Just…in general."

"Gin, you're such a pessimist. Why do you believe the worst of people instead of giving them the benefit of the doubt?"

"Hazard of my job, I guess. I see the worst people can do to each other, and it makes me…" *Sad. Scared.* "Cautious."

"Nothing wrong with caution in this day and age. Just don't become jaded. Is Riley still asleep? I wanted to thank him again for watching out for you last night."

"He had to leave. For work."

"You're *alone?*" Her mother sounded aghast.

"No. I have Zach. And the patrolman in the parking lot. And about four different locks on my door, which should be more than enough to stop an intruder."

"Someone should be with you."

"Megan is coming in a little while," Ginny lied and winced, waiting for the bolt of lightning to crash through her ceiling. But she didn't have the patience or energy to deal with her mother today.

"Well, all right. Tell Megan I said hello. I'll call later to check on you."

Riley had promised the same this morning. And then he'd kissed her goodbye. A chaste, tender kiss. The kind she remembered her dad giving her before she left for school as a kid. The memory brought a smile to her lips. Along with a mental image of Riley pressing kisses to their children's foreheads before they marched off to the school bus.

Disgruntled with herself, she shook her head and blew

her bangs out of her eyes. *That* fantasy was more than a little premature.

After hanging up with her mom, Ginny rolled to her side and let her thoughts drift to the strange twist her dream had taken. Riley as an abuser. A chill chased down her spine. What was *that* about?

Considering how many horror stories she heard every day from her clients, was it any surprise her brain had taken this dark path? Especially since one of the abusive men had turned his violence against her?

Zachary hopped up on the bed and trotted up to her. *If you're awake, then why aren't you getting up to feed me?* his gold-eyed stare asked.

Sighing, Ginny tossed back the covers and gave up the hope of sleeping late. She made her way to the kitchen and fumbled left-handed to feed the cat and prepare his insulin shot. She managed to poke her own finger as she tried to recap the syringe for disposal. Grumbling to herself over the handicap of her broken arm, she grabbed a cereal bar out of the pantry and ripped it open with her teeth.

When her phone rang again, Lagniappe Fire Department showed on her caller ID. A sweet pleasure flowed through her blood, and she grinned as she answered. "Hi, hot stuff. How's the fire biz?"

"Hi yourself, gorgeous. Pretty quiet this morning. How about there?"

"My mom called. I asked her, if she was coming over, to buy more condoms to replace the ones you and I used up last night."

Riley made a strangled sort of choking sound. "You told her *what?*"

Ginny chuckled. "Easy, fireman. She knew I was joking… I think. But she *may* show up here later with an economy-size box."

"Wow. I just…don't even know what to do with that." Humor laced his tone.

"Question for ya?"

"Shoot."

"How did you lock my dead bolt?"

"I found an extra key hanging on a nail in your cabinet. I'll bring it back tomorrow when I get off."

Ginny opened her cabinet. Sure enough, her spare key was missing. The odd flutter of uneasiness stirred inside her again. Not that she was exactly worried about Riley having the key, but…

A loud alarm sounded through the phone.

"Hell, that's a call. I gotta go."

Ginny's chest tightened as she remembered the terror of the women's center fire. Riley faced that sort of danger every day on the job. "Be careful," she croaked, worry clogging her throat.

She got no response. He was already gone.

She spent the next few minutes puttering around the kitchen, trying not to think about Riley going to a dangerous fire scene. She knew he was well-trained, wore protective gear and had the other firemen looking out for him, but…she couldn't squash the niggling anxiety. How did the families of firefighters do this every day?

After washing her countertop for the third time, she tossed the washrag in the sink with a grunt. Maybe a hot shower would relax her. She stripped her T-shirt over her head then wiggled out of her sleep pants and underwear. She was in the middle of trying to arrange a plastic bag over her cast and seal it off when her phone rang again. She jerked the bag off and snatched up the phone.

"Riley?" she asked, hope surging.

"Tell me what I have to do to get my wife back. I'll do anything." The male voice was gruff and full of emotion.

On the heels of her disappointment that the call wasn't from Riley, it took Ginny a couple beats to realize who the caller had to be. "Mr. Compton, is that you?"

"Tell me where Annie is. Where my children are. We're a family, and we belong together."

Ginny's heart sped to a gallop. She sat down on the edge of her bed and pulled the sheet around her. Talking to the man who had tried to smother her a couple nights earlier was surreal and frightening. Her nakedness made her feel all the more vulnerable. She started to hang up the phone, then hesitated.

What if she could glean some hint of where he was hiding, convince him to surrender, get some morsel of information that would help end the standoff?

Drawing a fortifying breath, she put the phone back to her ear. "You know I can't tell you where they are. I have to protect them. You've proved yourself a danger to them."

"No, I won't hurt them. Ever again. I love Annie. I love my kids."

"Where are you, Walt? Where are you staying?"

"Please, just…tell me how to get them back." His voice cracked, and Ginny's stomach turned.

She'd heard this sort of emotional plea too many times before and was immune to the manipulation. Still, on the off chance the man was serious about changing and righting his wrongs, she said, "If you really want to prove you've mended your ways, you need to turn yourself in to the police."

"Never," he growled. The fury in his tone, the radical change in his manner sent a chill up her spine. "The cops will never find me."

Ginny gritted her teeth. "Then I can't help you."

"Listen, bitch! This is your fault!" he snarled. "Tell me where Annie is *now* or you won't like the way I get you to talk. I can make you hurt. I'll make you suffer!"

Bile rose in Ginny's throat. She slammed the phone down, jerking her hand away as if his acerbic words scorched her fingers.

Pressing a hand over her racing heart, she took several gulping breaths before she could calm herself enough to think straight.

Hand shaking, she first checked the caller ID. It listed a number identified only as Pay Phone.

Not much help there. Unless…

Could the police trace the source of the call? Maybe.

She found the business card Detective Rogers, the officer in charge of her case, had left with her yesterday and dialed his cell phone. When he answered, she related the details of the call from Walt Compton.

Rogers promised to get the phone company to start checking their records for the number. Ginny thanked the detective and reconsidered her shower. She'd seen *Psycho* a few too many times to shake the jitters still dancing through her. She considered going over to her parents' house to shower and spend the afternoon. Or calling Megan to come over under the guise of having brunch together. But Ginny dismissed each of these options quickly. Depending on anyone else to make her feel safe was a cop-out. She had a police guard in the parking lot and locks on her door. She would be fine.

And she would not rely on anyone else to protect her, not when she taught her clients to find their inner strength and independence. She'd handle Walt Compton's threats on her own.

Mustering her nerve, she pulled the plastic bag back over her cast and headed to the bathroom.

She refused to let Walt's scare tactics mess with her head.

Monday morning, as Ginny headed out of her apartment building for work, she met Riley coming home from his twenty-four hour shift at the fire station. Her pulse did a Louisiana two-step when she spotted him walking in from the parking lot. When he entered the lobby area, letting in the brisk November chill, the shiver that raced over her skin wasn't entirely due to the cool draft. He wore a suede bomber jacket unzipped over a navy Lagniappe Fire Department T-shirt that hugged his broad chest. His tawny hair was still damp, as if he'd showered just moments before he drove home, and the crisp soap scent that clung to him echoed that assessment.

"Morning, 3C. Where you off to?" His eyes and his smile both warmed when he greeted her.

She moved close enough to slide a hand inside his jacket and give his chest a playful pat. "Well, it *is* Monday, hot stuff. Most of us civilians have regular eight-to-five business hours."

His smile dimmed. "You're working today? What happened to giving yourself time to rest and recuperate?"

She shrugged. "I rested all weekend. Besides, I have people that need me on the job, people I'm responsible for. And tons of paperwork to catch up on. Plus files that were lost in the fire to reconstruct, boxes of salvaged stuff from the office to sort through, info that has to be reentered into the computer—"

He laid a finger across her lips to silence her, but the heat from his intimate touch quieted her more than the gesture did. Breath snagged in her lungs, and her thoughts rushed back to the kiss they'd shared Saturday night. A kiss that so easily could have led to much more. She'd lost control, allowed the powerful attraction that crackled between them to sweep her up. In the heat and passion of the moment, she'd shown little willpower and poor judgment, both unforgivable. She'd spent most of Sunday alternately reliving the mind-blowing kisses, then castigating herself for being so weak-willed.

Most men she knew would have acted on that chemistry, would have sweet-talked her and pushed her for sex. And if she'd given in, she'd have woken the next morning feeling used and even more disappointed in herself.

But Riley had shown restraint when she'd lost her head. Had treated her with courtesy and respect. In hindsight, that consideration should have warmed and soothed her. Instead, it left her feeling a bit off-balance.

She prided herself on being able to read people, knowing why they acted as they did. Yet things with Riley didn't add up the way she expected…and she didn't like it. The unknowns about people were what could turn around and bite you on the butt.

"You want me to drive you?" Riley asked.

Ginny blinked. Case in point—she'd expected him to argue her need to stay home longer to recover, not offer to drive her to work.

She shook off the uneasy rustle of butterfly wings stirring inside her. "Naw, I think I can manage. Thanks."

"So where are you working from? I could take you to lunch."

"They found an empty corner in the basement of the parish courthouse. We'll be crowded, but we'll have everything we need. I just worry the ladies will be intimidated by the setting and won't feel comfortable coming to us there."

Riley quirked his mouth and nodded in agreement. "I can understand that."

Curling his hand around her shoulder, he shifted closer to her, pitched his voice to an intimate murmur. "So…about noon? I'll meet you on the front steps of the courthouse."

"Sure. Noon it is." She grinned, then rose on her toes to give him a quick kiss.

Riley had other ideas. He snaked his arm around her waist and pulled her flush against his body. He waited long enough to greet Mr. Hanniky in 1A as he stepped out of his apartment to retrieve his newspaper. Then Riley gave Ginny a kiss that she knew would stay with her through the morning. Deep and sweet and toe-curling.

She needed a few seconds after he broke the kiss to regain her equilibrium. "Wow. You're better than a cup of strong java for getting the blood pumping in the morning."

His answering grin was sexy and smug.

Ginny tore herself from his grasp and backed toward the door, her heart thumping a wild cadence. "I—I'm gonna be late. See you at lunch."

He winked and turned to head down the corridor to his apartment.

Ginny watched him walk away. His loose-limbed amble, which had mesmerized her before now, left her feeling unsteady, confused.

What was wrong with her? She couldn't continue to let her runaway attraction to him muddle her thoughts and skew her reasoning. She had to remain as clear-minded and objective as possible until she had a better picture of what lay beneath the surface of Riley Sinclair.

Even if he seemed to be everything she wanted, everything she'd been looking for, experience had taught her that surprises could come from out of the blue. She still had so much to learn about Riley. Yet the prospect unnerved her. The more time she spent with him the more uneasy she became, as if waiting for an inevitable disaster. What was she missing about him? No one was as perfect as he seemed.

Shoving past the lobby door into the nip of late autumn, Ginny mulled over the contradictory emotions swirling through her. She was accustomed to helping other people sort out their feelings. Unraveling and interpreting her own crazy reaction to Riley was nowhere near as simple. And that murkiness was as upsetting as anything else. She didn't like the sense that any part of her life was out of her control or beyond her understanding.

Discourse and analysis were her strong suit. Perhaps at lunch she could have an overdue heart-to-heart discussion with Riley and sort through her topsy-turvy emotions. Time had come to get to know the true soul of the man she was falling for. A smoldering chemistry just wasn't enough to warrant risking her heart.

Chapter 6

Riley was waiting on the courthouse steps by the time Ginny got off the phone with an especially distraught client. She was about to sneak up behind him and surprise him when an attractive brunette in a colorful business suit approached him and wrapped him in an affectionate hug. His face lit up when he greeted her, and he kissed her cheek.

Ginny hesitated, hanging back to watch the exchange. She refused to admit the pinch in her chest could be jealousy. Like she'd told her mother, Riley didn't belong to her.

Yet a quiet voice prodded her. *Be honest. You want him to be yours.*

But only if…

The conditional phrase that popped into her head unbidden startled her. Only if what?

She didn't get a chance to think the question through before Riley spotted her and waved her over. Ginny fixed a friendly smile on her face and walked down the stairs to meet him and the mysterious brunette.

"Ginny, this is Libby Walters. Her husband, Cal, has been a good friend of mine since our days at the fire academy. He was with me when we pulled you out of the women's center fire the other day."

Ginny used her left hand to shake Libby's hand, and they exchanged cordial greetings.

Libby motioned to her cast. "I'm glad that was the worst of your injuries. Cal said the fire was pretty bad, and you almost died. Thank heavens you're okay."

Ginny gave her a polite smile. "Because of Riley and your husband."

Riley cleared his throat and changed the subject. "Libby works here. She's an assistant D.A." He slipped a possessive arm around Ginny's waist. "That's in addition to being a mom. Cal's daughter, Ally, is five, and they have a new baby, Sara, who is…" He glanced to Libby to fill in the blank.

"Four months." The motherly pride and sheer bliss beaming in Libby's smile caused another pluck of unrest in Ginny, though she couldn't say why this woman's happiness unsettled her.

Echoes of the anguished woman she'd been counseling over the phone minutes before whispered in her head. Pushing the disturbing conversation aside, she mustered a smile. "Sounds like you have your hands full. My friend Megan just got married and is learning to balance motherhood and a full-time teaching job. Her five-year-old stepdaughter has bound-less energy and a reputation for her adventurous nature."

Libby nodded. "It's tiring, but I wouldn't trade my kids for all the world. Well, Riley says you're headed to lunch. Don't let me keep you."

After saying their goodbyes, Riley escorted Ginny to the street, where he'd parked his truck. As they drove to a nearby deli, she used the conversation with Libby as a launching pad for the discussion she wanted with Riley.

"So do you see yourself married with children in the future?"

He pursed his lips and raised his fingers from the steering wheel in an offhand gesture. "I suppose. Someday maybe."

His casual answer niggled at her unsatisfactorily. She tipped her head. "Is it something you *want* or just something you're resigned to as standard procedure?"

He raised one eyebrow. "Pretty heavy question for our first date."

"I thought Saturday night was our first date. Pizza and John Wayne. Remember?"

He grinned. "I thought you considered that glorified babysitting."

"And you haven't answered my question."

Riley gave an uncomfortable chuckle as he pulled into a parking space in front of the deli. "Can we save the third degree until I've had some lunch? I'm starved."

More avoidance and dodging. Ginny frowned as he got out. She opened her own door and slid down before he could make it around the front bumper to help her.

Once they placed their orders, she followed him to a small table for two by the front window. As they settled in, Ginny distributed the napkins and straws she'd picked up for them.

Riley tapped his straw out of the paper wrapper and poked it into his drink. "So Libby was inviting me to join their family a week from Saturday at the city park for a cookout. They're going to grill burgers. Wanna come with?"

Ginny smiled. "Sounds fun."

"Why don't you see if Megan and her husband want to come."

"You sure we wouldn't be imposing?"

"Not at all. Megan's stepdaughter is the same age as Ally. I bet they'd have fun playing together."

She nodded. "All right, I will. Caitlyn doesn't have many kids her age in the neighborhood. I bet she'd love to meet a friend her age."

"Great. I'll call Cal later to let him know and see what we can bring."

Their sandwiches arrived, and Ginny used the moment to form her next question, determined not to let Riley evade topics she felt were important for getting to know him.

"So…the marriage and kids question. What you want or just fulfilling an expectation of society?"

He sighed, his brow wrinkling. "You don't give up, do you?"

"Not easily."

He delayed by taking a bite of his club sandwich and chewing slowly. She waited patiently, as she did with her clients, her steady, expectant gaze telling him she was listening when he was ready to answer.

"When I find the right woman, I guess I'll want to marry. Right now, it's just a notion. A someday possibility that I've given only a little thought to." He waved his sandwich as if to say, *There. I answered.*

"Why not?"

Riley scowled. "Why not what?"

"Why haven't you thought about marriage much?"

He shrugged. "I just haven't."

She dragged a French fry through a blob of ketchup. "I know you said your dad died, but what was your parents' marriage like when you were younger? Were they happy?"

He shifted in his seat and avoided her gaze, both sure signs he was uncomfortable with the topic. "I don't know. I guess."

"Do you consider them role models? Would you want to emulate the relationship they had?"

He raised his eyebrows and shook his head. "Why are we talking about this? Where is 3C? I want to have lunch with her. Counselor Ginny asks too many questions." He smiled, but she read the uneasiness in his eyes.

"Why does talking about your family bother you so badly? So much of who we are is formed in our childhood, in the way we were raised, in our family dynamic. I just want to get to know you."

"I'm…a firefighter."

"That's what you do, not who you are."

He sighed. "It's all that matters at this point."

She shook her head. "I want to know more than that."

"Okay…I graduated from LSU, then joined the fire academy a month later. I like football, German beer, movies where things blow up, and…" He paused as he searched for another *like* to add to his laundry list.

"And John Wayne," she finished for him.

He aimed a finger-and-thumb gun at her. "Yes. See, you do know me."

"I could say the same about my brother Billy. That's all guy stuff. I want to know the Riley-specific stuff." She poked at her pickle spear, but frustration with their conversation squelched her appetite. "What makes you tick? What's in your heart and soul? Who are you deep inside?"

"This is definitely, oh…eighth or ninth date material, at least. Are you sure we should go there?" He pulled his lips in a lopsided grin that didn't reach his eyes.

Ginny frowned at her plate. "I'm sorry. I don't mean to push. I…well, it's important to me. I know I'm attracted to you and vice versa. I just want to know what I'm getting into before we take this any further."

When she glanced up, his eyes were a dark gray. His jaw tightened, and he drew a deep breath. "Why do we have to know more than the basics right now? That's what dating is for. We're attracted, so we go out or watch a movie together at your place. Little by little, we learn each other's likes and dislikes. We see if we click on more than a physical level. Nothing high pressure. No exploratory surgery on our second date. That's what I'm looking for. Those are my terms."

"Your *terms?*" Though his tone was friendly and non-threatening, his word choice sent a prickle down Ginny's back. Was he drawing a line in the sand?

He knitted his brow in thought. "Maybe that word is a bit of overkill, but I know what kind of relationship works for me and where I've gone wrong in the past. I don't want to make the same mistakes."

Ginny sat forward, her eyes fixed on his. Maybe he was going to give her some insight, after all. "What mistakes have you made in the past?"

He frowned. "We'd need longer than your lunch hour to get into *that.*" His expression softened with a charming grin. "So the Saints pulled out a miracle win last night. Did you watch the game? You a Saints fan?"

Her spirits sagged, and she scowled at him for changing the subject. But she let the diversion stand. She'd put enough of a damper on their lunch without pressing the issue any further. When counseling, she could only push so hard before her clients would balk and withdraw in self-defense. The key to making breakthroughs was pushing a little then backing off, giving them space to think and learn to trust her. Slowly she got the women to open up to her. Only then could she help them start the healing process.

Riley would trust her, open up to her more in time. She hoped.

To be fair, she hadn't shared much of her own life, her own history with him. She reached across the table and laced her fingers with his. "How about a trade-off? I tell you, 'Yes, I'm a lifelong Saints fan,' then move on to something deeper. Like…'My parents have been married for thirty-one years. Their home has always been full of love and warmth and laughter. They were great role models as parents and as an example of a marriage that worked. They had their disagreements, but they fought fair.'"

Riley was listening, his gaze locked on hers, an expression of genuine interest and tenderness softening the tension that had held him earlier.

Encouraged, she continued. "There was never any violence or manipulation between my parents, and they always let the other speak their mind, have an opinion, even if it differed from their own."

Riley lifted his eyebrows. "Sounds pretty near perfect."

"Yeah. Pretty close. I was really lucky. My parents raised us to be confident, capable adults by allowing us the freedom to make our own mistakes, while providing clear parameters and using their parental authority enough to make us feel safe. When my mom dotes on me, I know it is because she loves me. It still drives me crazy…."

Ginny grinned and rolled her eyes. "But Mom isn't the only one who tends to smother me. My dad can be just as bad in his own way. And growing up with two brothers made dating hell. Matt, the brother that's in college, used to give my boy-friends such grief." She chuckled. "You're lucky he's in Baton Rouge."

Riley tipped her a crooked smile that shot pure sunshine to her heart. "I can handle him."

She propped her chin on her left hand. "I'm sure you can. You'll probably meet him in a couple weeks, when he's home for Thanksgiving."

Riley's smile dimmed. "I need to be with my mom at Thanksgiving. She's alone now and…"

Ginny nodded. "I understand. But Matt will be home for about five days. I'm sure you'll catch him at some point."

Riley checked his watch. "It's getting late. I'd better get you back to your office before you turn into a pumpkin." He winked and took her plate. "You finished with this?"

"Sure." She sat back in her chair and watched him carry their trash to the garbage bin. He held up his hands to her, then hitched his head toward the men's restroom.

She nodded and sat back to wait while he washed up. Her gaze drifted to the pedestrians walking along the busy down-town street. A mother pushed a stroller by the deli window, and Ginny smiled at the tiny pink face of her toddler.

Riley's determination not to tell her more about his family or his father's death nagged at her. She tried to imagine what her life would have been like if her father had died, and she shuddered at the thought. It was too painful to consider for long. Riley had had a load of grief to deal with at a young age. No wonder it was difficult to talk about his past. But he also had buried emotions, suppressed pain he needed to come to terms with. She could see that truth in his quicksilver eyes. The question was, what more was he hiding behind his shuttered gaze?

Lost in thought, she automatically scanned the people and cars crowding the street, until she glimpsed a man with red hair standing near the bus stop across the street. He was staring straight at her.

Ginny's pulse lurched, and she sat forward in her chair, craning her head to try to get a better view around the bustling pedestrians and traffic on the street. A city bus arrived at the stop and obscured her view.

Ginny growled under her breath in frustration. She had to know if the man she'd seen was Walt Compton or a figment of her imagination.

Shoving her chair back, she hurried to the door of the restaurant and out to the sidewalk. The bus still blocked her view, and the flow of traffic made it impossible to cross the street at that moment.

She glanced up and down the street again, just to be sure she hadn't missed the man leaving the bus stop. Could she even be certain she'd recognize Walt? She'd only seen him twice. The first time had been at a distance, at the women's center before the fire. The next time had been a brief look in the dim light of her hospital room.

With a rumble and a puff of diesel exhaust, the bus pulled away, and Ginny searched the area around the stop. Only a pair of teenaged girls now stood by the small shelter.

Disappointment landed in her stomach like a rock. Her head still buzzed from the adrenaline that had jolted her system. If only she could be sure the man she'd seen was Annie's husband.

"There you are. Not thinking of ditching me, were you?" Riley's mouth quirked with humor.

"I thought I saw Walt Compton." She aimed a finger at the bus stop. "He was standing over there."

Riley's brow furrowed as he swept a glance up and down the city street. "Are you sure it was him?"

"Not one hundred percent. I noticed him because he had red hair. And because he was staring at me." She sighed. "Red hair is rare enough in men to make it plausible it was him, but…"

"Have you called the police yet?"

"No. I can't be sure it was him, and I don't want to sound like the boy who cried wolf, having them chasing after figments of my imagination. Besides, he must have gotten on the bus that was just here. He's long gone now."

Riley nodded toward his truck. "We could follow the bus. We could still track it down."

"Do you know how many city buses are milling around just in a five-block radius? How are we supposed to know which one he's on?" As if to prove her point, another bus chugged up to the stop across the street with a hiss of hydraulics.

"Maybe so. I still think you should report the incident." Riley unclipped the cell phone at his hip and held it out to her.

She waved the phone away. "I have Detective Rogers's business card at home. I'll call him this evening and tell him what happened."

Riley's expression was grim. "I don't like it. If this guy is following you—"

"We don't know that he is. The man I saw could have been anyone." She flipped her wrist to check her watch. "Right now I need to get back to work. I'm supposed to go see Annie and her kids at the shelter this afternoon. I'll ask her if she has a recent picture of Walt with her or knows where we can get one. I really need a better sense of who I'm supposed to be on the lookout for. I'd hate to hassle an innocent man just because he has red hair."

A muscle jumped in Riley's cheek. "Let me take you out to the shelter. Just in case Compton *is* following you."

Ginny shook her head. "Can't. The location of the shelter is secret. Has to be. For the women's safety."

Riley turned his hands up, his face the image of innocence. "I'm not a threat to anyone."

Ginny smiled. "Rules are rules. I can't tell you where the shelter is. I'll have Helen, one of our new counselors, ride out with me. We'll take her car and drive a circuitous route." She crossed her heart and held up three fingers. "Promise. I know how to watch and make sure I'm not followed."

Pressing his lips in a hard line, Riley stepped off the curb and opened the passenger door for her. "Just be careful. I don't like the idea of this guy being on the loose, knowing that he's gunning for you."

Ginny's lunch flip-flopped in her stomach. "Believe me. I'm not thrilled about it, either. But I know how to look after myself. I'll be okay."

He regarded her with a skeptical glance, then rounded the truck to the driver's side. As he climbed behind the wheel, he said, "Stop by my apartment before you go home tonight. I want to be the first one in your place this evening. Just in case."

She gave him a withering glance. "Not necessary."

He aimed his ignition key at her. "Do it, or I'll use the spare key I found in your cabinet to camp out in your apartment this afternoon."

She blew the bangs out of her eyes as she fastened her seat belt. "Unnecessary."

Riley smirked and cranked the engine. "But effective. What can I say? I care."

His words and the warmth of his smile stirred the same strange mix of longing and apprehension that she'd experienced so many times since Saturday night.

His kindness, his concern touched her, but her wild attraction to him also rang warning bells. Falling for his charms and his sexy smile would be so easy. She had to use her head around Riley and keep control over her heart.

As they drove back toward the courthouse, Ginny considered telling him about the call she'd gotten from Compton Sunday morning, but decided against it. Riley knew the threat against her and had already assumed the role of her personal guardian. A role that chafed her need for independence, while also making her feel more secure. Though she was grateful to Riley for his interest in looking out for her, she also didn't want to become dependent on him for her security and peace of mind. Her life, her safety was her own responsibility.

She frowned, realizing this was just another paradox where her handsome neighbor was concerned, and the ambiguity of her emotions nettled her.

With so much else in her life out of control at the moment, she needed to be certain about the direction of her relationship with Riley. So far, she didn't even have that.

"This is the most recent picture I have of him," Annie said, pulling a photo from her wallet. "I gave our last family photo to the police, but you can keep that one for now."

Sitting in the living room of the women's shelter, Ginny looked down at the handsome soldier in the military photo. She could easily see why Annie had been attracted to Walt when she met him. His broad shoulders, square jaw and firm mouth spoke of a firm resolve, and his dark eyes were hypnotic.

Ginny shivered. Appearances were deceiving.

Beneath his masculine good looks beat the heart of a cruel and violent man, a man who had intimidated, manipulated and beaten his wife.

Riley's handsome face flashed in Ginny's mind, and her stomach somersaulted. What mysteries lay beneath her neighbor's *GQ*-worthy appearance?

"In that picture, you can see where Haley gets her looks. She has his nose and mouth."

Ginny looked up when Annie spoke and offered a half smile. "But she got your freckles."

The dark-haired girl in question glanced up from playing dolls at their feet and grinned. "Mama calls my fweckles pixie dust."

Ginny laughed. "That they are!"

Annie closed her hand around Ginny's and pitched her voice lower. Her expression bore no humor. "Ginny, if Walt doesn't want to be found, the police won't find him. He was in the Special Forces. The military taught him to be invisible, to stay hidden. He trained to do covert reconnaissance, to survive with no supplies. He's smart and resourceful. If you saw him, it's because he wanted you to. He wanted to scare you, let you know he's watching you, following you. He wanted to intimidate you. Please be careful."

Ginny nodded. "I will. But you be careful, too. And if there is anything you think of, no matter how small, that you think will help the police locate Walt, call me. Anytime. If you need anything, phone. I'm here for you, Annie."

The woman nodded somberly. Glancing away, she twirled the strap of her purse around her finger. "I appreciate all you've done already. And the staff here. They've been so nice." She paused, sighed. "I know this is for the best. I couldn't let Haley grow up thinking it was okay for men to hit. Couldn't let Ben learn his father's bad habits." Annie stroked the peach fuzz on her infant son's head, and the baby gurgled and cooed. "It's just scary, not knowing where I'll go, what I'll do."

"The first step is to stay safe. We'll help you figure out the rest once Walt is off the street, where he can't hurt you." Ginny stood. "I have to get back to the office now, but I'll be in touch."

Annie rose and hugged her, and as she headed out, Ginny tousled Haley's hair. Every client was important to Ginny, but Annie and her small children claimed a special place in her heart. She wouldn't rest until she knew Walt was no longer a threat to his family. She could do no less for Annie.

"When he first tried to kiss me, I thought it was kinda nice. He was a good kisser, you know," Rose said. Ginny's newest client dabbed at her eyes.

From the hall outside her makeshift office in the basement of the courthouse, Ginny could hear the other members of the women's center staff leaving for the day. Several days had passed since she'd seen the red-haired man on the downtown street, and Ginny had not seen or heard anything else suspicious. But the idea of being alone in the office into the evening hours left her edgy.

And disappointed.

She had made plans to have dinner with Riley at his apartment and had been looking forward to the time alone with him.

Riley had worked his regular shift on Wednesday, as well as covering extra shifts Tuesday for a fellow firefighter whose son was home from school sick, and Thursday for a fire station across town that was short a man. Ginny had missed him these past four and a half days. More than she liked to admit.

"But then he started getting more aggressive," Rose continued, and Ginny refocused her attention on the young woman across from her. "He didn't listen when I said I wasn't ready to go further."

When Rose stopped to blow her nose, Ginny asked softly, "Did you say no? Were you clear in saying that you didn't want to have sex?"

Rose nodded. "I told him to stop. Over and over. I begged him. I was saving myself for the man I marry. But he didn't stop. He got angry and rough and…he hurt me."

Ginny's chest ached with sympathy for Rose, as it did every time a new client told her horrifying story. But listening to Rose, Ginny felt her stomach knot with anxiety as her brain conjured up a picture of Riley.

She thought of the kisses they'd shared. Riley was a good kisser, too. An excellent kisser. She couldn't imagine the man she knew turning violent, forcing himself on her.

But then…Rose hadn't expected as much from her boyfriend, either.

Donna hadn't expected as much from Jim Prather.

Annie hadn't expected it of Walt.

A chill skated down Ginny's neck.

"Afterward, he acted like it had been something I wanted, something we'd both wanted. He kept asking why I was so upset, why I was crying." Rose stared at nothing in particular, remembering and shaking.

Ginny sat forward to the edge of her chair and placed a hand on Rose's forearm. "If you said no, if he forced you to have sex against your will, it was rape. You did the right thing coming here. We can help you file charges against him and—"

Rose's head shot up, her eyes wild. "No, I can't do that! He'd be arrested. He'd…he'd never speak to me again. I'd lose him!"

Ginny blinked, stunned. And yet, sadly, not surprised by Rose's attitude, either. She'd heard the same devotion to scumbag boyfriends before, from other lonely, confused and hurting women. Ginny fought the twist of nausea in her stomach. She had to make Rose understand what was at stake, that she deserved better. "Rose, he raped you. Why would you want to stay with a man who would disregard your wishes, your welfare, your right to refusal? He hurt you. If you go back to him, it will happen again. If you don't turn him in to the police, he could go on to rape other women. He may have already raped other women."

The horror-stricken look on Rose's face wrenched Ginny's heart. She had her work cut out for her tonight. She would not leave until they had talked through all the ramifications of what had happened, what Rose needed to do to bring the man to justice and what medical care she needed to get. Ginny would set up regular counseling appointments for Rose until the young woman could sort through the turbulent emotions she faced and could appreciate and embrace her own self-worth. Rose needed her, and Ginny would stay until late into the night if necessary.

Steaks with Riley would have to wait.

No sooner had the thought sifted through her mind than a quick rap on her door reverberated through the office. The door opened, and Riley poked his head in the room. "Ready to roll?"

His gaze darted to Rose, and he winced. "Sorry. Didn't mean to interrupt. Helen told me to come on back."

At the sight of his golden hair, square jaw and warm gray eyes, Ginny felt her pulse flutter. "Rose, will you excuse me for just a moment?"

Rising from her chair, Ginny met Riley at the door and whispered, "I'm sorry. Something's come up that I need to handle. I'll be here pretty late, so I have to cancel. Maybe another night?"

Riley's face reflected his disappointment, but he nodded. "Sure. Tomorrow good for you?"

He reached up to run a finger along her cheek, and the light caress sent a delicious shiver through her.

"Probably. Depends on how things go tonight. I'll call you."

Riley cast a glance around the dim basement corridor. "Is anyone else staying late with you? I don't want you here alone."

When she took a deep breath to sigh tiredly, she caught the spicy scent of his aftershave, and another pang of regret for the spoiled plans jabbed her. "There's a guard on duty upstairs at the main entrance. We'll be okay."

"Not good enough. I'll wait out here for you."

She cocked her head and frowned. "Go home, Riley. I could be hours. You don't need to stay. I'll keep my office door locked." She crossed her heart. "Promise."

"Still, I—"

"Go home. I don't need a watchdog." She smiled and gave

him a wave. "Really. Go. Shoo." She took a step back, blew him a kiss, then closed her office door. Facing Rose, she said, "Sorry about that. Now…I wish you'd reconsider bringing charges. What he did to you was a crime…."

Hearing Ginny's office door open, Riley swung his legs down from the receptionist's desk where he had propped his feet and checked his watch. Almost 2:00 a.m. He dragged a hand over his bleary eyes and glanced toward the corridor, where he heard Ginny's and the other woman's voices.

"Get some rest," Ginny said as they rounded the corner to the reception area.

The woman with her glanced his way. And screamed.

Ginny gasped and clapped a hand to her chest.

The women's loud reaction jolted him from his groggy haze, as well.

"Riley! What are you doing here?" Ginny asked, her tone accusing.

Her client blinked and sent Ginny a nervous glance.

"Hi." Riley offered his hand to the skittish young woman. "Riley Sinclair. I'm Ginny's…"

He hesitated. What exactly were they?

"Neighbor," Ginny supplied as he said, "Boyfriend."

He gave her a subtle querying look when the young woman glanced away. Ginny responded with a scowl. "Why are you still here?"

"Because *you* still are."

"I told you to go home hours ago." She hiked her purse strap higher on her shoulder and frowned at him.

"And I chose to stay and make sure you two were safe instead." Riley walked around the receptionist's desk. "If you're ready," he said to Rose, whose eyes were wide and wary, "I'll walk you out to your car."

"O-okay." Ginny's client cast another uneasy glance his way.

"*I'll* see Rose to her car." Ginny started down the hall with a final stern glance at Riley. "You can go home."

Undeterred, he followed them to the elevator. "And after Rose leaves, who will walk *you* to your car?"

Ginny sighed, pivoted to face him and, taking him by the arm, pulled him a few steps away. "What are you doing? You know this babysitting mentality makes me nuts."

"Yeah, well, get over it."

Her spine stiffened, but he ignored her huff of indignation.

Riley shook his head. "There's no way I'm going to let you, or any woman I care about, work in an isolated courthouse basement, alone and unprotected, until 2:00 a.m. Or have you forgotten that Compton could be gunning for you?"

He saw the flicker of fear that Compton's name brought to her eyes, even if her posture remained stubbornly defensive.

The elevator bell dinged, but Ginny didn't move.

She took a deep breath and expelled it in a whoosh. "Look, Riley. I appreciate your concern, really. But I don't need a keeper. I don't want a keeper. Especially in matters that affect my job, my clients." She took a step closer and turned her back to the elevator, where Rose waited for her. Pitching her voice lower, she whispered, "The women I counsel have had nightmarish experiences with men. They don't need to find you lurking outside my office in the middle of the night when they don't expect it. You scared the beans out of Rose. That's not what she needs right now!"

Riley matched her quiet tone. "I'm sorry I startled her. But I won't apologize for trying to keep you safe. I have a duty to protect lives, and I take that duty even more seriously when it involves people I care about." He cupped a hand against her cheek and felt the shiver that chased through her. "I care about you, Gin. So you'd better get used to having me as your guardian."

Ginny squared her shoulders and took a step back from his touch. "I care about you, too, Riley. And I'd like to see more of you. But not at the expense of my privacy or my ability to do my job and look out for my clients' best interests. I need my space. I need my independence. I told you that from the start. Don't crowd me, Riley."

He clenched his teeth and shoved his hand in his pocket. "Looks like we're at a bit of an impasse."

"Looks like."

"Ginny?" Rose called. She held the elevator door open with her arm as it tried to close.

With a sigh, Ginny turned and stalked away.

Chapter 7

Riley said nothing else until they'd seen Rose safely to her car and on her way home. As he escorted Ginny across the shadowed courthouse parking lot, the cool autumn night reverberated with the stark silence between them and burrowed inside Riley with a chilling foreboding. His scalp prickled with a vague sense that they weren't alone, but when he scanned the area, he saw nothing.

When they reached her car, he caught her by the arm and turned her to face him. "What are we doing, Ginny? What have we got going between us?"

He brushed a flyaway wisp of her hair behind her ear. The security lights made the white-blond strands shine like silver. Her baby blues reflected the harsh halogen glow like diamonds.

In his chest, his heart gave a slow, tight throb. How had she gotten so deeply under his skin so quickly? And why did their current standoff frighten him so much?

"I thought we were onto something," he murmured. "I

know I feel a connection. I've never wanted a woman the way I want you. Are you telling me you don't feel that same heat between us? Am I really just another *neighbor* to you?"

The tension in her muscles eased, and the emotions in her face softened. "I don't know what we are, Riley. God knows, I'm attracted to you. And, yeah, someday, once we know each other better, I want to sleep with you."

His blood surged, and his nerves crackled in response to her admission. His gaze drifted to her lips. Memories of the taste of her kiss had teased him all day, and he was hungry for more of her.

"But a solid relationship has to be based on more than just sex," she continued.

He tamped his appetite for her kiss and cleared his throat. "Agreed."

She stepped closer and raised her hand to his chest, curling her fingers into his shirt. "I want to spend time with you, get to know you, explore the connection we have. But my life has been turned upside down thanks to Walt Compton. I'm confused right now. And…a little scared. About a lot of things. I need time to sort out what I feel, what I'm going to do."

Riley stroked a hand down her back, drawing her closer. "I understand that. But don't ask me to ignore my duty to protect you. The last time I did that—" A fist of emotion sneaked up to grab him by the throat. He gritted his teeth and swallowed. Shoved the gripping pain down again. He lowered his eyes from her sharp, intuitive gaze. "—I paid far too high of a price."

He blew out a cleansing breath and, closing his eyes, rested his forehead against hers. "Looking out for you is something I have to do. I *have* to."

What was it about this woman that had the power to resurrect everything he'd fought for years to bury? The idea of anything happening to Ginny scared him more and more with each passing day. She didn't want his help, his protection. So why was he forcing the issue? Why didn't he do as she asked and walk away while he could still salvage his sanity, his heart?

"Maybe we can find some kind of compromise." She slid her arms up around his neck, resting her cumbersome cast on one shoulder. With her other hand, she raked her fingers through the hair at his nape, and his skin felt electrified with sweet sensation.

"Such as?"

"You promise to give me the space I need to do my job, including anything that comes up concerning Annie and Walt Compton—"

He tensed and opened his mouth to argue, but she placed her fingers over his lips and plunged on.

"And I will promise to make more time to spend with you. I *want* more time to get to know you better. Time to explore this connection we feel…" She leaned into him, and the press of her body stoked the fires inside him.

As distracting as the sparkle in her eyes and the promise implied in her lopsided grin were, Riley couldn't agree to her demands. No way would he step back and let her handle Walt Compton without some level of protection.

You should have been here! I was counting on you! Didn't Jodi's death teach you anything? Echoes of Erin's cold rage from the night he'd failed to protect her blasted him with an icy regret, stinging guilt.

He refused to leave Ginny vulnerable. The cops were doing all they could, stationing a patrol car to watch her building and staking out Compton's usual haunts, but the police department had a whole city to protect. The officers had other murders, robberies and traffic accidents to handle on a shoestring budget and with limited personnel.

If Ginny was going to have the level of protection he felt she needed to keep her safe from Compton, Riley had to be able to guard her the way he saw fit, even if it stepped on her professional toes and crowded her need for autonomy. He couldn't, wouldn't neglect his responsibility to protect ever again. He'd lost too much in his life to forget the price of that mistake. But neither would he lie to her, make her think he was agreeing to her compromise.

Deflection, distraction was the tactic that had always served him best when he felt cornered—by his friends, by his mom, by Erin. He knew it wouldn't appease Ginny for long, but it might buy him more time to come up with a solution that worked for them both.

Sobering, he tightened his hold on her and pressed a soft kiss to the curve of her jaw. "I have to know you're safe, Ginny. I won't compromise on that."

She sighed lightly, and the tickle of her breath teased his senses.

"I am safe. I'm being careful." She angled her head to glance up at him.

Rather than argue the point, he placed nibbling kisses along her chin to the corner of her mouth. He'd spent much of the evening, as he waited for her to finish work, anticipating the chance to hold her, kiss her. "You taste good…so sweet."

"Riley, stop. I… It's hard to figure out—"

He interrupted her with a quick, butterfly kiss on her lips. "Yes?"

She pushed gently against his chest and stepped back. "It's just hard to think, to figure out what I need to do, when you kiss me like that. Don't get me wrong. I love your kisses, but this chemistry we have…it's confusing. It's distracting me from what I know I should do."

He pulled back far enough to meet her gaze. "So what are you saying?"

She hesitated, her mouth open like a fish but saying nothing. Finally, she wet her lips and shook her head. "It's after two in the morning. I've just spent a really wrenching eight hours with Rose, and I can barely see straight for fatigue. I don't know what I'm saying, and I'm far too tired to have this debate with you right now," she answered, her voice a husky whisper.

"Truce then?"

"Truce," she whispered, sagging wearily against him and closing her eyes.

"Just so long as we're straight on this point…" Pulling her against him, Riley dipped his head and captured her mouth. With firm pressure, he parted her lips with his tongue and swept the warm recesses beyond.

Her initial resistance melted in a heartbeat. She angled her head and moaned softly as he increased the gentle suction, imbibed the heady feminine taste of her. A gentle breeze stirred her baby powder scent, a feast for his senses.

He couldn't remember another woman's kiss ever pulling at him the way Ginny's did. The sexy duel of her tongue against his, the play of lips meshing and molding and the sizzle that raced through his veins were only a fraction of the pleasure her kiss brought him. Deep inside, a sweetness he'd never known swelled until it filled his chest with an almost painful longing.

He deepened the kiss, not fully understanding the need that drove him, made him want so much more than just the physical. More than passion, he wanted to claim her, to possess her. As if he could keep her safe, keep from losing her simply by branding her as *his* with his kiss. A cavemanlike sentiment, he knew. One she'd rebuff in a heartbeat.

Yet the haunting need clawed at him, nonetheless. And shook him to the marrow.

He sank his fingers into her silky hair and anchored her head between his palms as he gentled the kiss, soothing where he'd just ravaged.

His hand slid down her spine to cup her bottom and pull her hips more in line with his. He let his body's unmistakable condition speak for him.

"Yeah, I'd say we were in agreement on that point," he murmured against her lips.

He ducked his head to kiss her again but stopped when the eerie tingling sensation, the sense of being watched, chased over his skin again. Lifting his head, he squinted to see past the pool of light cast by the parking lot security lamps.

Searching the shadows, Riley swept his gaze around the dark courthouse lawn.

"What is it?" Ginny asked.

He frowned. "Nothing, I guess. Just realizing how little privacy we have here. Maybe we should save this for tomorrow night?"

Ginny glanced about them with a suspicious knit in her brow. "You're sure that's all? You didn't hear something?"

Riley ached an eyebrow. "Why? Did you?"

"I don't know. Maybe. But it could've been anything." She patted his chest and took a step back. "But you're right. I should head home now."

The chilly air that greeted him when she pulled out of his arms heightened the sense of danger that nipped at him.

While she unlocked her car door, Riley looked through her windows to check the backseat. He walked around to the rear, giving her Cherokee the once-over, wanting to satisfy himself that nothing was amiss.

And noted the odd angle at which the Jeep sat. When he circled to the passenger's side, he discovered why.

Returning to the driver's side, he caught Ginny's arm as she started to climb behind the steering wheel. "You have a flat."

Her forehead wrinkled. "What?"

"Other side. Up front. Flat as a pancake."

"Great. What did I do, pick up a nail?" She grunted in frustration. "I just bought these tires a month ago, too."

Without waiting for permission, he opened her back liftgate to take out the jack and wrench for unbolting the spare tire. He had her damaged tire off and the replacement on in a matter of minutes, but as he worked, he couldn't help wondering what she'd have done if he hadn't been there. The idea of her being stranded in the dark, abandoned parking lot at this late hour unsettled him.

Would she have struggled with her broken arm to change the tire herself, or would she have called him for help? Called a tow truck? Riley hated the idea of a stranger coming to her rescue, especially in the middle of the night.

Hated even more how vulnerable she'd have been if he hadn't been here.

Acid bit his gut.

Had that been the point? Had someone known she'd been working late and sabotaged her tire on purpose to strand her?

After tightening the last lug nut, Riley shoved himself to his feet and dusted the grit from the pavement off his hands. "That should do it. You're ready to roll."

"Thanks, fireman." She gave him a grateful grin. "Once again, you've saved the day."

As usual, his chest tightened following her unmerited praise. He dismissed it with a shrug, then hoisted the damaged tire into his arms. He wanted to take a closer look at it at home, in a better light. His instincts told him the damage had been caused by much more than a nail.

"You're going to follow me home, aren't you?" she asked, her tone more resigned than inquiring.

He gave her a tight nod. "Damn right."

He would even if he didn't live in the same building. He'd sensed something off from the time they'd reached the parking lot, and her flat tire only fueled his suspicions.

Hooking his arm through the tire to carry it, he stepped close to her and gave her one last resounding kiss. "Lock your car door. I'll be around in my truck in two minutes."

Riley hustled to the side street where he'd parked and loaded the tire in the truck bed with haste. He had no doubt that if he took even a few seconds longer than his promised two minutes to reach the courthouse parking lot, Ginny wouldn't be waiting.

* * *

"I took your tire down to the police department today." Riley worked beside Ginny in her kitchen the next night, preparing dinner.

She tossed the stem top of the carrot she was chopping for the salad into the trash and sent Riley a querying glance. "Why?"

"You didn't pick up a nail." He shook seasoning on their steaks, then met her gaze. "Your tire was cut. The gash was at least an inch long."

Her pulse stumbled. "It was sabotage?"

"That'd be my guess. And I think we both know who suspect number one is. The cops are looking for fingerprints or anything they can use to tie Compton to this latest incident."

Ginny continued chopping in silence, considering the ramifications.

"Other than just petty meanness, why would Walt slash my tire? What does he accomplish?" she wondered aloud.

"Think about it. You either would have been stuck changing the tire yourself, which with your broken arm could have taken quite awhile, or you'd have had to wait for someone to come change it for you. Either way, he delayed your leaving." Riley tightened his jaw, making the taut muscles in his cheek twitch. His gray eyes darkened to the color of storm clouds. "You'd have been vulnerable. Stranded. Easy prey."

Ginny swallowed uneasily. "But he wasn't there when I left. Nothing happened to me. He didn't jump out of the shadows."

"Because I was with you."

"Or…maybe it's a case of someone had the wrong car. Maybe it was just a prank by—"

"You don't really believe that, do you?" Riley screwed the lid on the bottle of garlic powder and slid it back onto her spice shelf. "Why won't you admit the danger this guy poses to you and accept the protection I'm offering?"

Ginny yanked open her refrigerator and took out a jar of

olives. "You can't guard me 24-7. And like I explained before, my clients would be intimidated by a big guy like you hovering over my shoulder. I wouldn't be able to do my job."

"So take some personal time off from work."

She gave him a scathing look and bumped the refrigerator closed with her hip. While Riley moved on to the can of black pepper, she steadied the olive jar with the fingers of her injured arm and tried to twist the lid off with her left hand. The jar slipped, but she caught it before it could crash to the floor. Trying a different tactic, she put the jar between her knees and gave the lid another firm twist. Still no luck. She couldn't get the proper leverage.

"Allow me." Riley reached down to remove the jar from between her legs.

"No, I'll get it." She clutched the olives to her chest, turning her back. "I'm learning how to do this sort of thing one-handed."

"A little secret…" Riley said, his tone laced with amusement. "The best way to get jars open with one hand…"

She peered over her shoulder at him and raised one eyebrow. "Yeah?"

"Use your good hand…to give me the jar." He tried again to take the olives from her.

She dodged, chuckling. "Not so fast! I'm not ready to surrender. Besides, you have your own situation to deal with."

With a nod, she directed Riley's attention to the counter, where Zachary had jumped up to help himself to the waiting steaks.

"Hey, buster!" Riley lifted the tabby from the counter, prying the meat from the cat's mouth. "Who invited you?"

"That's my chow hound, Zach. He's not supposed to eat table food, because he's diabetic and on a prescribed diet. Which of course means he steals scraps whenever he can." Ginny wedged the olive jar between her legs again and gave the lid another hard turn.

Riley held Zachary up to look him in the eye. "Hear that, pal? Steak is not on the menu for you."

Zachary meowed in protest.

"So noted." Riley set the cat on the floor.

The olives made a satisfying *pop* as the vacuum broke and the lid twisted loose.

"Ha! Told you I could do it!" With a gloating grin, Ginny set the jar on the counter.

"There's no shame in asking for help, you know."

She slanted a skeptical glance at him. "Are you talking about the olives or are we still on the whole you-as-my-body-guard schtick?"

"Take your pick."

She fished out an olive and stepped over to pop it in his mouth. "Next topic, please."

"Stubborn," he mumbled, giving the salvaged steak a disgruntled once-over. "You can have the steak your cat chewed."

"Okay by me." She gave Riley a quick kiss, tasting the salty olive on his lips. When she met his gaze, she read the worry in his expression and cocked her head. "I'll be fine, Riley. I know self-defense. I know how to be careful. I won't take unnecessary chances. I promise."

He plowed his fingers into her hair and, cradling the back of her head, drew her closer. "I'd never forgive myself if anything happened to you and I could have prevented it."

The shadows that darkened his eyes gave Ginny pause. Something more than simple worry for her safety was at play here. Perhaps she'd sensed it all along, but now the lines bracketing his taut mouth, the emotion clouding his expression, left no doubt.

"You're not just afraid for me, are you? Something happened. Something you think you should have prevented."

He tensed, and she knew she'd struck a nerve. When he tried to back away from her, she tightened her grip on his shoulders.

"Tell me what happened. What's made you feel responsible for me this way?"

"Forget it. I need to get these steaks on the grill, or we'll be eating at midnight." The smile he gave her was forced, grim.

"Riley, why is it so hard for you to talk to me?"

"How do you want yours cooked? Medium? Rare?"

Disappointment knotted her stomach. His refusal to open up to her spoke of an inherent lack of trust. And if they didn't have basic trust and openness between them, what hope did they have for building a relationship that worked?

The fluttering sensation she'd felt so often in her chest when she thought about Riley, about where their relationship might lead, stirred again. But tonight it was more of a thrashing beat. She inhaled deeply, trying to calm the disturbing cadence. "Medium is fine."

With a tight nod, he turned and headed out to her balcony with the steaks. Ginny stood alone in her kitchen, staring at the checked pattern of her floor for several minutes. Thinking. Wondering. Analyzing.

And fretting.

Riley had come to mean a great deal to her. Not only because he'd saved her life. Not just because he was handsome as sin and his kisses were pure heaven. She'd grown fond of his warmth, thoughtfulness and intelligence. He was good company. But everything she knew about him was superficial, one-dimensional.

And that was the crux of the matter.

What if there was more to him she hadn't seen? An irresponsible, unfaithful or untrustworthy side he'd managed to keep hidden. Or she'd been too blinded by his sex appeal to notice.

Her doubts stirred the wild beating of her heart to throb double time.

What if—

Her phone trilled, jolting her from the disturbing track of her thoughts.

She crossed to her phone, checked the caller ID.

Pay phone. Walt Compton had used a pay phone last time he called her apartment.

Adrenaline spiked her pulse. Fear froze her muscles.

The phone rang a second time. A third. Finally her answering machine picked up.

"Next time, Ms. West," Walt's voice growled through her machine. "I will always have another chance. And next time you'll be alone!"

With a click, the line went dead.

Chapter 8

Ginny spent the next week looking over her shoulder, jumping at her own shadow and hating her skittishness. When she gave the voice mail recording to the police, they confirmed finding Walt Compton's fingerprints on her slashed tire. Beyond that they had no new progress to report. Despite an ongoing all points bulletin for Annie's husband, he had managed to stay under the radar for more than two weeks. Annie had warned Ginny that Walt's military training and natural cunning would make him difficult to capture, and so far, she'd been correct.

The new evidence that Walt Compton was watching Ginny and waiting for a chance to strike convinced her extra precaution was in order. Depending on others to be with her all the time chafed her, yet whenever she left work for any reason, she took one of her coworkers or the courthouse security guard with her as she walked to her car. She didn't argue when her mother camped out at her apartment on the days Riley worked, and Ginny made a point of calling Annie at the women's center several times to check on her.

On Riley's days off, he insisted on staying on her couch. Ginny relented, as much because she enjoyed the time they spent cuddling to watch television as because Riley's presence gave her a sense of security she didn't feel any other time. Yet her personal security didn't translate into a safe feeling regarding the future of their relationship.

Riley continued to dodge questions about his past, his family and his previous girlfriends, and Ginny's sense of the relationship's impending demise grew stronger every day.

In an ostrich-style, head-in-the-sand way she'd have vehemently discouraged for her clients, she found herself avoiding topics she knew Riley hated her to bring up. With a restless gnawing inside her, she stuck to the safe subjects of current events, stories of the day's happenings at the fire station, and her family's plans for Thanksgiving. She knew that by delaying a deeper conversation, not pressing for more honesty, she was left with only the illusion of a working relationship. But she hoped that by giving Riley more time, he'd soon trust her enough to be completely open with her about whatever had happened in his past. If not, she was only postponing another heartbreak.

And when cuddling led to kisses and kisses led to erotic touches, Ginny battled her growing desire for Riley. She couldn't, in good conscience, enjoy sexual intimacies with him until she felt sure they had a similar level of connection and commitment.

Although he never pressured her, always respected her "no," she could see his mounting frustration with her sexual restrictions. The same frustrations kept her tossing and turning at night, kept her feeling off balance and achy with need.

Some days Ginny cursed her convictions and swore to throw caution to the wind that night. But by the time she saw Riley in the evening, her niggling doubts about their future and her yearning for a deeper emotional relationship would edge in again and reaffirm her decision not to sleep with him.

By the end of the week, the strain of wondering if and when Walt might strike again, her self-imposed celibacy and her growing concern over the superficial nature of her relationship with Riley had worn Ginny's nerves down. She looked forward to the picnic at the city park that she and Riley had planned with Cal and Libby. The temperate autumn weather, food and company of friends were a perfect recipe for relaxing and getting her mind off Walt's threats.

On Saturday, they met the others at the park around 10:00 a.m., and as they unpacked the cars, all the introductions were made. Megan Calhoun's stepdaughter, Caitlyn, in her never-met-a-stranger way, charmed the men with tales of her new cat's mischief, and Cal and Libby Walters's baby daughter, Sara, charmed Megan and Ginny with her coos and grins. The women took turns holding the infant and entertaining her with goofy faces and silly voices.

While nuzzling the precious baby's cheeks, Ginny was hit with an unexpected tug of maternal yearning. Her thoughts turned to her first lunch with Riley, and his deflection of the topic of marriage and children.

Ginny had always assumed she'd have children, but because of her busy job and a string of lousy luck with the men she dated, she'd shelved ideas of family for the time being. But seeing Libby's joy with her baby and knowing how happy Megan had been since becoming Caitlyn's stepmom, Ginny admitted she felt left out. With effort, she pushed the internal ache aside and tried not to spoil her day off with wistful longings.

Megan had brought her German shepherd, Sam, along for the day, and he was an instant hit with Cal's daughter, Ally.

"Can we get a dog, Daddy?" she asked, her blue eyes wide with excitement.

Cal and Libby exchanged an *uh-oh* look.

Jack Calhoun, Megan's husband, chuckled. "Been there. Done that. Good luck, partner."

"Uh, we'll see," Cal told his daughter as he grabbed a Frisbee from the picnic table to distract her from further dog requests. "Who's up for a game?"

"Me!" both of the five-year-olds sang out.

Megan offered to watch the baby while the rest of the adults engaged the little girls in a Frisbee match designed to wear the high-energy kids out before their naps.

Riley used the game as an opportunity to playfully grab Ginny and wrestle her to the ground. After three such grabs and subsequent stolen kisses, she laughed and wiggled to free herself from his grasp. "There's no tackling in Frisbee!"

"No? Well, there should be. Especially when you're playing against such attractive opponents." He flashed her a cocky grin.

Ginny smiled and gave him another kiss. "Uh, hot stuff? I'm not your opponent. I'm on your team."

"Oh. Right." He shrugged. "So call it a huddle."

She chuckled at his mock-innocent look. "You're so bad…."

With a devilish grin, he waggled his eyebrows.

"Hey," Jack called to them, "are you two playing Frisbee with us or not?"

"Yes!" Ginny shouted.

At the same time, Riley called, "Not!"

"Well, I don't know about you, but I need a break!" Libby said breathlessly. "Ally's running me ragged!"

"Let's play fetch with Sam now," Ally said.

"Yeah!" Caitlyn cheered, and Sam barked in agreement.

While Ally and Caitlyn romped in the grass with Sam and Megan, Ginny helped Libby set out the food and plates, and the men gathered around the grill to talk football while the meat cooked.

As she worked on lunch, Libby balanced her baby on her hip and kept an eagle eye on the grassy spot where the girls played with the dog and giggled together. "It's so good to see Ally coming out of her shell. She had so much to deal with in her early years, and Cal and I worried she'd always be skittish and clingy."

Ginny smiled and handed Libby a stack of paper plates from the grocery sack. "Given plenty of love and support, kids can be pretty resilient."

When Ginny thought of Annie's kids, the violence they must have witnessed in their home, her heart wrenched. She prayed Annie could find some peace soon and that her love would help her kids heal and flourish.

Libby spoke, drawing Ginny's thoughts back to the present. "Oh, Ally's got plenty of love. Cal dotes on her. She's got him wrapped around her little finger. Just like Sara here does." She kissed her baby's head.

Cal turned away from the grill. "Did I hear my name taken in vain?"

Libby's eyes lit up like a kid's at Christmas as her husband stepped up beside her. "Not at all. Just telling Ginny how much you love our daughters."

A wide grin split his face, and he skimmed his fingers through Libby's hair to capture the nape of her neck. "I love all three of my ladies. Heart and soul." He ducked his head to plant a deep kiss on Libby's lips.

Riley wolf whistled. "Get a room!"

"Better yet, get a plate," Jack said. "I think the burgers are done. Caity, Ally, come on and eat now!"

Cal took Sara from her mother's arms. "You eat first, Lib. I'll hold squirt for a while."

Libby thanked her thoughtful husband with another kiss and a loving stroke on his cheek.

The affection between the husband and wife touched Ginny but also prodded a raw wound in her soul. She averted her gaze from Cal and Libby just in time to see Jack help Megan to her feet, then haul her into his arms. They beamed at each other and shared some whispered confidence that made them both laugh.

Ginny was overjoyed that her friend had found such a caring and supportive husband. Megan deserved every bit of the happiness she had with Jack. But as with the Walters, watching the newlyweds chafed something deep inside Ginny.

To her horror, tears prickled her eyes, and her throat tightened.

"Excuse me," she croaked as she hurried off to another picnic table until she could compose herself.

She sank down on the bench of the vacant table and pressed the heels of her hands into her eyes. Dragging in a deep breath she tried to analyze what had set her off.

The crack of a twig signaled Riley's approach just before he spoke. "Gin?" His voice held a note of wariness as well as worry. "What happened? Are you okay?"

Still unable to speak without squeaking, she nodded and swiped the moisture from her cheeks.

He sat beside her and rubbed a hand over her back. His concern, ironically, just provoked more tears. No doubt her crying jag had Riley baffled.

She glanced over her shoulder at him and, sure enough, the look on his face was a blend of confusion and typical male tear-phobia. Ginny gave him a watery smile for his courage in what had to be intimidating territory for him. Weepy girlfriend land.

"I'm fine. Really."

His arched eyebrow said he wasn't convinced.

Ginny dashed a few more tears from her face and pivoted on the bench to face him. "I was watching how much in love Libby and Cal are. Thinking about how perfect Jack is for Megan, how supportive he's been, how happy she is with him and Caitlyn in her life."

"Then these are happy tears?" Riley cocked his head, his expression hopeful.

She sucked her bottom lip between her teeth. "Sort of. Sort of not."

He knitted his brow. "Sort of not?"

Ginny rubbed the fingers that poked from her cast and twisted her mouth, deep in thought. "It's just…I can't help thinking about Annie. And the lady who came in last week, Rose. And a hundred other women I've counseled. Women whose husbands or boyfriends promised to love them but…hurt them instead." Her voice cracked, and she stopped to draw a breath and wipe her face again.

Riley caught her hand in his and kissed her fingers. "You see a lot of pain in your line of work."

"Too much. I'm supposed to keep a professional distance, not get emotionally involved, but…how do you do that when a young girl with so much life ahead of her comes to you after she's been brutally raped by her boyfriend? Or when a mother gets beaten *in front of her children* by the man who's supposed to protect her!"

Ginny realized how loud and emotional she'd become, and she squeezed her eyes and lips shut. But the anger, hurt and sorrow that had been shaken loose from her soul wouldn't slip quietly back behind closed doors. Her shoulders shook as a sob tore free.

"When I see how loving and kind some men can be with their wives, it just cuts all the deeper that the women I see every day in my office suffer such pain. I try to explain to them that real love doesn't hurt. Love doesn't hit or intimidate or rape or burn you with an iron."

Riley's eyes looked suspiciously damp. "No, it doesn't."

She flung her left arm out, pointing toward their friends. "That is love. That's the kind of respect and affection Annie deserves. That all of them deserve."

Riley nodded. "I know."

"I want to do more for them, but…I can't take away their pain."

He wiped his thumb under her eye then stroked her hair. "No. But you do help. You get them out. You keep them safe.

You help them get back on their feet. You talk to them and listen to them and try to show them a better way."

Ginny noted the earnest sympathy in Riley's eyes, and a tiny smile lifted the corner of her mouth. "I didn't mean to imply I was doubting my abilities as a counselor. I know I'm good at my job."

Riley's forehead wrinkled, and he shook his head. "Then I'm lost. I don't know what you want me to say."

A fuzzy warmth spread around her heart that he was even trying to understand and boost her flagging spirits. She cupped his cheek with her hand. "You don't have to say anything right now. I'm just sounding off."

He flashed that lopsided grin. "So I should just nod and say, 'Yes, dear'?"

"And maybe find me a tissue. My nose is starting to run."

"How about a napkin?" He stood and pulled a wrinkled wad from his pocket. "I had just picked this up to start filling my plate when I saw you head over here."

"Thanks." She accepted the napkin with a smile of gratitude and blew her nose. "I just hate that jobs like mine even have to exist. And I know there are more *good* men in the world—decent, caring men—than there are Walt Comptons. I just wish every woman I counsel could know what it meant to be truly loved and cherished. Unconditionally."

Riley shook his head. "How do women like Annie end up with someone like Walt? People don't change overnight. There have to be signs of what these guys are really like when they get involved with them."

Ginny lifted a shoulder and sighed. "There usually are, if they know what to look for, how to read the signs. A little jealousy and possessiveness might be flattering to someone who has low self-esteem. They might excuse a short temper or occasional hostility as isolated events, not see the bigger picture. When you're in love, in a new relationship, in a situation that gives you something you think your life has lacked until then, it is easy to ignore flaws that shouldn't be over-looked."

Ginny's heart tripped as she heard her own explanation. Was that what she was doing with Riley? Had she missed male companionship, the pleasure of stolen kisses and the hope of a lasting relationship so much in recent years that she was blind to signs she should have noticed? Was she making excuses for Riley's unwillingness to open up to her because she wanted so desperately for the relationship to work?

A clammy panic settled over her again. Things had to change between them, or she'd have to have the guts to break up with Riley. She couldn't risk her heart to a doomed relationship.

"So you're saying, in effect, the people closest to the situation can't see the forest for the trees?" Riley asked, jarring her from her private brooding.

Ginny rubbed her eyes and took a cleansing breath. Personal pain twined now with the ache she felt for her clients, blurring the line between her private and professional life, muddying her issues with Riley even more.

"Uh, yeah." She cleared the emotion from her throat. "Typically, people see what they want to see. They get what they expect…at first, anyway. And some women have been instilled with the lie that they don't deserve any better. Life tends to be a self-fulfilling prophecy. If you expect disappointment, you get disappointment. If you expect failure, you get failure."

Riley tensed and snapped his head up.

Ginny dabbed at her eyes with the napkin, wondering what she'd said that touched a nerve with him.

She flexed her fingers and redirected the discussion toward a lighter topic. "As much as I fuss and groan about my family's smothering, I'm eternally grateful that I had the example my parents set, that I saw what a marriage with real love looked like." She paused and sighed. "I want what my parents have. Not that my dating record would prove that. I've dated so many losers."

Riley's brow dipped in a deep scowl.

She quickly pressed a finger to his lips to forestall a protest. "Present company excluded."

But Riley's expression remained grim. A muscle in his jaw ticked, and fire leaped in his eyes. "Did any of these losers ever hurt you?"

"Physically? No. Crushed expectations, disillusionment and bitter disappointment—yeah. My losers were of the didn't-tell-me-they-were-married-until-the-fifth-date variety. And the unemployed-and-stealing-from-his-elderly-parents sort. And those are just the two most recent. But…" She shuddered and a knot of emotion choked her when an image of Donna, beaten and huddled on her dorm bed, flashed in her mind. "My bad judgment *has* hurt people I care about." Ginny's voice cracked, and she took a fortifying breath. "It's bad enough I seem to attract the creeps, but I'll never forget how much my mistake cost my friend."

Riley's gray eyes honed in on hers, his brow creasing. He seemed ready to speak, but sucked in a deep breath and cut his gaze toward the street instead.

She sighed. "I don't know why I'm such a loser magnet. You'd think I could pick the bad eggs out of the crowd." She shook her head and gave a short, humorless laugh.

She glanced up at Riley, who wore a pensive expression.

The lines around his mouth firmed. "You deserve unconditional love as much as Megan does. You deserve what your parents have." He gritted his teeth, his face taut with emotion.

"Riley?"

"I don't want to hurt you, Gin. I don't want to let you down. But I don't know if I can give you what you expect, what you deserve."

Fingers of foreboding gripped her chest. She drew a slow, shaky breath. "What do you mean?"

"It's just that…I've never been good at…figuring out relationships. If you're looking for the kind of near perfection your parents have, I don't know that I can live up to your expectations. My track record isn't very impressive. I've…" He seemed to struggle for the right words. "I've let a lot of people down in the past."

The familiar quivering beat fluttered in her chest. Maybe he was finally ready to talk with her, share with her the kind of depth she wanted between them. "I don't expect perfection, Riley. I just want you to be honest with me, to be open with me. If there's a problem between us, we need to talk about it."

He said nothing for several moments, just stared across the open field where some kids had started a soccer game. His jaw rigid, his eyes swirling with clouds of emotion, he glanced at her. "Ginny, I—"

The trill of her cell phone cut him off.

Frustration stabbed her. She needed to have this conversation with Riley, no matter the outcome. She took her phone out of her pocket and set it on the table without checking the number. "Ignore it. What were you going to say?"

He scrubbed a hand over his cheek and chin. "Take the call, Gin. It could be important."

She doubted anything could be as important to her at that moment as finally getting Riley to open up to her, as bridging the distance between them.

He picked up her phone and held it out to her. He seemed almost relieved, as if the call had given him a reprieve from the discussion he so clearly wanted to avoid.

Sighing in defeat and disappointment, Ginny raked fingers through her hair, then took the phone from him. "Hello?"

"Ginny, we need you at the shelter. Fast! Annie is hysterical, and the situation is deteriorating quickly," Helen said, panic and concern rife in her voice.

Instantly, Ginny's pulse kicked up, and she went into crisis management mode. "What happened?"

"He's here, Ginny! Walt Compton found the women's shelter!"

Ice sluiced through her veins. "What? He's *there?* How did he find the shelter?"

She met Riley's gaze. His expression said he understood what was happening without her explaining. His body tensed as she sprang to her feet.

"I don't know," Helen said. "He tried to grab Annie while she was in the backyard."

"Have you called the police?" Ginny jogged toward her car, then remembered she didn't have her purse.

"We have." Helen sounded breathless, frightened. "They're on the way."

I need my purse, she mouthed to Riley, pointing back at the table where the others were eating.

While he hurried to get it, Ginny rubbed her temple and took a moment to collect her thoughts. "What happened to the cop who was supposed to be on guard in front of the house?"

"I don't know. He wasn't there when I went to get his help."

Ginny mumbled an unladylike curse. "Does Walt have a weapon? Our priority is to keep everyone safe."

"Not that I can tell. He—"

Through the phone, Ginny heard a crash, and Helen shrieked. "He broke the window. Threw a rock. Oh, God, where are the cops?"

"Helen, calm down! You have to stay in control. The women are counting on you to take charge and protect them until the cops arrive."

"Everyone is in the safe room except Annie and me. She insists on talking to Walt, trying to reason with him."

In the background, Ginny could hear male shouts. Ranting. Hostility.

"He's beyond reasoning. Get her in the safe room. Tell her to do it for her kids. And you get safe, too. I'm on my way!"

Ginny snapped her phone closed as Riley returned with her purse.

"I'll drive." He started toward her car without waiting for her.

"No! You can't go. I told you already the shelter location has to stay a secret."

Riley huffed in frustration. "Like it stayed a secret to Walt Compton?"

Tension crackled along Ginny's nerves. "I don't know how Walt found the shelter, but it doesn't change the rules. If anything, it's an example of why we have to have the rules! You can't go, Riley."

"Then you're not going, either. Walt Compton has threatened you, too, remember?"

"It's my job to go. I *have* to go. I don't have time to debate this with you, Riley!" She turned and started for her car, only to have him catch her arm.

"I'm a first responder and can keep the location a secret same as the cops can. I know the shelter's secret location is about protecting lives. Protecting lives is *my* job. Protecting *you* is something I have to do. I *am* going." The stony resolve in his eyes, his voice, his expression brooked no resistance and stopped her dead.

Those are my terms.

His bold words from their lunch two weeks earlier filtered through her head, mirroring the determination that now set his jaw and fired heat in his eyes. For weeks, he'd been gracious and accommodating, deferring to her preferences in movies and pizza toppings more often than not. But here, on the issue of her safety, he'd put his foot down, demanding his say in the give-and-take of their relationship.

A curious mix of irritation and respect swirled through her. His unyielding determination should have sparked her own stubbornness. Instead, she found his iron resolve admirable…and incredibly sexy.

"I'll drive. Let's go," he said, pulling her with him as he headed for her car.

Ginny shoved Riley's alpha male one-upsmanship aside as they rushed to the women's shelter. She had no idea what she might face with Walt Compton. She prayed the police would have the situation under control—and Walt in custody—by the time they arrived on the scene.

"I won't stay here anymore!" Annie wailed while she tried to quiet her crying baby on her shoulder. "You said I'd be safe, but he almost got me! You can't keep me here against my will!"

"Annie, listen to me. Despite what happened today, you're still far safer here, with our trained staff in residence, than you are trying to go it alone." Ginny sat on the end of the sofa at the women's shelter, hoping she portrayed the image of cool control she wanted to project to help soothe Annie's understandable anxiety. Inside, though, Ginny's own nerves were as frayed as the ratty blanket four-year-old Haley clutched like a lifeline.

When Ginny and Riley had arrived at the women's shelter, policemen were already on the scene. Walt Compton was not.

With the crisis behind them, Riley had returned to her car to wait, giving Ginny the time and space she needed to work.

Helen, still rattled by the incident, had told Ginny how Walt fled through the back bushes just moments before the police arrived. The police had searched the area and come up with nothing. The officer who'd been assigned to watch the shelter had admitted to leaving his post for several minutes to find a restroom and buy a hamburger, for which he'd been placed on immediate suspension.

Clearly, Walt had been casing the shelter and knew when the guard had left. To find the shelter, Walt must have followed a staff member from their home. Ginny didn't doubt the former Special Forces soldier's cunning or skill.

Ginny squelched her own disappointment and frustration with the sloppy police work and focused on calming Annie and considering their next step. "Until Walt is taken into police custody—"

"And when will that be? It's been *weeks,* and they haven't caught him yet!"

Ginny sucked in a steadying breath. "I don't know when they'll find him. They've promised they're doing everything they can to locate him. But he hasn't shown up at work or your home since the women's center fire. He's not registered at any local motels. When he's called me, he's used a different public phone each time. They've contacted all the friends you gave them to check. He's just managed somehow to stay off the grid."

"See?" Annie shook her head, her shoulders sagging with defeat. "It's like I told you. If he doesn't want to be caught, he won't be. He's too well trained in evasion techniques!"

"The police know about his training. They'll figure out a way to outmaneuver him." Ginny prayed she was right. Something had to be done to find Walt. Soon. "In the meantime, you have to stay here to stay safe."

"But he found me here!" Annie shrieked. "How can I stay now that he knows where I am? He'll be back. I know he will!"

Ginny's stomach roiled. She suspected that as well, but she didn't have a backup plan. Yet.

"Annie, there's always a trained staff member here, and the police have promised to up their patrols in the area and put a policewoman inside the facility if needed. You still have more protection here than—"

"No!" She shook her head. "I have to go. I'll leave town!"

"And go where? You have no job, no money, no family to stay with." Ginny hesitated. She hated to scare Annie any more than she was, but her client had to hear the blunt truth. "Annie, if you leave, you'll have no protection. You need to stay…at least until I can find somewhere else safe for you."

"Is anywhere safe? He said he'd find me no matter where I went." A desperate hopelessness filled Annie's eyes.

Ginny took a deep breath for composure. "Annie, he's just trying to scare you."

"Well, it's working. I shoulda never left him. It was a mistake. I—"

"No!" Ginny grabbed Annie's hand and squeezed her

fingers. "You did the right thing. I'll call some other safe shelters in nearby parishes and—"

"Safe shelters? That's what you said about *this* place."

Ginny glanced from Annie's tear-streaked, frightened face to Haley's wide-eyed gaze. The little girl stuck her thumb in her mouth, clutched her blanket to her chin and laid her head against her mom. The baby, Ben, still fussed, probably picking up on his mother's anxiety.

Ginny stroked Haley's silky hair and lifted her glance to Annie. "Give me two days. Just forty-eight hours. I'll find another place for you to stay until Walt is captured. I promise."

Annie's shoulders sagged. The anger and fear that had blazed in her eyes faded to a blank glaze of defeat. "What's the point? He said he'd kill me, and I know he will. Why should I bother running anymore?"

Ginny straightened her spine, and the hair on her neck bristled. With a gentle hand under Haley's chin, she tipped the girl's head up. "This is why. She needs you to stay strong. So does Ben. Don't give up on me, Annie. We've come too far."

Annie wrapped an arm around Haley's shoulders and drew her closer, kissing the crown of her head. "All right. Two days."

Chapter 9

"Damn it!" Ginny slammed her phone down and sent the file of papers on her lap flying across her living room floor.

Riley looked up from the sports magazine he was skimming and met her gaze. Frustration vibrated from her like waves of heat from an oil well fire.

"The shelter in Ouachita is full, too." She raked hair back from her face with her left hand. "I can't find a place for Annie anywhere, and I only have about two hours left on the forty-eight I promised her."

Riley crouched to gather up the papers she'd knocked away. He wanted to help ease her stress but was at a loss what to do. "You really think she's gonna hold you to that forty-eight hour deal? She was upset when you made that promise. Maybe she's calmer now and can see that she's in the best place for her already."

Ginny shook her head and took a sip of the red wine he'd poured for her, hoping it would help her unwind. "She called me earlier today for a status report. She's understandably spooked. If I can't find a new place for her and the kids, she's gonna try to leave town and go it alone."

Riley scowled. "She can't do that! She'd be a sitting duck."

After setting her wineglass on the coffee table, Ginny slumped down on the sofa and leaned her head back on the cushions. "I've tried to explain that to her. She won't listen. All she knows is that Walt is still at large, and he found her at the one place I promised her would be safe."

Riley put the stack of papers on the end table and sat beside Ginny. He pulled her legs onto his lap and started massaging her bare feet.

She moaned in bliss and curled her toes. "Don't do that. It feels too good. I can't think when you're distracting me with carnal pleasures."

"Haven't you earned a break? You've been working all afternoon. You've barely slept since Saturday."

She snagged the file from the end table and shook her head. "I'll sleep after I find a safe shelter with an opening for a woman with two kids." She sorted through the file, reorganizing the papers, then glanced up at Riley. "I know I'm not good company today. I'd understand if you wanted to go home."

He cocked an eyebrow. "Trying to get rid of me?"

"No. Especially if you're willing to keep doing that thing you're doing to my feet." She wiggled her toes. "You have magic hands, Riley Sinclair."

He slid his palm from her foot up her calf and under the hem of the boxer style sleeping shorts she wore. Her skin felt silky, warm and tempting. "My hands are talented in many ways." He flashed a grin as he stroked her inner thigh. "Shall I show you?"

She laughed and caught his hand. "I'm working."

"What if I told you I had a solution to your problem?"

Ginny lifted her head from the sofa cushions, hope and curiosity lighting her face. "You do?"

"Let Annie stay at my apartment."

She let her head fall back heavily once more. "No. Thanks, but…"

Disappointment stabbed him. Why couldn't she accept his help? So much about Ginny's situation with Walt left him feeling out of control and useless. The need to do more to protect Ginny and resolve the problems she had with Annie and Walt Compton gnawed at him. Ginny might not think she needed his help, but he couldn't sit by and see her get hurt. He'd made the mistake of letting his guard down with Erin, and she'd paid the price.

Shoving back the guilt that rose in his throat, he shifted on the couch to face Ginny. "Why *can't* Annie use my apartment? I'm not there one day or more out of three, because of work. And lately I've been sleeping here, so my place is hardly being used. There's already a cop stationed outside this building, watching the place for you, and since you're one floor down from my place, we can keep tabs on her, too."

"I don't know. Walt's already watching me. He knows where I live. It seems like bringing Annie here would put her more in the line of fire. If I can't find a shelter, I need someplace far from here, someplace out of the way that Walt wouldn't suspect or think to look for her."

"I'm not saying long-term. Try it just for a couple days. If you trust her, I'm happy to let her use my place until something else can be arranged. It will at least buy you more time to find a shelter opening."

Ginny narrowed a suspicious gaze on Riley and grinned. "And buy you a ready excuse to continue sleeping over here all the time."

He wiggled his eyebrows and stretched toward her, pressing her farther into the sofa cushions. "Darn. She's onto me."

The soft curve of her body fit perfectly in his arms, and he ached to feel her pressed against him, warm and naked. Desire zinged through him, making every nerve ending spark and his muscles tense in anticipation. He gave her a deep, wet kiss.

"Mmm." Ginny hummed softly as she threaded her fingers through his hair.

Riley traced the seam of her lips with his tongue, and she opened to him. He tasted the red wine she'd sipped and the warm sweetness unique to the woman melting in his arms. The mating of their mouths shot fire through his veins, and the sultry sound of her sighs heightened his hunger.

Having spent much of the past several weeks with Ginny, he'd learned her mannerisms. She tipped her head when deep in thought, and her voice warmed when she talked to her cat. He'd witnessed repeatedly the compassion, optimism and stubborn determination that made her a strong ally to her clients, and he knew the conviction and intelligence that made her eyes shine with a blue fire.

His physical attraction had grown deeper because of his familiarity with who she was beyond the curvaceous blond exterior that had first drawn him to her. She captivated him, body and soul. He wanted Ginny more every day, wanted to bury himself deep inside her and lose himself in the sweet oblivion of her kiss, her touch. His longing for her had become as much a spiritual desire as a physical one.

He slipped a hand under her sweatshirt to cup her breast. Her nipple beaded at once, and he groaned. Working his fingers to her back, he sought the clasp of her bra and managed to undo one hook before she shoved at his shoulder.

"Wait," she said breathlessly as she tore her mouth from his. She wiggled to get free from him.

Riley sighed and released her. He arched an eyebrow in query as he sat up, his body still crackling with need.

He'd been patient with the tempo she'd set for their relationship, but his self-restraint was wearing thin. Their weeks of sassy flirting and heated kisses were really getting to him.

But by sheer force of will, he held his desires in check. His own code of ethics dictated that Ginny had to decide the right time and place. He would not move any faster, push any further than she allowed. Even if the waiting killed him.

"Before we go anywhere with this—" She waved her hand to indicate the foreplay she'd interrupted. "—I think we should finish the conversation we were having Saturday."

He snapped his eyebrows together in question, narrowing a dubious gaze on her.

"At the park," she added. "Right before I got the call from the women's shelter."

His gut tightened as he recalled the topic of that particular conversation. Why had he said anything about his poor track record? Although he'd do anything he could to avoid hurting Ginny, she'd scared him with her talk of perfect parents and high standards. If he was destined to disappoint her, wasn't it better he warn her now? Give her the chance to leave him before things got too serious?

"You said you'd let a lot of people down. What did you mean by that?" Her head tilted, and her eyes narrowed as she pinned an expectant gaze on him. "Girlfriends you couldn't commit to? Your parents' expectations? Your boss? Your friends?"

Riley scrubbed a hand over his face. He felt trapped, cornered. Every survival instinct screamed for him to run, to deflect her questions and protect the truths he'd kept buried for years.

Yet he'd opened the door. He should have known Ginny would use that crack in his defenses to wheedle more information from him.

But the naked truth was too raw and cut too deep to open those wounds for her. He'd known going into this relationship with Ginny that her keen insights and inquisitive nature would corner him eventually, that she wouldn't be satisfied with half-truths and evasion tactics. A woman like Ginny needed to see all the way into his soul, needed to analyze and dissect, needed to lay everything out for examination.

But that level of scrutiny, that total, unguarded honesty was what he couldn't give her.

That was what he'd started to say at the picnic, what she was waiting to hear now.

Ginny was driven by a need to heal wounded souls, but his pain was beyond redemption. Nothing could change the past. No one could right the wrong he'd done. He knew, because he'd spent the last sixteen years trying.

What's more, his disastrous relationship with Erin had taught him too clearly that knowledge was power. Erin had used his deepest feelings and her knowledge of his painful past to manipulate him, to control him, to hurt him. How could he risk giving another woman that kind of power and influence over his emotions, over his very heart and soul? He couldn't.

He sighed and pushed himself off the sofa to pace.

"Riley, please talk to me. I listen to people for a living. You can tell me anything that's bothering you. And there's not much you could say that would shock me, if that's what you're worried about. I've heard just about everything from my clients." She turned her palms up, signaling her openness to what he was withholding.

"Ginny, I'm *not* one of your clients." He took a deep breath when he heard the tension and frustration in his tone. He didn't want to start a fight, but he had to make her understand his need for privacy. "Look, I didn't come to you looking for advice or help. I don't want to talk about anything more than what DVD we're going to rent tonight and what to eat for dinner. I'll tell you about my day and listen to you talk about yours. I can debate politics with you or discuss sports or talk current events."

Ginny sighed and stared down at her lap.

"But I don't do the kind of heart and soul tell-all conversations you seem to need. I'm just not wired that way."

Everything from her slumped posture to her frowning expression shouted her disappointment with him, more clearly than if she'd yelled at him. Knowing that he'd already let her down in such a basic way cut him to the quick. Failing someone else he cared about was the last thing he wanted.

"What kind of relationship do we have, then, if we don't have that intimate level of honesty and trust? What kind of future are we supposed to build based on superficial things like what toppings we like on our pizza?" The hurt in her quietly spoken question arrowed to his heart.

"I don't know. I care about you, Gin. But…" He balled his hands into fists, not sure how to finish the sentence, or how to move forward with her.

If he were smart, he'd walk out now and not look back.

But knowing Walt Compton was still a threat to her safety, Riley refused to leave her unprotected. That had been the second lesson his experience with Erin had taught him. When he failed, people got hurt.

"Ginny, who I am isn't about what I can or can't tell you about my past or my deep dark secrets and feelings. Who I am *now* is what should matter. And who I am is in everything I do and say and the way I live my life. Getting to know each other on a basic level of shared interests and everyday life *is* important, because life is about the choices we make every day."

His first clue that Erin had a skewed view of their relationship had been her total disregard for their lack of common interests. They'd had no real basis for their relationship other than one tragic day as teenagers—the day Jodi had died.

Ginny met his gaze, her heart in her eyes. His chest contracted so tightly that breathing was impossible.

He moved back to the couch and brushed the hair from her cheek. "For me, a relationship is about how well you get along with another person, every day. How well you can just…*be* with them. No pressure, no strings. That's all I have for you right now, Ginny. It may be all I ever have. That's why at the park I said I was afraid I'd hurt you, that I'd let you down. I know you want more from me."

"Riley, I don't—"

A sharp knock sounded on her door.

Ginny tensed, glancing toward the entrance, but she made no move to answer it. Her expression told him she wasn't nearly through with this conversation. But he'd said all he intended. If he had to walk out, go back to his own apartment tonight to make that point to her, so be it.

Another knock sounded.

"Ginny?" a woman's voice called.

Rolling her eyes, Ginny finally pushed herself up from the couch. "My mother."

Seeing his mistress move from the couch, Zachary hopped down from the windowsill where he'd been napping and trotted over to his food bowl.

"In a minute, chow hound." Ginny let Hannah in, giving her mother a hug as she entered.

"Oh, darlin', are you all right? Megan told me you left your picnic early the other day because of that Compton man. What were you thinking?"

"Right now I'm thinking Megan has a big mouth," Ginny mumbled.

Hannah scowled. "She cares about you and worries. Just like I do." Her mom held out the brown paper bag in her hands. "Homemade potato soup. I made extra the other night because I knew it was your favorite. I can heat it up if you want."

"Sounds good to me," Riley said.

Hannah turned, her face brightening. "Riley! I didn't see you there. How are you, honey?"

"Doing well, thanks."

Waving a finger at him, Hannah set the sack on the counter and opened it. "While I've got your ear, I wanted to invite you to come eat dinner with us Wednesday night. Both of you. Matt gets in from LSU Wednesday, and we're having a family dinner. Then, of course, you're welcome to come back on Thanksgiving, too. Henry makes the best Cajun fried turkey in the state!"

Zachary meowed plaintively for attention.

"Hey, buddy." Hannah leaned over to pick the cat up and scratch his head.

Ginny dumped the soup in a pan and turned the burner on.

"It smells great, Mom. I've been working all weekend, and pizza and cereal were getting old."

"Oh, hon, you really should eat better. You're getting too thin." Hannah turned back to Riley as Ginny gave an exasperated grunt. "So can we count on you for dinner Wednesday, Riley?"

"I wouldn't miss it."

"Great!" Hannah patted his cheek as she walked out. "Take care of her for me, Riley. I'm counting on you to keep my girl out of trouble."

Though Hannah's parting shot was delivered in an airy, almost teasing manner, her words reverberated in Riley and settled like rocks in his gut. The request rang with the echoes of old promises made…and broken.

When I'm gone, you'll be the man of the family. Promise me you'll take care of your mom and Jodi.

He forced a brittle smile for Hannah and told her what he'd told his father. "I will."

It was a promise he didn't plan to break a second time.

Later that night, Ginny called the shelter and reported her lack of progress to Annie. She half expected the young mother to be packed and gone when she phoned. Instead, Annie was waiting for her call, resigned to staying in the women's shelter. "Ben's started running a fever. I can't justify taking off while he's sick. He needs medicine, and the shelter's got a nurse on staff in case he gets worse."

"Then you promise you're going to stay put for now? At least through Thanksgiving?"

"For a little while," Annie said noncommittally.

"Good." Relief loosened the knots that had kinked Ginny's muscles and cramped her lungs all weekend. She released a silent, cleansing breath. "Let the kids have a traditional turkey dinner, and next Monday I'll double-check all of the same places. I'll even try some shelters in Arkansas if I have to. We'll find something. Or the cops will catch Walt. Keep the faith, Annie. Everything will work out." Ginny almost had herself believing. She simply refused to quit until Annie was completely safe. One way or another.

On the Tuesday afternoon before Thanksgiving, Ginny left work late. She'd spent extra time with a college-age client facing her first holiday alone after leaving her emotionally abusive family. Driving home, Ginny took a roundabout route and kept a sharp eye out for any vehicle that could be following her. She saw none, but wouldn't breathe easily until she was in her apartment with the door locked.

She frowned, realizing Walt had succeeded in making her jumpy and unsure of herself.

At her apartment building, she stopped to say hello to the police officer who'd spent the last three weeks staking out the parking lot and surrounding premises.

"Can I bring you down a cup of coffee?" Ginny asked.

Officer Holden smiled but declined. "You have my cell phone number in case of trouble, right?"

Ginny nodded and pulled her jacket tighter as a nippy breeze stirred the evening air. "On speed dial."

The officer winked. "All right then. You get inside where it's warmer. Good night, ma'am."

Ginny gave him a wave and hurried toward the lobby, where she picked up her mail before heading upstairs. She stopped by Riley's apartment to break their date for that evening. She was too drained, both mentally and physically, to be good company. What she really needed was time away from Riley to sort out her feelings for him, a little distance from the sexual energy that muddled her thoughts.

"Rain check?" she asked, when his face creased in concern. "All I have the energy for is a hot bath and an early bedtime. I'm sorry."

Riley cocked an eyebrow, his unwavering gray gaze hard and stubborn. "Not a chance. You go on to bed, but I'm still coming over. Let me just turn off my TV and grab a magazine."

"You don't—"

"But I am."

She knew better than to argue when he got that steely look in his eyes. And she could still have her bath and go to bed while he read on her couch. Why pick that battle when they had the bigger issue of his unwillingness to be open with her and discuss the painful past he was harboring? "Whatev. See you in a few."

When Riley disappeared into his apartment, Ginny trudged upstairs. She kicked off her shoes as soon as she walked through her door.

Zachary ran out from his favorite sleeping spot in her pile of dirty laundry and almost tripped her in his rush to the kitchen to be fed.

"Hmm. You are due for a meal and a shot, aren't you, Zach-boy?"

"Rrow!"

Chuckling at her pet, Ginny dropped her purse on the sofa and headed to the kitchen to pour the cat his supper. While Zach ate, she fixed his insulin shot. She'd squatted behind her pet to give the shot while the cat was distracted with eating, when a shadow fell over her.

She glanced behind her. "Riley?"

"Guess again." Walt Compton glared down at her, one of her butcher knives in his hand.

Ginny screamed, sending Zachary scurrying, and she lurched to her feet. As she rose, she knocked the hand holding the knife with her casted arm.

Walt stumbled back a step but quickly caught his balance and surged toward her again.

She struck out with the only weapon she had.

The syringe of insulin.

Ginny thrust the needle forward, jabbing it in Walt's eye.

He roared in pain and anger. After plucking the syringe out, he clutched a hand to his injured eye. "You'll pay for that, bitch!"

Ginny was trapped, cornered between her kitchen cabinets and Walt. Her apartment phone was out of reach, and she'd dropped her purse with her cell phone on the living room sofa. She had to use her wits.

She snagged the toaster from the counter and tried to smash it against Walt's head. He deflected the blow and swung at her with the knife.

Twisting out of the path of the blade, she scrambled for something, *anything* else to throw at him. A banana. Spoons and spatulas from her utensils drawer. The dish towel. The oven timer. She sent one item after another hurtling at him in a continuous assault.

Walt ducked or deflected each missile, but the distraction kept him busy enough not to stab at her again for a few precious seconds.

When Ginny ran out of things to throw, the anger that burned in Walt's eyes sent a frisson of fear skittering down her spine.

"You've interfered in my life, in my marriage for the last time. I gave you a chance to convince Annie to change her mind, but I'm tired of waiting." He took a slow, menacing step closer, and Ginny shrank back against the counter.

"You and your cronies can't protect her forever. The police will give up eventually. And then what?" Spittle formed at the corner of Walt's mouth, and his eyes grew more wild and irrational. "Annie is as good as dead. She should have never left. Should've never taken my kids from me!"

Ginny pushed herself up on the counter, the weight on her injured arm making her wince. Sitting on the counter, she scooted a few inches farther away from Walt.

"Annie left because you were beating her! She was afraid you'd hurt the children. You had your chance to make things right, to get help."

Walt tensed. "Shut up!"

When he raised the knife again, Ginny aimed a well-placed kick to his groin. As he folded in pain, he slashed down in a wild arc and stabbed the counter, near enough to her leg to catch the fabric of her skirt.

While he grimaced and grabbed at his crotch, Ginny planted a foot on his hip and shoved. He staggered a step, off balance.

She seized the chance to launch herself off the counter. The cloth of her skirt tore as she made her escape.

But Walt spun and grabbed the back of her shirt as she scrambled for the door, the phone, another weapon. Anything.

The pan she'd heated her mother's soup in was still in the drying rack by the sink, and she grabbed the handle.

Spinning, she swung at Walt's head with a grunt of effort. This time when he raised his arm in self-defense, the weight of the pan smashing his hand sent the knife clattering to the floor. Quickly, Ginny kicked the blade out of his reach.

Growling in rage, Walt grabbed her left wrist and yanked her arm behind her back. Shoving her forward, he slammed her against the wall. The force of the blow knocked the breath from her lungs. Again he thrust her into the wall…and again. Ginny bit her tongue, and her mouth filled with the metallic taste of her blood.

"I'll teach you to stick your nose in my business and screw with my family!" Walt snarled in her ear.

"Ginny, where are you?"

She blinked, uncertain whether she'd really heard Riley's voice, or if she'd conjured it in her desperation.

Walt's grip on her arm tightened. His fingers dug into her skin. He grew still and silent, as if deciding his next move.

She struggled for a breath, desperate to give Riley warning of what he'd walked into. "Riley!" she rasped.

With a shove, Walt released her and turned to flee.

She crumpled to the floor, choking on her own fear and frustration. "Stop him!"

Chapter 10

Riley had just stepped into Ginny's apartment when a man came barreling out of her kitchen. The intruder knocked into him and rushed past him for the door. Stunned by the turn of events, Riley needed a beat to realize what had happened.

When he heard Ginny's strangled cry from the kitchen, his pulse spiked. Given the choice of chasing down the intruder or making sure she was all right, her welfare won hands down. He snatched up her apartment phone from the end table as he hurried to the kitchen and punched in 911.

When he rounded the corner to the kitchen, Ginny was on the floor, holding a bleeding lip. His heart leaped to his throat. "Gin, how bad are you hurt? How'd that guy get in here?"

She waved a hand toward the door. "Go after him! That was Walt! Stop him!"

"Not until I know you're all right." His hands were already roaming over her face and arms, searching for evidence of injury. "I need to report a break-in and assault," he told the emergency operator.

"I'm okay!" Ginny slapped his hands away and struggled to stand. "Get Walt before he disappears again!"

When she pushed herself to her feet, she wobbled, and Riley caught her before she fell. "You're not okay. You need to be checked by a doctor," he countered, then told the operator, "Belle Bayou Apartments on Fourth Street."

Ginny wrenched her arm from his grip and staggered to the living room.

"We need an ambulance. A woman's been hurt," Riley told the operator as he shadowed Ginny.

After rifling through her purse, she flipped open her cell and dialed in a number. As she waited for an answer, she headed for the open door. "Damn it, why isn't Officer Holden picking up? God, please let it mean he saw Walt and caught him."

Seeing Ginny on her feet and cognizant, Riley shoved the land line in her hand and rushed to the door. "You stay here and lock the door!"

She nodded. "I'm fine! Go!"

Riley rushed out to the parking lot and scanned the area. He saw no one except Ted Cooper, a college-age kid who lived two doors down from him.

"Ted, did you see anyone come out of the building earlier? Running from the area?"

"No, dude. Why?"

Riley gritted his teeth. "Break-in at 3C."

"Damn. Not cool."

"No, not cool at all." Riley spotted Officer Holden's cruiser and jogged over to speak to him. As he neared the vehicle, Riley realized the driver's side window was broken, and a chill skated up his spine.

Picking his pace up to a run, Riley cast a wary gaze around the vicinity of the police car but saw nothing.

When he reached the cruiser, he peered inside…and tensed. Officer Holden lay sprawled across the front seat with blood seeping from his temple.

"He got the jump on me." Officer Holden sat at the end of the ambulance and shook his head slowly, grimacing. "He had a baseball bat or something. Smashed the window and—" He motioned to his temple. "That's all I remember until I woke up."

Detective Rogers nodded and flipped his notebook closed. He looked up at Ginny. "I guess that's all for now. If you think of anything else, call me. Night or day. We *will* nail this bastard. I won't rest until we do."

"Thanks." She twisted her lips in a moue of frustration. Walt had escaped. Again. She kicked the tire of the nearest car and gritted her teeth.

Riley caught Ginny by the arm and gently pulled her aside. "I'm taking you with me to my mother's over the holiday. I want you out of town. I want to be close, so this jerk can't take another shot at you."

"I'll be perfectly safe at my parents. I'll even stay over at their place for a few days, if it will make you feel better."

In truth, it would make Ginny feel better, too. Walt had gotten past the police guard. Had gotten inside her home. Had been waiting for her.

A prickly sensation crept through her. Not even her home felt safe anymore. She shuddered, and Riley pulled her into his arms.

He rubbed the chill bumps on her arms and held her tight. "I want you with me. I have to be sure you are safe, and I think getting you out of town for a few days is what's best. Please don't fight me on this."

Snuggled against his wide, warm chest, Ginny finally felt the cold that had sunk into her bones begin to ease. She hated to admit that she was growing accustomed to having Riley's protection. She didn't want to become dependent on him, fall into the trap of relying on him for her sense of security. She taught her clients to find their inner strength and be self-reliant in matters of personal safety. She encouraged them to use common sense and precaution. How could she do any less?

But maybe in this case, the smart thing was to leave town. Was it running from the problem or was it prevention?

Ginny inhaled the clean laundry scent of Riley's sweatshirt and thought of home. She'd never missed a major holiday with her parents and brothers. Breaking that tradition would be hard.

But what might she learn about Riley if she met his mom? What insights would she gain by visiting the home where he grew up? She could justify spending Thanksgiving with Riley if she didn't call it hiding, cowering.

"Are you sure your mother wouldn't mind me coming uninvited?"

"I'm inviting you. And my mother loves company of any kind. She's a real social butterfly."

"All right. I'll go with you to your mom's house for Thanksgiving. But we spend tomorrow night with my family. Deal?"

Riley peered down at her with warmth in his eyes. "Look at us, dividing up holiday time between our families like a…real couple."

A real couple.

Ginny quirked a grin, but inside, a swarm of bees buzzed through her veins. She tightened her grip on Riley's shirt.

"Next you'll be fussing at me for not stopping to ask directions," he said, stroking a finger down the length of her nose.

She swallowed hard to loosen her throat and forced a note of humor into her tone. "I thought firemen were supposed to know every street, have the whole city map memorized."

"We do." His grin became smug. "That's why I don't stop for directions."

He dipped his head to steal a kiss. The touch of his lips left her head feeling woozy and her skin warm and flushed.

By all indications, they were rapidly moving forward in their relationship.

But moving forward on Riley's terms. She still knew so little about what made him tick. The picture she had of him had great gaps where his history, his family and his deepest desires and dream should have been.

Those voids of knowledge yawned like black holes, ready to swallow her. She'd already come too far into the relationship, grown too fond of Riley to escape unscathed if something dark and ugly should crawl out of one of those holes.

She'd seen too many Jim Prathers and Walt Comptons in her line of work to put all of her hopes, her heart, her life at the mercy of a first impression, a superficial connection.

The more involved she became with Riley and the deeper her feelings for him grew, the louder the doubt demons screamed in her head and the stronger the flutter pulse of panic gripped her chest. She feared it was already too late to save her heart.

On Wednesday evening, after Ginny had introduced Riley to her brothers and her father, she and Riley joined her parents in the kitchen as the final preparations were made for dinner. Ginny took advantage of the captive audience to announce, "Riley has invited me to go with him to stay with his mother over Thanksgiving. I accepted."

Hannah blinked, clearly surprised by the change in plans.

"I knew my mom would love to meet Ginny, and…well, I just want to get her out of town, want her to lie low for a while." Riley frowned. "Compton came to her apartment. Threatened her again."

Hannah gasped.

"What?" Ginny's father, Henry, abandoned the carrots he'd been chopping and faced Ginny. "Did he hurt you?"

"No. Riley showed up, and Walt took off."

"Then the police didn't get him? He's still on the loose?" Hannah asked.

Ginny sighed and pressed a hand to her stomach. The subject of Annie's husband always stirred the acid in her gut and left her feeling off balance. Not even being surrounded by her family and Riley made her feel truly safe any longer. "No, Walt hasn't been found yet."

"So…what are the cops telling you? What are they doing? What leads do they have?" her father asked, concern puckering his brow.

"They've got uniforms watching my apartment, the Comptons' house, Walt's workplace, and they're following up on every lead that is phoned in. They've tracked down the phones he used to call me and asked if anyone in the area remembered seeing him. They get small tips but nothing pans out." She pushed a strand of hair behind her ear. "Annie told me the other day that while Walt was in the military, he trained to do covert reconnaissance. He's smart, and he knows how to hide."

"Oh, dear," her mother whispered, sinking into a chair. "In that case, I'm glad you're leaving town with Riley. There'll be other Thanksgivings for you to share with us, but you have to stay safe now."

An alarm buzzed behind Ginny, and everyone in the room flinched a bit.

"That's the corn casserole." Hannah went to the oven and took out a large bubbling pan. "Henry, time to start the meat grilling."

"Aye, aye, Captain." Her husband took the marinating meat from the refrigerator and nodded to Riley. "Why don't you grab a couple of beers from the cooler and join me out back while I sizzle these up?"

"Sure thing." Riley gave Ginny's shoulder a light squeeze, then grabbed two bottles of beer and followed her father out to the back porch.

After twisting the cap off both bottles, Riley handed one to Henry and took a sip of his. "I saw your new Mustang. It's a beaut."

"Thanks. Hannah says men are just boys with more expensive toys. She may be right."

Riley laughed politely, then took another sip of beer.

"I have to say I was pleasantly surprised to hear Gin was bringing you along today," Henry said. "I can count on one hand the number of Ginny's boyfriends I've ever met. It's encouraging to know she's serious enough about you to bring you to meet her family."

Riley lowered his beer bottle slowly. "I don't know that it means Ginny's serious about me. It was your wife who invited me."

Henry nodded as he started arranging the chicken on the grill with a pair of tongs. "Hannah can't stop talking about you. She thinks you hung the moon."

"Because I was the one who pulled Ginny out of the women's center fire?"

"That. And because she sees integrity and kindness in you. Ginny has a history of dating men who…well, don't live up to their initial promise, you might say."

"So I've heard. But…I can't say I'm doing much better. I'm trying to give her what she wants and needs, but she…" Riley hesitated, remembering this was Ginny's father he was talking to, and looked for the right words to finish his sentence.

"She's hard to please. Is that what you were going to say?" Henry asked with an easy smile.

"Well…"

"Don't forget, I raised her. I know how picky and demanding she can be. Which tells me if she likes you, you're doing a lot right. Regardless of who made the invite, Ginny wouldn't have agreed to bring you here if you didn't mean something special to her."

Riley didn't voice his skepticism, but he also saw this moment for the opportunity it was. Maybe Henry could help him figure out what he was doing wrong with Ginny, why things between them seemed so complicated. "Yeah, I guess hard to please is what I mean. It's like the rules keep changing.

I've tried to protect her since this whole thing with Compton started, but she says I'm smothering her."

Henry grunted and poked at the chicken.

"She wants me to talk about all kind of personal stuff to, quote, 'know who I am,' but she doesn't want to hear that I like the Saints and that I've been with the fire department for seven years. It seems sometimes that the more I try to make her happy, the more she withdraws, the more she asks of me." Riley sat on a lawn chair and stared at the ground near his feet. "I'm not sure I'm the man she thinks I am. I don't know if I can be who she wants me to be."

Henry took a seat across from him and drank a swig of his beer. He was quiet for so long, Riley grew uncomfortable. Had he said too much?

"She wants you to talk about your *feelings?*" Henry said the *f* word with a definite sneer in his tone.

Riley looked up, startled. "I don't—"

"Hannah does that, too. Drives me nuts. I don't know why women think relationships have to be analyzed to death."

Riley released a breath that was half laugh, half relief. "Yeah."

"Ginny's all the worse because of her job." Henry chuckled. "I feel for you, man."

Riley pulled a loose corner of the label on his beer. "I think part of why I'm having a hard time making her happy is because she's got such a high standard. I mean, she's told me what her childhood was like, how perfect your marriage is. I think she's looking for that same perfection in me, and I can't compete with the example you and Hannah set."

Henry scoffed and waved his beer in dismissal. "Hogwash. No marriage is perfect. Certainly not mine and Hannah's. Don't let Gin's misconceptions and idealized memories mess with your head."

Riley squeezed his bottle so hard he though the glass might shatter. "What…misconceptions?"

Henry took another pull on his beer and cast a sideways

glance at him. "A couple years after Gin was born, Hannah and I separated for about six months. Almost got divorced."

Riley's face must have reflected his shock. Henry lifted his eyebrows and shrugged. "Hannah had had two miscarriages in one year and was worried she might never have any more children. We saw several specialists with no luck. They couldn't tell us why she was losing the babies. The stress wore us both down, and finally I'd had enough. I walked out. Definitely not my proudest moment. I still loved Hannah, and I adored my daughter, but the tension in our house was too much. After we both had time to cool down and take stock of things, we gave it another shot."

Riley leaned toward Henry, fascinated by what he was learning. "So what was different the second time? How'd you make it work?"

"We went to a counselor who helped us set up a system for handling our grievances so that our stress level doesn't build up like it did before. Hannah insists that we talk about everything now. How we *feel* about everything—from the way we raise our kids to what we eat for dinner." Henry heaved a sigh and shook his head. "I have to tell you, it was exhausting at first. Uncomfortable for me. But I did it because I loved Hannah and it was important to her. Because there was merit to talking out our differences. Ginny was too young to remember the separation. Parents shield their kids from unpleasantness in a marriage, for the most part. So I can understand her thinking everything was all rosy."

Henry shifted on his chair to face Riley, and pinned him with a serious gaze. "But don't kid yourself Riley. Every relationship takes work. No one is perfect. Don't let my daughter back you into a corner where you think you have to be perfect to make your relationship work. Just do what you can. But remember— when you love someone, sometimes you have to do what's hard, you have to make sacrifices and leaps of faith to make things work. Just be up front with her, be faithful, be the man your mama raised you to be. You'll be fine." With a tight nod, Henry tipped up his beer for another sip, signaling the end to his lecture.

Then with a sputter, he set the beer down and launched out of his chair. "Dang it, son, you let me ramble on and nearly burn the chicken!" He flipped the meat over, and it sizzled and smoked. "Grab that tray for me, will ya? I think we're about ready to eat."

Riley picked up the platter from the picnic table and carried it to the grill. "I appreciate you telling me about you and Hannah. You've given me a lot to think about."

"You're welcome. But don't overthink it. Ginny can make things harder than they are by overanalyzing. If you two care about each other, don't let situations build up. Say what's on your mind, put your cards on the table and deal with it. Period. By all indications, you're a good man, Riley. Ginny is lucky to have found you."

He grinned and shook his head. "I'd say I'm the one who was lucky to find her."

Henry's smile spread wider. "You're right about that. C'mon. Let's get this chicken inside. I'm starved."

Chapter 11

Thanksgiving morning, Riley and Ginny headed out to his mother's house. After a thirty minute drive from the city, they reached his rural childhood home, nestled in the woods at the edge of Lagniappe Lake. The oaks, gums and maples shading the house had turned dazzling shades of gold, red and orange, and the late autumn sun made the leaves glow like fire on the branches.

He parked his truck in front of the house and escorted Ginny to the porch.

"It's beautiful out here. If I had a place like this where I could escape on weekends, I'd visit all the time. It's so quiet," Ginny said.

"Yeah." He glanced around the yard, remembering. "But when you're a restless teenager, all the peace and quiet translates to boredom and isolation. The nearest neighbor is two miles and the closest store is twelve miles. I couldn't wait to leave for college."

"Yeah, but you know better now."

He opened the screened door and knocked. "I told you, I'm a bad son. I know I should visit her more, but…I don't. I get busy. I forget to call…."

Ginny wrapped her arm around him and snuggled closer. "Don't be so hard on yourself. My mom says the same thing about Matt. Maybe it's a son thing."

Riley's chest tightened. He knew, for him, there was more to it. He shoved down the bitter taste of guilt that rose in his throat and shrugged.

When his mom didn't answer his knock, he tested the knob. Locked.

Ginny sent him a narrow-eyed gaze. "She knew we were coming, didn't she? Are we early?"

"I talked to her this morning. She knew." He noticed a piece of tape stuck on the door and glanced down to find a folded sheet of paper at his feet. "Wait, Holmes. Here's a clue."

He read the note aloud. "'Dropped a whole carton of eggs. Ran to town for more. Gotta have eggs to make my dressing and pecan pie. Key's in usual spot. Back soon. Love, Mom.'"

"Good luck to her finding a store open on Thanksgiving," Ginny muttered.

"She will or she'll die trying. She's stubborn that way." He grinned and tweaked Ginny's chin. "Like someone else I know."

She raised her pale eyebrows. "Careful with the comparisons to your mother, there. Dangerous ground."

Riley raised his hand. "'Nough said."

"So you know where the key is, right? The usual spot?"

"Yeah." He stepped off the porch and shoved his hands in his pockets, inhaling the crisp morning air. "But I think I'd rather show you the lake. Our boat. Follow me."

Taking her hand, he headed down the rutted dirt road that led to Lagniappe Lake. When the waterfront came into view, his gut swirled with acid, and his lungs constricted with dread.

As hard as it was facing the pain the lake evoked, he forced himself to take this pilgrimage each time he came home. In remembrance of what he'd lost. As penance. As punishment.

"Um, Riley...I'm not going anywhere." Ginny's voice lifted him from his reverie.

"Huh?"

"You're squeezing my hand like you think I'm gonna make a break for it."

"Oh." He flashed her a quick smile of apology. "Sorry."

"Are you okay?"

He shrugged. "Why wouldn't I be?"

"You tell me."

Instead, he nodded toward the long wooden dock that extended out into the deep waters of the lake. Far enough out to accommodate mooring the family's small cabin cruiser. Far enough out for swimming.

Far enough out for drowning.

He gritted his teeth and tugged Ginny forward. "There it is. The *Arielle*. My father's boat and weekend hobby. I can't tell you how many hours I spent with him working on that boat, keeping it clean and in good repair."

Ginny slowed to a stop and stared. "Holy cow, Riley! That's not a boat. That's a ship! A yacht!"

Riley scoffed. "It's not that big. The size of the aft deck just makes it look bigger. The living space and head combined are smaller than your kitchen."

"But it *has* a living space. That's no simple fishing or ski boat like the families I knew as a kid had." Ginny started forward again at a faster pace until she reached the end of the dock. "Can I go on board?"

Her face shone with the excitement of a child at a birthday party. He tried to see the cruiser through her eyes. The wide, weathered deck with its waist high safety railing, the mildewed cushions of the side bench seats and the rust-stained storage compartments.

Compunction plucked at him. His mother wasn't all he'd

neglected in recent years. What would his dad think if he could see the sorry shape of his beloved *Arielle?*

Riley offered Ginny a hand as he helped her climb aboard. He followed her to the door of the cabin, which she opened to peek inside.

"Careful, the stairs are steep." He put a hand under her elbow as she started down.

She sniffed. "It smells like lemons in here."

Riley took a whiff as he glanced around the tidy interior of the living space. "More like lemon-scented cleaner." He shook his head. "I think my mom must have been straightening things up in here. Guess she knew I'd show the boat off to you and wanted it to make a good impression."

"Well, you can tell her I was impressed long before I even saw the living quarters. It's awesome."

Riley lifted a hinged countertop. "Under here is a two-burner stove and the sink. Over there is the head. And this table lowers like this…." He folded in the legs of the small Formica table and laid it atop brackets between the bench seats at thigh height. "Then these cushions fold out to make a mattress and…voilà! A bed."

Ginny laughed. "You really could live out here!"

"I did. I camped in here with friends a lot during summer vacations. And my dad and I took trips out in the Gulf a couple times before he got sick." Happy memories of times spent on the *Arielle* with his father and friends rose to ride shotgun with the darker memories that had his gut in knots.

Ginny's shoulder brushed his as she moved past him to take a closer look at the head. "It even has a—ow!" She bent and grabbed her toe.

Riley edged around the bed to see what she had kicked. "You okay, Gin?"

"I stubbed my toe on this—whatever it is." She bent to pick something up. "This very…um, *colorful* rock."

Riley grinned when he saw what she held. "Oh, my God. I

haven't seen that thing in years." He chuckled and took the softball-size, garishly painted rock from her. "My paperweight."

Ginny snorted. "Paperweight? Isn't that a little big for a paperweight?"

"It's a *lot* big for a paperweight. But I didn't know that in first grade when I made it for my dad for Father's Day. He actually kept it on his desk for a while before it got relegated to doorstop status." Riley smiled and placed the rock on the floor near the cabin door. "Jodi used to say it looked like a rainbow threw up on it." He cocked his head and appraised the doorstop. "And she was right."

Ginny moved closer to him and tipped her head. "Who's Jodi?"

Riley jerked his gaze up to meet hers, not realizing until that moment what he'd said. His stomach bunched, and his heart performed a tuck and roll. "My sister."

Ginny's face brightened. "You didn't tell me you have a sister. Will she be here this weekend?"

Bile rose in his throat, and he had to swallow hard before he could speak. "No. She…she's dead."

Ginny blanched, and Riley turned away, unable to face the sympathy that welled in her eyes.

It was his fault Jodi would never spend another holiday with her family. Would never graduate from college or marry. Would never have kids.

Grief squeezed his throat as he stared out the cabin window to the calm green waters of Lagniappe Lake.

When you love someone, sometimes you have to do what's hard, you have to make sacrifices and leaps of faith to make things work. Henry West's advice whispered in Riley's mind, and he drew a deep breath for the strength to do what he had to do.

"She died when she was fourteen…and it was my fault."

Ginny tried to speak, but the air backed up in her lungs. She shook her head in denial and tried to process the bombshell Riley had dropped. When she could finally speak, she stuttered, "Oh, Riley, no. Wh-why would you say that?"

He spared her a brief glance before turning back to the tiny window that let a thin gray light into the living quarters. "Because it *was* my fault. She was my responsibility, and I neglected her. I failed her…and she died." He nodded toward the window. "Right out there. Near the end of the dock."

Ginny couldn't move, couldn't tear her gaze from the agony molding Riley's face into a mask of pain and grief. Compassion raked her heart with sharp tines. "H-how? What happened?"

"Coroner thinks she hit her head on the dock while she was diving." He spoke softly, slowly. Drawing a deep breath, he continued staring out the window with a zombielike stillness. "She had been doing flips and dives earlier, but…I wasn't paying attention to her like I should have. A neighbor was with us. A girl…Erin…and I was too busy trying to impress her to pay attention to my little sister. We weren't supposed to swim alone. It was a cardinal rule for us."

Lost in his memories, he drew his eyebrows together in a deep, troubled frown. "It was my job to watch out for Jodi while she swam, but I didn't. And…she drowned." His voice cracked, and he paused to squeeze his eyes shut. Ball his fists. Grit his teeth.

The pain etched in his face, vibrating from him in waves, wrenched Ginny's emotions and stole her breath. She forced her limbs to move. Quietly, she approached him, placed her hand on his back.

At her touch, he flinched, and his nostrils flared as he sucked in another deep, shaky breath. He sent her a brief, startled glance, as if he'd forgotten she was there, then looked away again. She saw the moisture that filled his eyes, and tears of shared pain for his suffering stung her nose.

She stroked her hand over his back, felt him shudder. "Riley…oh, sweetheart…I'm so sorry. I…" Her throat clogged, and she struggled for a breath before she could go on. "You can't blame yourself. It was an accident—"

"A preventable accident!" he snapped, whirling toward her. "If I'd been watching her like I was supposed to, I could have saved her! I could have pulled her from the water before she drowned."

"Maybe. But—"

"When my dad died, I became the man of the family." He thumped his chest with his fist, his voice full of the pain-born anger and frustration she knew he held for himself. "It was my *duty* to protect my sister, and I failed! Jodi is dead because of me!"

Ginny stepped closer to him, placed a soothing hand on his chest. "You can't keep blaming yourself like this, Riley. It will eat you up inside. Destroy you."

And in that instant, it clicked into place. Now that her initial shock had worn off, she saw that *this* was what she'd seen shadowing his gaze when she brought up his family. This was why he danced around the topic of his past, kept her at arm's length from his emotions. He'd been carrying a load of guilt and grief so heavy that it crushed him. He could live with himself only by burying the pain as deep as he could.

He shook his head, curling his lip in disdain, then backed away from her touch. "No. I can never make up for what I did. I can save a hundred other people's lives, and it will never bring Jodi back. Letting her die was…unforgivable."

Riley turned toward the window, blinking, breathing hard, clearly fighting not to give in to the tears puddling in his eyes.

Ginny's empathy for his anguish squeezed her chest with a viselike grip. She absorbed the hurt and misery that radiated from him as if they were physical blows to her gut. To her soul.

She'd heard so many tales of tragedy through her job at the women's center, and she always felt a sympathetic sadness for her clients' situations.

But Riley's internal struggle with his guilt, the wounds

left by his sister's death gouged to her marrow. His pain was her pain.

Because she was falling in love with him.

Her heart gave another sharp twist as that truth washed through her. With a strangled sob, she allowed the tears that had been hovering in her eyes to flow down her cheeks. Never had she felt so helpless in easing another's pain.

When she'd found out Jim had battered Donna, her own guilt had morphed into a purpose, a new career path. Donna's primary pain had been physical, but Ginny knew the deep gouges emotional pain like Riley's could leave on a life.

She had been trained to counsel, to comfort, to guide people toward healing. But she was at a loss where to begin easing Riley's grief. She was far too emotionally involved with him to see his suffering objectively.

His body language screamed, *Stay away. Leave me alone.*

But he'd been alone in his anguish for too long. She wanted desperately to find a way to share the burden he'd carried for years. To let him know he wasn't alone anymore.

Moving up behind him, she wrapped her arms around his waist. Her cast made the embrace awkward, but she didn't care. She rested her cheek on his broad back and wept for him from the depths of her soul. She cried the tears he stubbornly held in check, unable to stem the wellspring of emotion once she'd started.

She felt him tense, felt his hand cover hers. Felt him grow still. A few seconds passed as her tears soaked his shirt, then he pivoted within the circle of her arms. He caught her chin and tilted her head up.

Stormy gray eyes searched hers, concern written in the creases in his brow, the hard line of his mouth. He wiped her damp cheek with his thumb, obviously upset over her tears. "Ginny? What... Why—?"

"Because you're hurting. When you hurt, I do, too. And I don't know what to do to heal your pain."

The muscle in his jaw jumped, and he frowned. "It's not your job to heal my pain. I don't expect you to try to fix me. This is my problem, my responsibility, my—"

She silenced him with a kiss.

"No," she said, her lips still brushing his. "It's mine, too. Because I care about you, Riley. You've become a part of who I am. I won't let you go through this by yourself."

He sighed heavily, resting his forehead against hers and pulling her closer. "Ginny…I never wanted to burden you with this. I never meant for you to find out. I wanted—"

"To suffer in silence. I know." She stroked the side of his face with her hand and raised her gaze to his. "Thank you. For sharing this with me." She brushed another soft kiss over his lips and slid her arm around his neck. "I know it was difficult. It means a lot to me…that you trusted me enough to tell me."

He said nothing for several moments. He simply stood with his forehead against hers, his arms around her back, and Ginny gave him the time he needed to sort out his thoughts. She threaded her fingers through the hair at his nape and felt the steady thud of his heartbeat against her chest.

"Jodi was my best friend," he whispered, his voice a rasp. "I miss her…so much."

This time when Ginny pulled back to meet his eyes, she found moisture had leaked from his eyelashes onto his cheek.

And her heart split wide open.

"Oh, Riley…" She drank in his tears as she pressed her lips to his cheeks, his eyes, his mouth.

He returned her kisses with an urgency and passion that dissolved her defenses. She tasted the need behind his deep, searing kiss, and her body answered with an equal longing to be with him, be part of him, be joined with him. Physically. Spiritually. Emotionally.

Riley speared his fingers into her hair, anchoring her close as he drew on her lips. His breath mingled with hers, reminding her that this man had once, literally, breathed life into her.

She recalled the moment she'd opened her eyes, locked gazes with him and known an unearthly connection, an awareness that had shaken her to her soul. That had comforted her. Calmed and reassured her.

Now she tried with her kiss, with her touch, to infuse him with even a fraction of the life-sustaining gift he'd given her. She ached for a way to heal his wounded heart, revive his hope and nourish his soul. Her own heart longed to reinforce the bonds of trust and affection he'd offered her by sharing his darkest memories, his deepest hurt with her.

When she broke away to gulp in oxygen, he moved his lips across her cheek to her ear, her eyes, her jaw, trailing tender kisses that sent shivers of anticipation over her skin. His hands moved restlessly from her hair to her shoulders, then skimmed down her spine. His fingers slipped under her sweater to caress the sensitive hollow at the small of her back.

From low in her belly, warmth exploded through her body in a tingling rush, and she gasped at the onslaught of sensation. Ginny's fingers curled into Riley's shirt, and she worked the fabric up, pulling it over his head.

He finished guiding the shirt off his arms and dropped it at his feet. His eyes locked on hers. The questions and emotions in his gaze mirrored the ones ricocheting inside her.

Surprise for what her boldness implied.

Desire and expectancy.

Uncertainty and heartbreaking need.

Was she sure she was ready to take this step?

Holding his gaze, she gave him a tiny nod.

He inhaled a sharp, shaky breath. Riley's eyes flashed hot…yet mellowed with tenderness at the same time. But before she could give that duality more thought, he turned and snatched a sheet from a small cabinet over the bed. With a flick of his wrists, he spread it over the mattress.

Ginny swept her sweater over her head and let it fall on the floor next to Riley's shirt. When he turned to face her, she heard his breath catch. His gray eyes darkened to the color of smoke, and the fire in his gaze made her blood heat and her heart race.

Without a word, they undressed each other slowly, stopping occasionally to share another kiss, a lingering gaze, a soft caress. When Ginny was down to just her satin panties and Riley his boxer briefs, he scooped her into his arms and laid her on the bed, following her down and covering her body with his.

Ginny held her breath, and she shivered in the cool November air. Anticipation and yearning rippled through her, along with the nip of nerves. She hadn't been with a man in years, hadn't dared to open herself to the emotional and physical costs such intimacy required.

She strummed her fingers up the bumps of Riley's spine, then across the wide muscled span of his shoulders. He kissed her forehead gently as he settled on top of her, bracing most of his weight on his arms.

"Ginny," he whispered, her name no more than a sigh.

He brushed a light kiss across her lips, then moved lower, his mouth exploring the curve of her throat, the valley between her breasts, the dip of her navel. His lips and fingers worshiped her, aroused her, memorized her.

She closed her eyes and lost herself in the heady sensations that thickened her blood and made her body hum with need. When Riley skimmed her panties down and pressed a kiss over her womb, electricity sparked through her. With a mewl of pleasure, she arched her back to meet his lips and beg for more. He tossed the last of her clothes in the pile of others on the floor and stood to strip off his briefs.

Ginny's mouth grew arid and her breathing shallow and quick. Riley's naked body was a masterpiece of nature that could rival the work of the greatest sculptors. He was taut muscle, lean lines and rigid strength. Her warrior protector, her wounded soldier, the man who'd found a way into her heart.

Realizing how much Riley meant to her, the bond they

were forging in this moment, Ginny felt her pulse spike. A flicker of fear spiraled through her. How could she give so much of herself to him and not end up hurt? There was a lot still left unsaid between them. She forced herself to swallow the nagging doubt and focus on the warmth in Riley's eyes.

After fishing a condom from his wallet, he covered himself and moved back to the edge of the small bed. She reached for him and twined her legs with his as he settled between her thighs.

"So beautiful," he murmured as he captured her mouth again. His hand stroked behind her knee, along the inside of her leg until he reached the juncture of her thighs.

Ginny raised her hips, seeking the completion her body craved. She released a ragged sigh when his fingers caressed her, pushing her closer to the edge of her control, firing shimmering sparks through her veins. She stroked her hands to his buttocks and nudged him closer, opening wider to accommodate him. She was shaking, strung tight, ready to shatter. But she refused to let go too soon.

"Riley…I…want you inside me…when I—" Her words were a breathless gasp, lost in a feathery moan when his lips nipped her sensitized breast. When she grew impatient and slid her hand between them to fold her fingers around his thick shaft, he answered with a husky growl. Wrapping her legs around his hips, she guided him inside her and nearly fell apart from the first probing touch.

But Riley resisted, slowing the pace. He eased inside her with a careful, erotic stroke. Filling her, stretching her, joining their souls. She clutched her arms around him, shaking as he withdrew, then slid home again with the same sensual, patient pace. Riley quivered with restraint, but the caress of his body inside her sent her spiraling into sweet oblivion. Tightening her hold on him, she cried out as the pulsing waves of bliss engulfed her. She felt him tense, fighting his own release as her body milked his. When the last ripples of sensation faded, she raised her gaze and found him watching her with a piercing intensity and affection warming his eyes.

He smiled and pressed a kiss to the tip of her nose. Holding her gaze, he moved inside her again with the same slow, seductive pace as before. Renewing the heat within her. Sighing his pleasure. And finally joining her as they shattered in each other's arms.

Chapter 12

"Shouldn't your mother be back from the store by now?" Ginny whispered, while drawing tiny circles on his chest with her fingernail.

Riley groaned. "Probably."

"We should go."

"In a minute," he said, letting his own fingers trail along her cheek, trace her lips. "I'm not ready to let you go yet."

She smiled coyly and kissed the finger he brushed over her mouth. He studied the play of sunlight from the cabin window as it danced in her eyes and made her hair shine. He grinned, thinking how different sex with Ginny had been from what he'd imagined. He'd always figured, based on their flirtation, their sizzling chemistry and the heat of the kisses they'd shared, that their sex would be a lusty affair, wild and sweaty. Maybe just a little raunchy.

But the sex they'd just had hadn't been about sex at all.

They'd been making love.

Riley sucked in a deep breath and released it slowly as all the implications of that realization washed through him.

"Bad news," he murmured.

"What?" She rolled toward him, resting her cast on his chest as she pushed up on her left elbow. Her position afforded him a spectacular view of her breasts. He almost lost his train of thought.

"That was the only condom I brought."

"To the boat or…for the weekend?"

He winced. "Yes."

She grinned and dropped a kiss on his lips. "Good thing I plan ahead then, huh?"

He arched an eyebrow. "Oh?"

She flashed an impish grin then snuggled back down in the nook of his arm. "Really. We should go."

"Soon." He wasn't ready to leave the peaceful bliss of simply holding Ginny close and relishing what they'd shared. She continued to surprise and amaze him.

His emotions had been jagged and raw after offering up the ugly truth about Jodi's death. But instead of being repulsed by his revelation and condemning him as he'd expected, Ginny had cried. She'd offered love and acceptance, taking on his pain as her own.

Still, a thread of panic wound through him. By giving up this piece of himself to her, he'd handed her the tool to shred his heart if she chose. He'd given her access to the deepest part of his soul.

If she, like Erin, chose to use this painful time in his past against him, use it to manipulate him, she could hurt him far worse than Erin ever had. Because he'd grown to care deeply for Ginny. More than he'd ever cared for another woman.

Swallowing hard to tamp down the niggling concern, Riley closed his eyes and inhaled the baby powder scent of her skin, savoring the moment. The *Arielle* rocked gently as small waves lapped at the boat.

"Riley?"

He opened his eyes to slits to peer down at Ginny. He sensed the change in her mood immediately, saw the worry lines that creased her forehead. His chest tightened. "Yeah?"

"Have you ever talked with anyone about what happened to Jodi?"

A sick feeling settled in his gut. "Besides you?"

"Yeah."

He sighed. He *so* didn't want to go down this path again. "No."

"You should."

"No."

"Riley—"

"No! It was hard enough telling you. I'm not going to talk to a stranger about it. I'm handling it fine without anyone poking around in my head, psychoanalyzing me."

She propped herself on her elbow again and gazed at him with concern. "But you're hurting. How can you say you're fine? You can't keep that kind of hurt bottled up. You need to talk about—"

"No…I don't." He pushed away from her and swung his legs off the bed.

Her pity made his teeth hurt. Pity was the last thing he wanted…or deserved. The only reason he'd told her anything was because she'd have likely found out from his mother this weekend anyway. Then she'd have been mad that he hadn't told her. He cared about Ginny, so he'd taken her father's advice and tried to give her the truth she wanted. But he should have known she wouldn't be able to let the subject rest. He'd spilled his guts to her, opened a vein and bled his deepest pain for her. And it wasn't enough.

He wasn't sure he could ever be everything Ginny wanted and needed. She saw him as a hero. She was looking for the perfection she believed her parents had.

He was no hero. Anything but perfect.

He was doomed to fail her, disappoint her. Let her down.

Raking fingers through his hair, he sighed. "Please, Ginny. Let it go. I told you because I wanted you to know, to understand who I am, what I am. But I can't talk about it anymore. Don't…" He ground his back teeth. Rubbed at the throb of pain behind his eyes. "Don't ask for more."

She moved up behind him and looped her arms loosely around his neck. Propping her chin on his shoulder, she held him silently.

After a moment, she scooted around to sit beside him. She lifted her left hand to finger-comb her hair. "I don't suppose you have a hairbrush down here. I'm a mess. Your mom is going to take one look at me and think, *Hussy.*"

Relief that Ginny had let the topic go, at least for the time being, eased the knot of tension in his chest. He handed her her bra and panties from the floor and quirked a smile. "My mom is going to love you…." He snagged his briefs and jeans and sent her a side glance. "Hussy or not."

"Unh!" She boxed him on the shoulder and laughed. "You rat!"

Despite the grin she gave him, he still saw the shadow of worry and sympathy in her eyes.

A leaden weight settled in his gut when he realized how much had changed between them just in the last hour. They'd made love, but was that physical bond enough to save their relationship? She now knew his ugliest secret, and he already felt the strain it put on them.

He'd brought Ginny home with him for Thanksgiving to keep her safe. But by the end of the weekend, would the ugly truths he shared with her manage to drive a wedge between them or destroy the fragile faith Ginny had in him?

Maureen Sinclair welcomed Ginny into her home with a warm hug and a graciousness that made Ginny feel immediately at ease. Riley had inherited her soft gray eyes, dark blond hair and bright smile. Though the years had left their mark on her with tiny lines around her eyes and mouth, Maureen Sinclair was still a beautiful woman.

She fussed about the kitchen, giving both Riley and Ginny jobs to do as well, and by late afternoon they were sitting down to a sumptuous Southern feast. Turkey with corn bread dressing and giblet gravy, cranberry relish, sweet potato casserole, green beans with fried onions, and both pumpkin and pecan pie.

When Ginny tried to help with the dishes, she was shooed out of the kitchen to watch football in the family room with Riley.

Later that evening, they played cards, flipped through family photo albums and watched the romantic comedy DVD Maureen had rented earlier in the week.

Despite the dramatic turn their relationship had taken that morning on the *Arielle,* Ginny refused Riley's invitation to share his bed. She felt odd sleeping with him with his mother just down the hall, and she wanted a little time to herself to take stock of the new direction of their relationship.

She was glad she'd come home with Riley this weekend. She had a better understanding of who he was and where he'd come from, not just because of his revelation about Jodi's death, but because of the loving, easygoing way he interacted with his mother. Maureen had also shared insights about her son as they perused old family photos.

Just remembering the emotion and warmth in his eyes as he'd made love to her made Ginny's skin prickle with a flush of arousal and her heart swell with affection. She'd been moved by the exquisite tenderness and care he'd shown as her lover.

Yet for all the new information she had about Riley and the new physical bond they shared, his revelation about his sister's death raised more questions for Ginny. Questions she knew Riley would be loath to answer. Questions she felt compelled to resolve for her own peace of mind.

Ginny fell asleep with those nagging queries swirling through her head. That night, she slept better than she had in weeks, feeling a certain distance from Walt Compton's threat and her clients' troublesome situations. Exactly why Riley had brought her out to the lake house.

The next morning, following the scents of freshly brewed coffee and homemade cinnamon rolls, she padded barefooted into the kitchen and greeted Riley's mother with a sleepy smile. "Good morning."

Maureen glanced up from the eggs she was beating to a froth. "Morning, Ginny. Coffee is ready if you want a cup."

"Please."

"Help yourself. Mugs are over there." Maureen nodded toward a rack on the countertop.

"Is Riley up yet?" Ginny asked, pouring herself a steaming mug of the savory brew.

"Sure is. He headed down to the lake to tinker with his boat a bit before breakfast."

Ginny sipped her coffee, then frowned. "His boat? He told me the *Arielle* was his dad's."

"It was. But his father willed it to him before he died. The boat is Riley's now."

Ginny raised the mug to her lips for another sip, pondering why Riley hadn't mentioned that. Wondering if it had been more than a simple omission.

Carrying her mug to the opposite side of the counter from where Maureen worked, she took a seat on one of the bar stools, deciding whether to join Riley down at the boat.

"Riley tells me you're a counselor at the Lagniappe Women's Center." Maureen's voice pulled her out of her musing.

"Yes, ma'am. I've been there for eight years."

"Admirable work. But difficult at times, I'm sure. Seeing the terrible things some people go through."

Ginny nodded. "But also heartening, when I see them rise above their circumstances and make a new life for themselves. A better life." Her thoughts shifted to Annie, praying she would have the chance to build a better life for herself and her children.

"Riley also says you've been having trouble lately with the husband of one of your clients. That this man has threatened you. Come to your apartment. Even tried to kill you. How frightening!"

She glanced up and met the worried-mother expression Maureen wore. Ginny gave her a reassuring smile. "I've had a few scary moments, but I'll be fine. The police have stepped up their hunt for him. They're bound to catch him soon."

Maureen wiped her hands on a towel, then took a skillet down from a cabinet. "Riley is worried about you. He doesn't think you're taking your safety seriously enough."

Ginny's hand tightened around her mug. "He's been very supportive of me throughout this ordeal with Walt Compton. But Riley can be…"

She hesitated. Should she even broach the topic with his mother? She didn't want to sound critical. Ginny chose her words carefully, hoping Maureen might help give her some perspective on how to handle Riley when he was overbearing. "Well, he's superprotective. Borderline smothering at times. As much as I appreciate his concern, he's driving me crazy with his hypervigilance and constant worrying about me. I know how to take care of myself. I value my independence, and all his protectiveness is starting to feel…cloying."

Maureen glanced up and held her gaze for several seconds without saying anything. Ginny held her breath, fearing she'd said too much and offended her.

Dropping her eyes, Maureen poured the eggs into the skillet and stirred slowly. "Has Riley told you about the day Jodi died?"

Ginny's pulse stumbled, and she nodded. "Yesterday, just after we arrived. He blames himself."

Maureen lifted a startled look. "He does?"

"You didn't know?"

"I…I knew he'd taken Jodi's death especially hard when it happened. But I thought it was because he'd been there at the time. Because he'd been the one to pull her out of the lake. Because they'd been so close when they were younger. I didn't realize he—" Sighing, she pressed a hand to her mouth and closed her eyes. Shook her head. "It wasn't his fault. I never blamed him. Why—?"

Maureen didn't finish the question. Instead, she gave the eggs a brisk stir.

"He's carrying around a lot of guilt and pain." Ginny stared into her mug as if it held the answers she wanted. "He needs some resolution, some way to forgive himself for what he sees as a failure on his part."

Tilting her head, Maureen gave Ginny a heartbreaking look. "Then you understand why he's so protective of you? He worries about you because he cares. He's overprotective because he's scared of losing you, like he lost his sister. Afraid if he lets his guard down for even a moment that you'll be snatched away from him or that you'll be hurt. Jodi was gone in an instant of his inattention, and Erin was assaulted while he was gone to work. No wonder he's trying so hard to keep you safe."

"Erin?"

"He hasn't told you about Erin?"

"No." A chill skated down Ginny's spine. So there was more Riley hadn't told her. She'd sensed as much.

Maureen sighed and shook her head. "Well, when he's ready, I'm sure he'll explain. It's not my place, so…"

Ginny's chest squeezed as she wondered what new bombshell Riley might be withholding. Then her thoughts shifted to the rest of what Maureen had said about Riley's reasons for being so protective. Ginny hadn't made the connection, though she should have. Between their lovemaking and all the Thanksgiving activities, she hadn't taken the time to consider all the ramifications of how Jodi's death still shaped Riley's perspective and actions.

Her breath lodged in her lungs.

Maureen removed the eggs from the heat and turned off the

burner. "Honey, when my husband died, I thought I had to be strong for my children and self-reliant so I wouldn't be a worry or burden to my friends. I wanted to be the steel magnolia that Southern tradition teaches gals like us to be. I tried to do everything for myself, thinking that asking for help was a sign of weakness."

Maureen walked around the end of the kitchen counter and sat on a bar stool beside Ginny. "But a wise woman from my church helped me see things differently. She reminded me that love can only blossom when it flows both ways."

Ginny nodded. She knew that concept well enough through counseling her clients. Too often she'd seen how unrequited love led to rejection and heartache.

"So my friends' offers of help, the food they brought after the funeral…these were expressions of their love for me and my kids. If I denied them the chance to express the love and concern they felt while I was grieving, I destroyed an opportunity to let my relationship with that friend grow."

Ginny furrowed her brow as she considered what Maureen was saying.

"When you reject people's offers of help, you're also rejecting the love they want to show you. Think about how you feel when someone you care about is hurting. Your offers to help them come from a deep affection and concern, a heartfelt need to ease their pain. Right?"

Ginny thought of her years counseling Megan through her rape trauma. Of the pain she'd seen in Riley's eyes only yesterday. Of all the women she'd worked with over the years.

"Sure. It happens almost daily in my job."

Maureen covered Ginny's hands and met her gaze with a motherly gentleness.

"When you accept help, you're not weaker because of it. You're building stronger bonds with the people who love you, with people who want to share your pain and make things better for you. Love is as much about how we interact with others as it is a feeling in your heart."

Ginny blinked as something inside her shifted. "I've never looked at it that way before. But it makes sense. I know how I feel when my friends are hurting."

Maureen smiled. "Then let Riley help you. Let him do what he must do because of the love he has for you. He needs to feel he's not just sitting on the sidelines while you're going through a difficult time alone. Let him love you. And what you have together will grow stronger."

Let Riley love her? They'd never put a name to the feelings they had for each other. And somehow, calling what they had *love* scared her silly.

Annie and Walt had loved each other enough at one time to get married, have children. Megan's first fiancé had claimed he loved her, then, when a stranger raped her, he'd abandoned her and broken her heart in her darkest hour. Jim Prather had sworn he loved Donna before he took out his rage on her over a trivial matter.

If Ginny let herself love Riley, how could she be sure he wouldn't change his mind, wouldn't turn against her, wouldn't break her heart? How did she trust that love was truly what he felt, truly what *she* felt? If she could be such a bad judge of character, how could she be sure of any matters of the heart?

She swallowed the sour taste that rose from her stomach.

Maureen touched her arm. "Ginny? Are you all right?"

She glanced up. "What…what makes you think Riley loves me?"

Maureen laughed. "Oh, honey. A mother knows. It's in his eyes whenever he looks at you."

"Really?"

She nodded. "And since he moved out to go to college, he's brought home exactly one lady friend to meet me." She aimed a finger at Ginny. "You. That says a lot."

Ginny's stomach flip-flopped, and she gnawed her bottom

lip as she thought about the glow in Riley's eyes as they'd made love. She'd seen more than lust in his gaze. More than a sense of duty to protect her.

A warm reassurance swelled inside her, like the peace she'd known when she'd revived at the fire scene and had met Riley's piercing gaze. Her heart pounded an eager rhythm.

"So how about having some of these eggs before they get cold? And I have cinnamon rolls ready to come out of the oven." Maureen scooted off her stool and headed back around the counter.

"Uh, no. I…think I'll get dressed and join Riley down at the boat."

Maureen braced a hand on her hip and looked at the eggs. "Okay. I'll keep breakfast warm until you get back."

Ginny held her gaze and smiled. "Thank you. For…"

She hesitated, fumbling for the right words.

Riley's mother returned an understanding grin. "You're welcome, honey."

Ginny hurried back to the bedroom to change into a denim skirt and long-sleeved, cotton sweater. She jammed a few condoms in her pocket, then raced out of the house and down the bumpy dirt lane to the lake. To the *Arielle.* To Riley.

As she clattered down the dock to greet him, he looked up from the motor he had taken apart. Wiping his hands on a towel, he lifted a corner of his mouth in a sultry smile that spiked the heat and anticipation already tripping through her veins.

"Hey there. You sleep well?"

"I did. Like a baby. You?"

"I was kinda lonely, actually. Kept thinking about you, just down the hall…." He offered her a hand, which she held as she climbed aboard the *Arielle.* "Did Mom send you to get me for breakfast?"

"She's holding it for us. I came to…keep you company." Ginny flashed him a coy grin and pulled the condoms from her pocket. "I brought these."

Riley's eyebrows shot up, and he gave her an appraising look. "You say my mom is holding breakfast?"

She grinned. "We probably have about thirty minutes before the food is ruined."

Riley tossed the towel aside and gave her a wolfish grin. "We'd better get busy then."

Ginny yelped, then laughed as he scooped her up and carried her down the steep steps into the living quarters of the *Arielle*. Kicking the door closed, he set her down and held up his hands. "Don't move. I just have to wash up."

While he scrubbed his hands in the tiny sink, she dropped the condoms on the counter and shimmied out of her panties. When he turned, drying his hands, she twirled the panties on the end of her finger. "Time's a wasting."

A throaty growl rumbled from him as he crossed to her in two large steps. Their mouths met and meshed. Ravaged. Her hands roamed impatiently over his chest and shoulders, face and hair. Riley had his jeans off and a condom on in record time. When he lifted Ginny, his hands under her bare thighs, she wrapped her legs around him, and he backed her against the door.

Yesterday, they had been slow and careful, tender and sweet. Today, neither had patience for anything but this heated, frenzied joining. He sank into her, and she arched her neck, her pleasured cry mingling with his. Their teeth clicked as he kissed her. The thrusts of his tongue, deep into her mouth, mimicked in perfect rhythm the coupling of their bodies.

When she climaxed, Ginny dug her fingers into Riley's shirt and clung to him. He shuddered and released a ragged sigh as he joined her.

His gaze zeroed in on hers, and the myriad emotions burning in his eyes seared her heart, branded her. Even though their lovemaking had been hot and fast, the feelings they'd awakened yesterday were still just beneath the surface, still just as intense.

Perhaps more so.

She saw so much about Riley in a new light. Things she

should have recognized sooner. But she'd been so busy protecting her independence and trying to pry him open like a clam she found on the beach that she'd missed the obvious.

Then, like the slap of the cold lake against the boat's hull, all her new doubts and questions surged forward, demanding attention. A nip of cool apprehension swirled through her blood, and she shivered.

Riley let her legs slide down his until her feet touched the floor. He groaned and gave her another deep kiss. "I'll never be able to look at this boat the same way again. I may have to rename it the *Ginny.*"

Sorting through the questions in her head, she glanced around and addressed the topic at hand. "Why didn't you tell me this was your boat? That your dad left it to you."

Riley leaned back enough to give her a speculative glance. "How'd you—?" He cut himself off and shook his head. "Just how much did you and my mom discuss while I was out of the room?"

"Enough."

He narrowed his gaze as he put his clothes back on. "Should I be worried?"

She forced a grin and kissed his cheek. "I don't think so. In fact, she helped clear up a few things for me."

Ginny straightened her skirt and glanced around the small cabin, picturing Riley as a boy, bonding with his father as they worked together on weekends or lived in the tiny space on long fishing trips.

And inspiration struck, sidelining the questions she had for Riley.

"Annie," she muttered under her breath as the idea took shape, and she began analyzing the notion for pitfalls.

"What?" Riley paused to glance up at her.

"Annie could stay here. On your boat. It's plenty remote, and Walt would have no reason to think of her being here. She'd be safe…."

Riley glanced around and nodded. "Sure. I don't see why not. It's got everything you need. A bed, a stove, a bathroom, a—"

"No." Ginny shook her head and discarded the idea. "What would she do for heat? It's getting a lot colder at night and… and the water…" She waved a hand toward the window with its view of the lake.

"The water?"

"She's got an active four-year-old daughter and a crawling baby. It just seems kinda dangerous to have two young children living here." Ginny puffed out a sigh. "But it opens other possibilities. If I could find someone with an RV camper or—"

"My mom."

Ginny blinked. "Your mom has an RV?"

"No, but she has all those spare bedrooms. And you've seen for yourself how much she loves company."

"I don't—"

"You don't have an opening at another shelter, and you know Annie is antsy to get out of the Lagniappe shelter. If you're safe out here, away from town, she would be, too. You could alert the local law enforcement to post a guard at the driveway, and she wouldn't be alone, because my mom would be here with her."

"You're not worried about bringing potential danger to your mother's house? What if Walt does find Annie out here?"

Riley sighed and scrubbed a hand over his one-day beard. "My mom has lived alone a number of years, and she's pretty savvy about safety. She even took a class to learn how to shoot my dad's handgun. If we made sure there was a police guard posted, I'd be comfortable with the arrangement. But the decision would, of course, be up to my mother."

Ginny gnawed her bottom lip and considered the offer. Finally, she gave a nod. "All right, let's go ask her."

"Mama, look at that big boat!" Haley Compton squealed and bounced excitedly from one foot to the other as they neared the shore of Lagniappe Lake the next day. "Can I go look at it?"

Annie smiled at her daughter. "All right, but be careful, honey. Stay on the dock." She glanced at Ginny as they strolled down to the lake, and tears filled her eyes. "I haven't seen her this happy in months. Thank you. Thank you both." Annie turned to include Maureen in her appreciative gaze.

Maureen held Ben and dabbed at the baby's drooly mouth. "I'm glad I could help. Your kids are darling. It's been a long time since I had small children around at Christmastime. The look on Haley's face when she saw my Christmas tree was priceless and so heartwarming."

"It is a beautiful tree," Ginny agreed. And seeing it through Haley's young eyes had touched every adult in the room. Even Riley had seemed moved.

"We're going to have fun," Maureen said as they reached the end of the dock. Riley's mother bumped foreheads gently with Ben. "Aren't we, little man? We'll bake cookies and make decorations for the house and string popcorn and watch all the old classic Christmas movies."

Annie made a bittersweet hiccuping sound that drew Ginny's attention. The young mother's eyes were red, and she held her fingers to her lips. "I can never repay you for all of this. It means so much to me."

Maureen sent Ginny a knowing glance, then told Annie, "I'm happy to do it. I get as much out of helping as you do. Really. It is a blessing to feel needed, to be able to give something back for the times others helped me."

Warmth filled Ginny's chest, and she smiled at Maureen. Riley's mother had truly turned her family tragedies into wisdom and strength. Ginny felt sure Annie would learn a lot from Maureen about overcoming difficulties and persevering with grace and hope.

The crunching of dry leaves signaled Riley's approach, and Annie quickly swiped at her eyes.

"Okay, ladies, everything is out of my truck and waiting in the spare bedrooms to be unpacked. I checked the front drive on the way down here, and the local sheriff has posted a patrolman. I think you're good to go." He turned to his mother and pitched his voice lower. "If you need *anything,* anything at all, call me. If you so much as get a sniff that something is wrong, call the sheriff. Don't play the martyr. Don't overthink it. Okay?"

"I'll be fine, honey," Maureen said.

"Promise me."

She leaned in and kissed his cheek. "I promise."

The telltale twitch of his jaw muscle spoke of his concern and doubts. An overprotectiveness, Ginny now understood, born out of loss, guilt and grief.

She stepped closer to him and laced her fingers with his. "Let's give them the space they need to settle in now, okay?"

With her footsteps thumping on the dock, Haley ran to meet the group of adults. "Can we go for a ride in the boat?"

"Not today, sweetheart," Annie said, taking Ben back from Maureen.

When Haley stomped her foot and pouted, Riley released Ginny's hand and squatted in front of the little girl. "Tell you what. I'll be back out here in a few weeks for Christmas, and I'll take you for a ride then."

Haley's freckled face brightened. "Yeah!"

He tweaked her nose and grinned. Seeing his rapport with the child stirred Ginny's maternal longing. He lacked the awkwardness many single men had around other people's children.

Ginny's heart twisted. She knew Haley would need lots of good male role models in her life to fill the void left by her father's cruelty.

"Until then," Riley said, "you can play house on the boat if you want to, as long as you have your mommy or Mrs. Sinclair with you. Okay?"

Haley bobbed her head. "Okay!"

Before they left, Ginny pulled Annie into a tight hug. "Keep the faith. Better days are ahead. I'll keep looking for another shelter, the police will keep looking for Walt, and in the meantime, help your daughter have a memorable Christmas. Okay?"

Annie nodded and sniffled as tears leaked onto her cheeks. "Thank you, Ginny."

With one last concerned glance at his mother, Riley put his arm around Ginny's waist and escorted her back up the dirt road to his truck.

Chapter 13

Over the following two weeks, Ginny's life was calm, quiet, happy.

Too much so.

She felt as if she were waiting for the proverbial other shoe to drop. Though Annie and her kids had settled in well at Maureen's and no one had seen or heard from Walt since he'd attacked Ginny in her apartment, Ginny sensed he was lurking in the shadows, regrouping, planning his next big move. She knew better than to believe he had given up. The silence was as unnerving as his threats. She felt as if she were sitting in a sniper's crosshairs, waiting for the trigger to be squeezed.

Meanwhile, the Lagniappe Women's Center was given a new office to work from, a small house donated by an elderly woman's family after she moved in with her daughter. Unfortunately, as the holidays approached, the number of clients needing the center's help also increased, a sad irony of the season.

Ginny had her cast removed, and regaining the use of her right arm was a huge relief.

Her new physical relationship with Riley was bliss. Yet for all the satisfaction of their sex life, she still couldn't shake the nagging sense that there was a gaping distance between them.

Riley had not yet told her anything about Erin or the assault his mother had referred to. When Ginny asked him who Erin was, he'd given her a startled look, a shrug, and muttered, "An old girlfriend." She'd pressed for more information, but he'd become sullen and defensive.

"Why does she matter to you? She's in the past. She means nothing to me anymore. Forget about her."

But Ginny couldn't forget. His evasiveness only fueled her curiosity and concern. Who had battered Erin? Surely not Riley…

When he was ready, he would explain, his mother had assured her.

But no matter how many times Ginny tried to rationalize her anxiety, dispel her jitters, the truth was she grew more restless and frightened the deeper her feelings for Riley grew. The more she cared about him, the more her heart was at risk. The further they went without her resolving her confused feelings, finding answers to her questions and soothing the disquiet in her soul, the more she feared the relationship would end badly.

Her busyness at the women's center gave her ample excuse to bury her head in the sand and push aside the uneasiness. But running from a problem never solved anything. She was breaking every rule she'd ever given her clients for maintaining a healthy, open relationship with a man. She knew her days of pretending everything was fine and avoiding a decisive confrontation were numbered.

One morning, a week before Christmas, Riley lay beside her in the wake of their lovemaking and smiled at her con-

tentedly. He traced the line of her jaw with one finger. "So…
what are you doing today?"

"Um…Christmas shopping." She tilted her chin up so she
could meet his gaze. "With your mother."

He arched an eyebrow. "My mom?"

"Um-hmm. She called the other day and asked if I wanted
to meet her for lunch and an afternoon of shopping. She wants
to get Annie and the kids a few surprises and asked me to help
pick out a couple of things." Ginny paused. "Why? What did
you have in mind?"

"Well, shopping…for a ring."

Her breath snagged. "A ring?"

He gave her a lopsided grin. "An engagement ring. What
do you say? Wanna marry me?"

She sat up in the bed, struggling for breath. The uneasy
flutter she'd felt building in her chest for weeks escalated to
a pounding panic.

"Ginny?" Riley reached for her as she bolted from the bed,
then braced her arms on her dressertop, wheezing.

Wrapping the sheet around his waist, he crossed the floor
to her. "Ginny, what's wrong? Say something."

She shook her head slowly, her limbs shaking. "I…I can't
marry you. I—"

Riley's expression fell, and he furrowed his brow. "Why
not? We're good together. I thought you felt the same way I do."

She angled her head toward him. "And what is it…you
feel…exactly?"

Riley blinked, stepped back. He scrubbed a hand over his
face, his expression stunned. "I…I love you."

"You hesitated. You're not sure."

He gave a short, humorless laugh. "I am sure. I'm just
confused why you have to ask. Don't you feel the same way?
The past couple weeks, we've—"

"Forget the past couple weeks! You're talking about a commitment. A *lifetime* commitment."

His eyes narrowed. "I thought you wanted to get married. You said once that you wanted the same kind of committed relationship Megan and Jack have."

"I do!" She swallowed hard, the bitter taste of fear rising in her throat. "Someday."

Black shadows filled his face, and his jaw tightened. "But not with me. Is that what you're saying?"

When she saw the hurt in his eyes, a slicing ache shot through her. "Maybe with you. I don't know. But I'm not sure I know you well enough to say—"

"Bull!" Fire crackled in his gaze as his expression hardened. "You know me plenty well. You're just scared!"

"Damn right, I'm scared!"

Riley jerked as if slapped, then stared at her. "Scared of what? Of me?"

"Yes. No! I don't…" She snatched her robe from a chair and jammed her arms in the sleeves, tied the belt at her waist. Tears leaked from her eyes, and her thoughts tangled around each other.

"What are you afraid of, Ginny?" Riley rasped, his voice little more than a whisper.

She whirled to face him, her hands balled at her sides. "I'm afraid of being wrong! Wrong about you. I'm afraid I'll wake up one day and discover I've married Walt Compton."

Riley's eyes widened, and he sputtered, "You think I could be an abuser?"

Ginny buried her face in her hands and growled in frustration. "No! I don't mean that! I…" Her knees shook, and she sank onto the edge of the bed, scrambling to make sense of what she didn't really understand herself. "It's just that… when Annie married Walt, she was in love with him. She never thought he'd turn on her. She believed in him and trusted him and—"

"But there were probably signs of his true nature she didn't see. Right? You said yourself, people don't change that drastically overnight." Riley tightened the sheet around his hips and sat down next to her. His eyes were dark and intense, searching hers for comprehension. "You said there were always little signs, personality traits that could indicate a more violent or controlling nature. So she just ignored the signs or didn't recognize them, right?"

Ginny drew a shaky breath. "Maybe. Probably, but that's not—"

He took her hand, squeezed it. "Have you seen any of those signs in me? Do you *really* think I could *ever* hurt you?"

She closed her eyes. "No, but—"

"But nothing! I would never hurt you, Ginny. *Never.*" The conviction in his tone sent shivers down her back, while also warming her inside. Her head and heart agreed that she was physically safe with Riley. He was no Walt Compton.

But…

"Who was Erin, Riley?"

His eyebrows snapped together. "I told you. She's an ex-girlfriend. Emphasis on the ex. What does she have to do with this?"

Ginny raised her chin. "Because I know there's more you're not saying. Why won't you tell me what happened with her?"

He shook his head. "Why can't you trust me when I say you know all that matters about her? Don't you know that I—"

"No! I don't *know* anything." Her voice cracked on a sob, and she raked the hair back from her face with her fingers. "You won't answer my questions, and I can't trust my instincts anymore. Anything could happen. God knows, I've been wrong about men before! Ask Megan about some of the losers I've dated. Ask my college roommate about the creep I fixed her up with, a jerk who bloodied her nose and left handprint bruises on her arms!"

Riley flinched, horror flashing over his face.

"My judgment has been *so* screwed up before. I-—I just have to be sure this time. Marriage is a huge step, and I want to be sure the man I marry is everything I think he is. I don't want any surprises. I want you to talk to me, be honest with me. I want—"

"What your parents have?"

Hearing the harsh edge in his tone, she snapped her gaze up to his. "Yes. What's wrong with that?"

"Nothing, if you're willing to accept the truth about their marriage." He hesitated and scrubbed a hand over his face.

Her heartbeat stumbled. What was he saying?

His steely eyes pierced hers as he sighed and continued, "You have an idealized picture of them. You want to hold the man you marry up to an impossible standard. But no relationship is perfect, Gin. Not even your parents'."

"I know they're not perfect, but they—"

"Separated when you were a baby. Almost got a divorce."

She wrinkled her brow and stared at Riley, a knot lodging in her throat. "No, they didn't."

"Yes," he said softly. "They did. Your father told me about it when we had dinner with them before Thanksgiving."

Ginny felt as though she'd been kicked in the chest. Tears burned her nose and puddled in her eyes, while denials screamed in her brain. "No." She shook her head and stumbled away from the bed, hugging herself. "I would have known."

"How? You were a baby."

"They would have told me…later."

"Not if they wanted to protect you from the truth."

A sob hiccupped from her chest. "You're lying."

Her world shifted, leaving her grasping for something solid to cling to. Pain raked her chest, left her heart bleeding and raw.

Riley rose from the bed and tried to pull her into his arms, but she twisted free and backed away.

"Ginny, I didn't tell you about your parents to hurt you. But you deserve to know the truth. Especially if you think a perfect, fantasy marriage exists. In the real world, people fight, people get hurt. Even your parents. Even Megan and Jack.

What matters is that your parents loved each other enough to work things out. They found a way to make their relationship work. And so can we."

She spun to face him, uncertainty slashing through her. "Can we? I've been trying to deepen our relationship from day one, and I've met nothing but resistance from you. At least my parents talk to each other about the things that matter."

Riley scowled. "We talk!"

Ginny sighed and shook her head. "About movies. About football. About pizza toppings and our day at work. But when I've asked you about anything more personal, you've stone-walled and evaded and kept a distance between us. No matter how hard I tried to understand you and move past the super-ficial layer you showed me, you wouldn't let me in."

His jaw tense, he aimed a finger at her. "Not true. I told you about the day Jodi died! I've never told anyone else about that, but I told *you*. Do you have any idea how hard that was for me?"

"I appreciate how difficult it was. But even that day I knew you were holding something back about her death. Just like you won't tell me about Erin now. I need to know about her, Riley. Please! She was assaulted by someone, wasn't she?"

Riley blanched. "Who told you that?"

"Your mother. But that's all she said. I want to hear the truth from you. I want it now."

Riley's face hardened. Disappointment and pain, anger and frustration firmed his jaw and sparked in his eyes.

"Fine. Here's the truth. Erin is the girl I was flirting with the day Jodi drowned. I saw her a few years later, and I thought I'd be safe dating her. Because she already knew about Jodi, I assumed my past wouldn't be an issue with her. It was some-thing we both knew but didn't have to discuss. I was wrong."

Ginny held her breath, swiped the tears from her cheeks.

"Erin used how I felt about Jodi's death to manipulate me for her own purposes. A former boyfriend of Erin's had been harassing her, getting hostile. She was scared of what he might do. But she knew I was a fireman, knew I had guilt over Jodi's death, and she saw the chance to make me her personal bodyguard. She never had any feelings for me, never cared about what shared interests we might have, where our relationship might go. She used every opportunity to insinuate that I could make up for neglecting Jodi by saving her from Doug."

Riley paced to the far side of the room, then turned back. "I grew to resent her and the responsibility for protecting her she imposed on me. We had no real affection for each other, only a warped illusion of a relationship based on her needy clinging and manipulation and my guilt."

Ginny's heart twisted. "Oh, Riley—"

"I left her alone one morning after arguing about the day Jodi died. I went into work, left her by herself at her apartment." He sighed, and his brow creased with self-censure. "A few hours later I had a call that she was being taken to the hospital. Doug had caught up with her and made good his threats. I'd failed to protect her, like I'd failed to protect Jodi. No matter how I felt about her using me or the distance in our relationship, she needed me. She was counting on me, and I let her down." He gave his head a firm shake and snapped his mouth shut.

After a few strained moments of silence, Ginny whispered, "What happened to Erin wasn't your fault any more than Jodi's death was. Surely you know that."

"Do I? I'd made promises. Promises that I broke. People trusted me, and I let them down. I failed Erin, just like I failed my father and—"

Ginny gasped. "Your father?"

Riley gritted his teeth and turned away.

"There *is* more you haven't told me about Jodi's death. Isn't there?"

Acid flooded Riley's gut. Taking a deep breath, he gathered himself and pivoted back toward Ginny. He stared into her tearful, searching eyes, and his hands began to sweat.

He'd bared his darkest memories for her, exposed his pain and guilt to her scrutiny. And it wasn't enough. Would he ever be able to give her all she needed, or was he destined to fail her?

"I don't know what else I can say," he said wearily, "what else I can offer as proof of my love and commitment. But… maybe it doesn't matter. You've already convinced yourself I'm going to fail you, haven't you? You're always going to have questions I can't answer. I'm always going to come up short in your eyes because you expect something from me I can't be."

"Can't? Or won't?"

Riley turned up his hands. "The end result is the same." He shook his head. "I didn't tell you these things before because I didn't want to be picked apart like a science experiment. But even when I've bared my soul to you, you ask for more. You won't be happy until you've scraped me raw and dissected every pain-filled piece of my life, will you? You said yourself that you get what you expect out of life and people. You *expect* me to let you down, don't you?"

She looked stricken, crushed. Moisture beaded on her eyelashes. "I don't want to. But how can I believe in you when you keep secrets? When you erect a wall between us? How can I ever be sure I haven't made a mistake in trusting my heart to you?" Tears streamed down her cheeks, each one like a fist in his gut, an accusing finger pointed at him.

Promise me you'll take care of your mom and Jodi.

But he hadn't. Jodi had died on his watch.

Maybe Ginny was right not to trust him. Maybe he was destined to let her down. He'd failed his father. Failed Jodi.

Riley curled his fingers into his hair and blew out a harsh breath. Took a step back from her. "I can't do this."

Her eyebrows snapped together in a deep frown. "What?"

"Maybe you're right to not have faith in me. God knows, I live every day with the fear that I'll screw up and someone I love will get hurt. You want to know the whole truth about the day Jodi died? It's this—when my dad got sick, I promised I'd take care of the family after he died. But I didn't keep that promise. I didn't protect Jodi. And...I couldn't live with myself if I ever failed you the same way."

She sucked in a sharp breath. "Riley, no—"

"I love you, Gin, but I don't think my love will ever be enough for you. You need more than I can give you. You deserve better than I can offer." Numbly, he picked up his shirt and began to dress.

She watched him with a stunned disbelief freezing her face. Tears tracked down her cheeks. "That's it then? You're just going to walk away?"

"I don't know what else to do, Ginny. I don't know how to be what you need, and you can't believe in the man I've shown you I am. How do we bridge that gap?" He took his keys off her dresser and dropped them in his pocket. "I'm sorry."

He stepped closer, placed a finger under her chin to tilt her mouth up for a gentle kiss. He tasted the salt of her tears, heard the sob that caught in her throat.

"Riley, don't..."

His own heart shattering, he turned and walked out.

Ginny knocked, then opened her mother's front door. "Mom? Are you home?"

She heard footsteps from the back of the house, then her mother rounded the corner from the kitchen. "Ginny! What a nice surprise. I was just—" She stopped midsentence and tilted her head. "Honey? What's wrong? You look like you've been crying."

Ginny pressed her lips together, fighting the tight pinch of tears rising again in her throat, and nodded. "I think I blew it. I think I lost Riley." Her voice came out as little more than a squeak.

Hannah lifted a hand to her lips and knitted her brow. "Oh, Gin. What happened?"

"We had a fight. No, not really a fight." She shook her head, replaying what had transpired in the last hour. "The ironic thing is…it was one of the best discussions we've ever had. We were more honest and open about our feelings and our fears than we've ever been. But…he left."

"For good?"

"I—I think so."

Her mother drew her into a hug and squeezed her tight. "Oh, sweetie. I'm so sorry. Maybe once you both have time to calm down and think things over…"

Another part of her conversation with Riley tripped through Ginny's mind, and her heart lurched. She curled her fingers into her mother's sweater. Fresh tears prickled her eyes. "Mom, Riley said Dad told him you two almost got a divorce when I was a baby. That you separated. Is…is that true?"

Her mother pulled back and gaped at her. "He told—?" She closed her eyes and let out a slow, careful breath. "Come sit down, honey. Let's talk."

Ginny followed her into the living room and sat next to her on the couch. "Where are Billy and Dad?"

"Hunting. It's just us girls." Her mother put a throw pillow on her lap and patted it. Like she had as a little girl, Ginny curled on her side, putting her head on her mother's lap and her feet up on the sofa.

Hannah stroked her hair and took a deep breath. "Riley is right about your dad and me. We didn't tell you because… well, we wanted to shield you. It would have only undermined your sense of security as a child, and when you were older…it seemed like a moot point."

"What happened? Why did you split up?" Ginny wiped at the moisture on her cheek and sniffed as her nose started running.

"Long story. All of it irrelevant now. The thing you need to know is, we loved each other enough not to give up on what we had. We fought for our marriage and waded through the bad times because we had something worth keeping." She paused and tucked a wisp of hair behind Ginny's ear. "Do you love Riley?"

Ginny angled her head to look up at her. "Well…yeah. But—"

"Is he worth fighting for?"

"Yes, but what if—"

"Virginia Elaine West, don't analyze it to death. You've found a good man who loves you. Embrace that. Be happy."

"How? He says he can't be what I need him to be, and I don't know how to get past my fear that…that maybe he's right."

Her mother scowled but didn't interrupt.

"Mom, I see so much pain at work. So many women who gave their hearts to men who weren't what they appeared to be. How are you supposed to know if a guy is really all he seems or if he's just a ticking time bomb? How do I know Riley won't show a different side of himself after it's too late? Like Walt Compton. I've picked so many losers in the past. How do I trust my own judgment? I'm scared of getting hurt, scared of becoming one of the women I counsel. Scared I can't see Riley clearly because I *want* him to be the man for me. What if I'm confusing lust for love? What if I'm letting my heart blind me to something I should be seeing? What if—"

Her mother's laughter cut through her tirade.

She sent Hannah a sharp glance. "What's so funny?"

"I'm sorry, honey. I know I shouldn't laugh, but you sound just like me. The week before I married your dad, I was going nuts trying to dissect our relationship and prove to myself I was with the right man. You inherited your overeager analytical mind from me."

"Riley accused me of dissecting him. I don't mean to, I just… So how did you satisfy yourself that Dad was the right one?"

"I didn't."

Ginny sat up and glowered at Hannah. "What?"

"Marriage doesn't come with guarantees. And as you now

know, we had our problems. I had to look at what I *did* know and make my mind up based on that."

"Like what?"

"Like…I knew your father was hardworking, caring, honest. He has integrity and ambition. I knew he was a great kisser and—"

"Anh!" Ginny raised a hand. "Don't go there. TMI."

Hannah chuckled. "All right." She wrapped an arm around Ginny and hugged her close again. "I knew I loved him. I knew I hated the idea of life without him. He made me happy. I had something with him I'd never felt with another man before. We…*connected* somehow…on a level I couldn't explain."

Ginny thought of the moment she'd opened her eyes at the scene of the fire and seen Riley's face hovering over hers. Her panic and confusion had evaporated the moment she'd met his eyes. She'd sensed something then, a gut level assurance that she was safe. A supernatural connection. An inner peace like a homecoming.

"Soul mates," she whispered.

"Something like that," her mother said. "What you need to do is forget all the analyzing and searching out hidden problems that aren't there for a minute and look at what is in front of you. What do you *know* about Riley?"

Where did she start? Riley had so many wonderful traits. She'd felt a connection with him from the beginning, but she'd let her doubts and fears shout down those instincts. She'd kept him at arm's length, fighting his offers of help and protection. She'd demanded he tell her all his secrets and most private emotions, thinking that would create an intimacy between them that would allay her fears. Instead she'd made him feel awkward and inadequate.

So how did she silence those fears that held her back and take the leap of faith, allowing her to unconditionally give her heart to Riley?

Who I am is in everything I do and say and the way I live my life.

Riley's assertion percolated through Ginny's brain, stirring a warmth and peace that flooded her veins.

But before she could pin down any truths or conclusions, her cell phone trilled, and she scrambled through her purse for it. "Riley?"

"Not Riley. But close," a female voice answered. "It's Maureen. I was just thinking about the new Mexican restaurant that opened in town and thought maybe we could meet there for lunch instead of the deli. Are you game?"

Ginny gasped and checked her watch. She'd forgotten her plans to meet Riley's mother. She really wasn't in the mood to have lunch or to shop, but she hated to disappoint Maureen. "Uh, yeah…I'm game."

"Great! See you there in…what? Thirty minutes?"

She wiped her face and gathered her purse. If she hurried, she could meet Maureen in time. "Sure. Thirty minutes. See you then."

Ginny disconnected the call and glanced at her mom. "I forgot I'd promised Riley's mother I'd help her with some Christmas shopping this afternoon." She stood and smoothed the wrinkles from her shirt. "Wanna come with?"

"No, hon, I'll pass. I have a few projects to finish before the guys get back. You have fun."

"All right. I'll call you later. Thanks, Mom." Ginny gave her mother a kiss on the cheek and rushed out to her Cherokee. She made it back to her apartment with only enough time to change clothes and run a brush through her hair. She gave Zachary a quick pat as she ran for the door again. As she was headed out, her apartment phone rang, and, praying it was Riley, she snatched it up. "Hello?"

"You're good at hiding people, but I'm better at finding them." The hair on her neck rose. "Walt?"

"I have Annie. I'll turn myself in and let her go, if you meet my terms. If you don't, I'll kill her and take the kids. You'll never see me again."

In the background, Ginny could hear the frightened cries of a woman, the whimper of a baby. Her heart kicked up in a panicked rhythm.

Walt must have waited until Maureen left for their lunch together to ambush Annie. At least Ginny hoped Riley's mother was safe.

Dear God, please!

"H-how did you find them? I—"

"Because I'm smarter than you. Wasn't hard to figure out. So do we have a deal or am I going to kill the bitch?"

Ginny swallowed hard, forced her voice to sound calm. "What are your terms?"

"I want a meeting. You come here. Alone. Then you'll hear my terms."

She clutched the receiver with a death grip, her head swimming. "L-let me talk to Annie."

"Soon enough. You have thirty minutes to get here or Annie dies. If I see even a hint of a cop or that fireman of yours, Annie dies. Instantly. No questions asked. No negotiating. It's real simple, doll. Don't screw this up."

"But I—"

A click and a dial tone cut her off.

Her hand shaking, she replaced the receiver. Thirty minutes. It would take every minute of that time to drive out to Maureen's house. Ginny ran for the door without a second thought. She had so little time to reach Annie and prevent a disaster.

Chapter 14

Ginny jogged to her Cherokee, climbed in and gunned the engine. Heart pounding, she sped toward the parking exit. As she passed the policeman on guard duty, she hesitated. Could she signal him? Have him call in Walt's location?

No police, Walt had said.

Her throat tightened. How could she risk it?

How could she not?

But if Walt saw the cops and killed Annie…

Knowing the clock was ticking, Ginny mashed the gas pedal again. She could call in backup when she reached the lake house. She could warn the sheriff's deputy stationed at Maureen's driveway. She wouldn't go in alone, but she needed time to think through all the repercussions before she did something rash and got Annie killed for her efforts.

Walt was no dummy. He hadn't evaded the police this long by luck. His Special Forces training had served him well, and Ginny couldn't be rash in dealing with him or he could disappear again. Or worse, could make good his threats against Annie.

Ginny wiped her damp palm on her jeans and wove through traffic.

Biting her bottom lip, she checked her car clock. She'd already used eleven minutes.

When she hit the two-lane highway out of town, she ignored the speed limit and hauled out toward Lagniappe Lake. Every mile put her farther from Riley.

Her chest tightened as she remembered the harsh words they'd exchanged. Yet the discussion had been among the most honest and revealing they'd ever shared. Was she, because of her fear of getting hurt, demanding an impossible standard from Riley?

Tears burned her sinuses and squeezed her throat.

With a deep breath, she shook off her thoughts of him. She needed to focus on Annie. On the dangerous situation with Walt.

Again she checked the clock. She had only five minutes left.

Down the road, she saw the mailbox that marked the driveway to Maureen's house. The patrol car was parked along the shoulder, as promised.

She had to at least warn the sheriff deputy what was happening.

And why hadn't he seen Walt or heard anything from Maureen's house?

Her pulse hammering, Ginny signaled her turn, lowered her window and pulled up alongside the cruiser.

The officer looked up, lowered his window and smiled.

Then shifted his gaze. Scrambled for his weapon.

Too late.

An arm snaked around Ginny's throat, and a gun appeared in front of her. Before she could even gasp in surprise, the weapon was fired out her window in a deafening blast.

Once. Twice.

A dark hole appeared in the sheriff deputy's forehead, and he slumped against the steering wheel.

Nausea swam in Ginny's gut. Terror coiled around her heart.

"Thanks for the ride," Walt hissed in her ear, his arm choking her. "Down the driveway. Now. Don't try anything stupid, or I'll pop you, too. Got it?"

Shaking to her core, Ginny pulled into the drive and parked in front of Maureen's house. She didn't see Maureen's car and prayed that meant she'd left for their lunch. The lunch Ginny wouldn't make.

Had Annie heard the shots? Called for help?

"Out. Nice and easy." Walt jabbed her with the gun.

She mentally kicked herself for not checking her car more carefully when she'd gotten in. But she'd been so distracted, so worried about Annie, in such a hurry…just as Walt had planned, no doubt.

She cut her eyes to her purse on the passenger seat. Her cell phone was in plain view. Flicking a glance to the rearview mirror, she met Walt's menacing glare. His eyes darted to her cell.

He lunged forward and grabbed the phone. Hurled it out the open door into the woods. "That would count as something stupid. Just do what I say, and you might see tomorrow. Now get out!"

Self-reproach for her gullibility stiffened her muscles, and she gritted her teeth as she climbed out. "You said you had Annie. I heard her in the background."

Walt scoffed, shoved her forward. "Funny how most women and babies sound alike. Background noises can be taped, faked. A psychological trick and fundamental Special Ops tactic. And you took the bait. Hook, line and sinker."

Ginny's stomach rolled. She'd not just led him to Annie, she'd hand delivered him. He'd tricked her into rushing out to protect her client, knowing Ginny would be distracted and frantic. And he'd stowed away in her car.

Holding her arm in a viselike grip, Walt dragged her to the back door. He made short work of getting inside. One hard kick splintered the wood around the dead bolt. A second kick knocked the door open and allowed him inside.

"Annie!" he shouted. "Get out here or your friend takes a bullet!"

"Stay hidden! Call 911!" Ginny countered, earning a skull-jarring smack in the temple from the back of Walt's hand.

"Shut up!" He shoved her forward, toward the kitchen.

Pain ricocheted through her head. She blinked her vision back into focus. Despite the costs, she had to do whatever it took to give Annie a fighting chance. Had to make up for her careless mistake that had led danger straight to Annie and her kids.

Could she wiggle free of his grip, grab the phone and call for help? Ginny struggled against his iron grasp as he dragged her through the kitchen.

A note on the counter, written in neat block handwriting, caught her attention and Walt's at the same time.

Maureen—

I've taken the kids down to the lake. Haley wanted to play house on the boat, and Ben likes the rocking of the waves for his nap. Back before dinner, Annie

Walt jerked Ginny's arm, scowling. "Where's this boat?"

"I—I don't know," she bluffed, but the crack in her voice gave her lie away.

His dark eyes narrowed, and his face hardened with rigid, angry lines. "Take me to the boat *now,* or I'll shoot you and wait here for Annie and the owner of the house to come home."

Through the open back door, the faint sound of a girlish squeal filtered in from outside.

Walt glanced at the door, then yanked Ginny's arm. "Let's go."

She stumbled as he tugged her along, back out to the driveway. He looked down the rutted dirt road toward the lake. Sniffed the air.

Ginny inhaled as well, analyzing the fishy and stagnant muck scents that spoke of the nearby lake.

Determination set a deep scowl on Walt's face, and he poked the gun in Ginny's ribs. "I've about had it with your lies and interference. I'd shoot you now, but I have other plans for you."

Ginny swallowed the bile that inched up her throat. She had to stay calm, think. Her life, and Annie's, depended on it.

Walt shoved her forward again, down the road toward the lake. "Nobody screws with me and my family. Nobody," he growled close to her ear. He squeezed harder on her arm until a numb ache radiated down to her fingers. "You're going to see what your meddling caused. I'm gonna make you watch while I kill Annie."

Riley answered his cell phone on the first ring. "Ginny?"

He'd been restless for the last few hours, unable to reach her at her apartment or on her cell. He regretted the things he'd said, the way he'd stormed out of her apartment. Wasn't this just the way things had played out with Erin? An argument. His leaving. Her unprotected.

Riley cursed his stupidity.

"I take it that means you don't know where Ginny is." The familiar voice that answered wasn't Ginny's.

Riley suppressed the swirl of disappointment. "Mom?"

"Hi, honey. I was hoping you'd heard from Ginny lately. She was supposed to meet me almost twenty minutes ago, and she hasn't showed. She's not answering her cell, and I'm getting worried."

Sitting forward on his sofa, Riley frowned. "It's not like her to be late. Are you sure she knew when and where you were meeting?"

"Yes. I just talked to her less than an hour ago to confirm. She said she was on the way."

Anxiety kicked his pulse up a notch. Too many things had happened to Ginny in the past month for Riley to write this off. And all of the trouble she'd had centered around one man.

Walt Compton.

"Mom, I don't like this. I've got a bad feeling something's happened." He surged to his feet and ran out to the corridor. "I'm going to check her apartment. Call me back if she arrives."

"All right. Riley, be careful."

"I will." He snapped his phone closed and jammed it in his pocket as he ran down the stairs to the third floor.

If something had happened to Ginny, it would be his fault. He should never have left her alone this morning. He'd let his hurt and frustration with their relationship color his judgment. He knew the danger she was in from Compton, and still he'd stalked out like a sullen child, leaving her vulnerable. Exposed.

Sprinting to her apartment, he pounded on the door. "Ginny! Ginny, open up!"

He tested the knob. Found the door unlocked. A chill skated through him.

Ginny would never have left the door unlocked, especially not with the threats against her. He pushed the door open, peered inside cautiously. "Ginny?"

He heard nothing. Saw nothing.

She was gone, and the unlocked door told him she'd left in a rush, been preoccupied.

Something was definitely wrong.

That *something* undoubtedly meant Compton.

Riley sucked in a deep breath as fear for Ginny's life clambered through him.

He had to think, reason. Compton was ultimately after Annie. Annie was at his mother's house. But his mother wasn't home. His mother was waiting in town at some restaurant for Ginny.

Could Compton have found Annie? Riley didn't know how that was possible, but he knew better than to underestimate the former Special Forces soldier.

The best place to start looking for Ginny was at the lake house.

Cold fear slithered through Riley, and his gut knotted with self-censure. He'd already done the one thing he'd sworn not to.

He'd repeated the mistake he'd made with Erin. With Jodi.

He'd failed to protect someone he loved. And now Ginny could be in danger.

He just prayed he could find her and Compton before it was too late.

"Annie!" Walt shouted as they approached the lake.

His wife and daughter were on the deck of the *Arielle,* and Annie's head jerked up.

Haley, too, glanced their way, her face brightening. "Daddy!"

The little girl rushed toward the dock, but Annie caught her arm. "Haley, no!"

"He has a gun!" Ginny called, desperate to give Annie the warning that could spare her life.

"I said shut up!" Walt snarled and whacked her across the cheek again for her efforts.

"Walt, no! Leave Ginny alone! This is between you and me," Annie sobbed, clutching Haley to her side.

"Then she should have minded her own business. She's a part of this now, and she's gonna pay!"

Ginny shook off the blow and scrambled mentally for anything that could buy them time, a way to get away from Walt, a way to call for help. Did the boat have a radio? Surely it did, though she didn't remember seeing one. If Annie could get it and call for help...

"Where's Ben?" Walt shouted.

Annie's telltale glance toward the steps to the living area were answer enough. "He's napping."

"Get him. I'm taking him with me." Walt waved the gun as he gave his orders.

"No!"

They were nearing the dock now, and Ginny knew she had little time left to plan.

If she could distract Walt, would Annie have time to untie and push the boat away from the dock? Would they drift far enough that Walt couldn't reach them?

Ginny would try anything at this point.

Walt aimed the gun at Annie, his face tense. "Get my son! Now!"

Ginny seized her chance. The element of surprise. With a sharp twist, she spun toward him and kicked hard at his knee-cap. Then, with an upward arc of her arms, she hit his wrist. The gun flew from his grasp.

"Bitch!" he growled, digging his fingers deeper into her arm and yanking her up against his rock-hard chest.

"Ginny!"

Despite Walt's painful grip, Ginny turned toward the dock, toward Annie. "Untie the boat! Push off! Get out of here!"

"No, I—" Annie shook her head.

"For your kids! Now! Hurry, An—" A hard blow landed in Ginny's gut, and the air whooshed from her lungs. Walt released her arm as she crumpled to the ground.

She watched him stalk across the gravel to retrieve his weapon. Mustering all her strength, Ginny clambered to her feet and ran. Away from the dock. Buying Annie time.

Walt followed and was on her in seconds, tackling her.

She fought like a wildcat, scratching and flailing and kicking for all she was worth. He deflected her blows easily and seized her again. When he grabbed her arm, hauling her roughly to her feet, pain shot through her, radiating up her shoulder.

He jammed his nose in her face and barked, "If you try anything like that again, I'll shoot you in the leg and let you bleed."

A whimper formed in Ginny's throat, but she forced it down. She would not show him her fear.

Walt dragged her back toward the dock, and she dug in her heels, fighting, doing whatever she could to slow him down. But his massive strength was too much for her.

As her feet hit the wood planks of the long pier, she heard Walt curse, and she glanced up.

Annie had managed to untie the *Arielle,* and the afternoon breeze was helping push it out into the lake. Walt quickened his step, making Ginny stumble along behind him.

The stern end of the boat was only a couple feet from the dock. Walt released Ginny's arm and ran the last few steps, leaping to the gangway opening at the end of the cabin cruiser.

The *Arielle* rocked wildly when he landed. Annie screamed. Ginny's heart rose to her throat.

Walt was alone on the drifting boat with his wife and kids. Immediately, he seized Annie by the hair, got in her face.

Ginny didn't take time to debate the situation. Annie needed her help.

Using the adrenaline that surged through her to fuel her muscles, Ginny backed up a couple steps, charged forward and lunged across the widening gap of water. Miraculously, her foot caught the edge of the boat deck, and she grabbed the railing for dear life.

Walt aimed his gun at Annie's head, and Ginny rushed him, tackling him from behind. The blow knocked him off balance. His feet slipped on the deck, and he crashed to his knees, taking Annie and the gun down with him.

Ginny stomped on his wrist, then kicked at the gun. The weapon skittered across the deck.

Annie gasped and scrambled for the weapon. Walt was right behind her. Her hand closed around the gun seconds before Walt could snag it. Rising to her knees, she hurled it into the lake.

Her husband roared in frustration and attacked her from behind. Pinning his wife against the railing, he delivered one slap after another to her cheeks.

Nausea swamped Ginny's gut, but as she scurried to help Annie, she heard a wail from the living quarters steps.

She turned to see Haley rushing up the stairs.

"No!" Ginny cried, grabbing the girl and shoving her back. "Go inside and stay there! I'll help your mom. I promise."

Whining fearfully, Haley cast a tearful glance to her parents as Ginny guided her back down the stairs and shut the door.

Then she turned again toward Annie and Walt.

Icy dread swam through Ginny's veins, and panic choked her. She had to do something.

Now.

Or Walt would kill his wife.

Riley's body thrummed with adrenaline as he raced up to the turnoff to his mother's lake house. The sheriff's cruiser was still parked at the end of the drive.

That had to be a good sign, didn't it?

Rolling down his window, he pulled off the road, alongside the deputy's car—and his heart pitched.

Blood splattered the front seat, and the officer was slumped onto the steering wheel.

Riley jumped from his truck and pulled the man back from the wheel to check his vital signs.

But the hole in his head made clear the futility of the effort. Riley's anxiety racheted up several clicks. Snatching out his cell phone, he dialed 911 and reported the murder, the need for police assistance….

"And an ambulance," he added as acid curled through his stomach and rose in his throat.

Slamming his truck into gear, he roared up his mother's driveway. Ginny's Cherokee was parked in front of the house, the driver's door still open. Not a good sign. Leaving his engine running, he raced to the front door.

Locked.

As he sprinted to the back door, he gave the emergency operator the address, repeating it to be sure she got it right. He found the back door gaping open, the wood splintered.

"The back door has been kicked in. Compton must be inside," he reported.

"Sir, go back to your vehicle and wait for the police to arrive."

"No. I can't wait! He could kill them! I have to do something now!"

"Sir, do not—"

Riley didn't wait to hear more. Without disconnecting the call, he slid the phone in his front shirt pocket.

Breath suspended in his lungs, Riley moved inside cautiously, uncertain what he'd find. He took a knife from his mother's butcher block as he crept through the kitchen. Pausing, he listened for sounds of a struggle. The house was deathly quiet except for the muffled voice of the operator from his cell.

"Sir? Are you there? Hello? Sir, don't enter the house…."

Spotting the paper on the counter, Riley lifted the note and read.

He pulled out the phone again as he ran back to his truck. "The lake! Tell the officers they're down at the lake. All the way down the road to the dock. Hurry!"

Despite the emergency operator's instruction to stay on the phone, he tossed his cell phone, the line still open, toward the passenger seat. Wheeling onto the dirt road that led to the water, he gunned the engine and bounced down the rutted lane at a breakneck pace.

Heart in his throat, praying he wasn't too late, he squeezed the steering wheel, fighting to keep the truck on the road at the high speed.

When the narrow lane ended at the muddy shores of Lagniappe Lake, Riley slammed on the brakes, and his truck skidded to a stop.

Throwing the door open, he scanned the water as he jumped out of the truck. The boat wasn't at the dock. Wasn't in view.

"Ginny!" As he ran forward, the vessel came into sight in an inlet behind a stand of trees to the right of the dock.

He released the breath he held. The *Arielle* was there. Close to shore. For a split second, relief pierced the tension winding his gut in knots.

Then he spotted the trio on deck.

Without hearing a word they spoke, he understood the direness of the situation as Walt lashed out at his wife, knocking her so hard she crumpled to the deck.

Fury bit Riley's gut.

When Walt moved toward Annie again, Ginny launched herself at him, jumping onto his back and clawing at him. Icy terror washed through Riley, seeing Ginny, knowing the danger she was in.

In the span of precious seconds, a little girl charged out onto the deck from below, racing to Annie's side. Walt flung Ginny off his back, and she landed against the life jacket storage bin with a crash.

Riley ran toward the water's edge, his heart in his throat as he followed the ever-changing scene on the boat. While he shucked his shoes and bomber jacket, preparing to swim out to the *Arielle,* Walt grabbed his daughter's shirt and yanked her back from her mother with a vicious tug.

"Don't touch her!" Annie screamed, scrambling forward.

"Want her?" he taunted. "Come get her!"

Seizing his daughter under her arms, Compton lifted her over the side of the boat.

"No!" Annie wailed.

Horror froze Riley. A memory of his sister's body floating facedown in this same lake flashed in his mind.

Then Walt dropped the girl into the frigid lake.

Chapter 15

Annie screamed.

Ginny stumbled to her feet. Terror made her limbs leaden.

"She can't swim!" Annie sobbed as she charged to the side of the boat.

Ginny staggered to the railing. Eyes wide and stricken, Haley flailed helplessly in the water, her face sinking beneath the icy waves.

Walt grabbed Annie and shoved her to the deck again. Falling to his knees, he raised a fist to strike his wife once more.

Reacting strictly by instinct, Ginny grabbed the first thing she could. She hurled her shoe at Walt. And missed.

"Haley!" Annie cried, despite the barrage of blows her husband swung at her.

Pain ripped through Ginny's chest. She had to save the little girl. But doing so meant Walt would almost certainly kill Annie.

Tears burned her eyes, and a sob tore from her throat as Ginny faced the desperate choice she had to make.

She could only save one life.

She couldn't do it all. Couldn't do it alone. She needed help. She needed Riley.

From the shore, Riley read the split second indecision, the anguish in Ginny's expression, and knew the painful dilemma she faced. He'd experienced similar no-win choices on the job. Emotion clogged his throat. Before he could clear the constriction and call out to her, she sent a final sorrowful glance to Annie, then climbed over the railing of the boat. Located the girl. And dived into the lake.

Panic flashed through him, seeing Ginny in the water, remembering Jodi's pasty death mask when he'd pulled her from the depths.

But the mournful wail from the boat deck recalled him to his duty. Annie needed help.

And he wouldn't let Compton get away again.

Bracing himself for the numbing cold, he launched himself into icy waves. The shock of the frigid water stole his breath. Focusing on his goal, he swam out to the boat, found the ladder at the stern and hauled himself up and over the rail.

Walt never saw him coming.

Ginny gasped as painful needles of cold stabbed her body. She knew she had to get Haley out of the water quickly, or the icy lake would claim the child's life. The Louisiana winter might be temperate, but cold nights had brought water temperatures down to dangerous levels.

"Haley!" She scanned the spot where she'd last seen Annie's little girl and caught a flash of red beneath the glassy green water. Ginny dived under and swam to the sinking child. Wrapping her arms under Haley's, she gave a strong scissor kick to propel herself back to the surface.

Haley gagged, coughed, then gulped a breath.

"Hang on to me, Haley! I've got you!"

The frightened girl clutched at Ginny's neck, forcing her under again.

Ginny battled her way back up and tried to shift the child. "I've got you, Haley! Don't fight me. I won't let go! I promise."

"Mama!" Haley whimpered.

Ginny spared a heartsick glance toward the boat, expecting to see Walt gloating over Annie's battered body.

But Walt was far from gloating. He was struggling for the upper hand in an old-fashioned street fight with a tall, brawny blond man.

Riley!

Ginny's heart leaped. The joy of knowing Riley was here, that he was helping subdue Walt and save Annie, lasted all of a heartbeat. Then fear for Riley's life grabbed Ginny by the throat.

Walt seized Riley's neck and pinned him to the railing.

Sending up a prayer for Riley's safety, Ginny rallied. Her priority was still getting Haley, and herself, out of the icy water.

Already her legs were becoming stiff and numb. While she could still move, Ginny stroked and kicked as hard as she could, dragging Haley with her. The nearer she got to shore, the more still the child became. A growing anxiety gnawed Ginny's gut.

"Haley! Stay with me, baby!" she panted. "I'll have you out…and warming up…real soon."

Reinforcing adrenaline shot through Ginny when her foot hit the mucky lake bottom. She fumbled to stand up, then carried Haley the rest of the way to dry land. Spotting Riley's bomber jacket by the dock, she hurried to get it for the shivering girl. Ginny's tired and frozen legs wobbled, and she stumbled as she jogged toward the dock.

When she snatched up Riley's jacket, she inhaled the spicy aroma of his cologne and the mellow scent of suede. The familiar smells coalesced in her chest and tugged at her heart.

Riley had come to help her. He'd been there when she needed him. With his help, this nightmare could finally be over.

Tears prickled her eyes as she rushed back to Haley and

wrapped the coat around her thin shoulders. Once Annie's daughter was bundled up, Ginny peered deeply into her wide, dark eyes. "You're going to be all right, Haley. Okay? I have to go back to the boat and help your mom now." Shivering, Ginny glanced up and spotted Riley's vehicle. "See that truck? Go sit inside it. You'll be warmer there." Ginny's teeth chattered, and she wished she could climb into Riley's truck herself. But Annie was still in danger. Riley was at risk. Walt had to be stopped.

She hugged Haley tightly. "Stay in the truck until I come back. Lock the doors. Do you understand?"

Haley bobbed her head and staggered to her feet.

Trusting that the child would obey, Ginny gritted her teeth and waded back out into the chilled lake. It took every bit of energy and willpower she could muster to dive back into the icy water and swim toward the boat.

But her duty to save Annie compelled her. Her determination to end Walt's reign of terror pushed her. And her deep concern for the man she loved fueled her weary, icy limbs.

The man she loved.

Ginny missed a stroke as the words ricocheted in her brain. If she'd had any doubt before, she didn't anymore. Riley hadn't let her down. He'd been here when she needed him most. And she *had* needed him.

Admitting that she needed someone else, depended on him when the situation grew dire, didn't mean she was weak or vulnerable to manipulation. It simply meant she was human.

And like everyone else, she had an internal longing, an innate need to share her life with someone. Not by giving up her identity or her power or her independence, but by forming a stronger bond, a more powerful unit, a spiritual union of two souls.

She and Riley made a dynamic *team*.

Ginny pushed aside all the repercussions of this revelation, focusing her renewed energy on lifting her arm for the next stroke and the next. Kicking her legs. Blocking out the numbing cold.

When she reached the boat, she grabbed the rung of the swim ladder and pulled herself out of the lake with trembling arms. She rolled over the edge of the deck and collapsed in a shivering heap. The bumps and grunts of the continuing struggle between Riley and Walt drifted back from the front deck.

Along with the baby's cry.

Ginny's chest squeezed. The need to assure herself Ben was not in harm's way gave her the spike of energy she needed to clamber to her feet and stumble weakly toward the bow.

Anxiety bit her when she spotted the two men, both sporting bloodied faces and masks of angry determination. Riley held Walt in a modified wrestler's arm lock, pinned against the cabin wall.

Ginny swallowed the cry that sprang to her lips, afraid that calling Riley's name would only distract him and undermine his concentration.

She turned her attention to finding and helping her client.

Annie lay motionless and bleeding near the door to the living space. Wincing at the icy prickles in her legs, Ginny hobbled to her side.

"A-Annie!" She gently nudged her shoulder.

The battered woman peeked through swollen eyes. "Haley?"

"She's fine." Ginny's voice cracked, and she had to draw a calming breath to continue. "She's on shore. Where are you hurt worst? What can I do?"

"Ben," Annie whispered.

Ginny hesitated. She didn't want to leave Annie again, not as badly injured as she clearly was, but had to be sure the baby was safe. "I'll be right back."

The baby was still in the portable crib, though crying for all he was worth. Heartbreaking as it was to leave the sobbing child, Ginny at least knew he was safe and warm. She gave

Ben his pacifier and a stuffed bear, which soothed him a bit, then snatched the quilt from the bed for Annie.

After climbing back to the deck, Ginny tucked the quilt around the woman, while her own body shook with paroxysms of bone-deep cold. She was about to return below for a blanket for herself when a pained grunt called her attention back to the fighting men.

The momentum had shifted in Walt's favor. Ginny gasped as he pounded Riley in the gut, then shoved him when he bent over in pain. Walt stooped to grab Riley's leg and heaved him up onto the railing.

Riley hooked an arm around Walt's throat just as his own weight carried him over the side. Off balance, the two men disappeared into the water with a splash.

"Riley!" Ginny screamed.

She rushed to the rail and watched in horror as the struggle for dominance continued in the water.

Blood stained the lake, and the icy temperature was obviously sapping the strength of both men. Neither would last long if she didn't act. Fast.

Riley might be the most capable and heroic man she'd ever met, but he was human. He had his limits. The frigid lake and Walt Compton would take him from her if she didn't find a way to help. She searched the deck, her thoughts racing as she tried to come up with a plan.

At the bottom of the steps to the living area, the colorful doorstop Riley had painted in first grade caught her eye.

And she knew what to do.

Riley couldn't do much to fight Walt off in the lake. Swinging an effective punch underwater was pretty much futile. Still, he grappled with Compton and fought to keep his head and Walt's above the surface. Cold seeped through his muscles, sinking to his marrow.

He heard Ginny call his name, but resisted the urge to look

for her, knowing even the briefest distraction could give Compton the upper hand.

He tried everything he knew to subdue Walt, twisting his legs around Compton's, tugging his arm behind his back. But without leverage in the icy lake, Compton managed time and again to wrench free and lob another punch, though the water helped lessen the impact.

The man's strength and tenacity were amazing. Riley had long ago passed fatigued and was well into exhaustion, so he knew Walt had to be functioning purely on adrenaline and a stubborn refusal to be turned over to the police.

The lake's glacial temperature contributed to Riley's rapidly growing weariness. If he couldn't gain the upper hand soon, they could both be overcome by hypothermia and drown. The choking sense of defeat that had suffocated him since Jodi's death constricted his lungs again, harder now that he faced his own mortality.

But his life wasn't the only one that hung in the balance. Ginny, Annie, even Walt could die if Riley didn't find a way to turn the tide in his favor. The idea of losing Ginny struck terror in his heart and revived his will to fight.

He sensed Walt weakening, succumbing to the cold. But even as he thought he might take advantage of the man's slackening grip, Compton surprised him. With a spurt of strength, he snaked his arm around Riley's neck and pulled him beneath the water.

Walt's arm crushed Riley's windpipe. Water closed over his mouth and nose. The cold sliced through Riley with icy talons.

Darkness crowded his vision. His lungs ached for oxygen. He felt his heart throb painfully in his chest.

If he died now, Ginny would never know how deeply he loved her, that he *was* committed to her—no matter what. He'd been crazy to walk out on her, but his own fear of failure had kept him from seeing what she truly needed from him. Ginny deserved reassurance that he cared enough to fight for her, that he was devoted to her and that he would do anything in his power not to let her down, not to break her heart.

And now he might die with those truths unsaid.

Ginny deserved more. Much more.

Feet slipping on the wet deck, Ginny hurried to the steps and retrieved the painted rock. Her arms were numb and tired from her swim in the cold water, and climbing back up the steps carrying the rock took a surprising amount of energy. She trembled from the weight of the softball-size rock as she hefted it to the railing.

Ginny groaned at the thought of going back into the cold water.

She located the men again, and panic seized her chest when she realized Walt had a choke hold on Riley and was keeping his face under water.

Horror punched her gut, stole her breath. Riley was drowning. Dying.

"No!" she sobbed. "Riley!"

Wasting no time, she swung her legs over the railing, hugged the rock to her chest and launched herself into the lake. She swam closer to the men, struggling not to sink with the heavy rock.

Her leg muscles screamed in pain and fatigue as she treaded water long enough to drag the rock up, over her head. Gasping for breath, she swung it down onto Walt's skull. He jerked, went limp, and began sinking in the murky water.

Seconds later, Riley burst to the surface, coughing and sucking in a huge lungful of air. He swiped the water from his eyes and cast a look around him.

"Riley!" Ginny wheezed. Breathing was rapidly becoming harder.

"Where's…Compton?" Riley asked as he gulped air.

She glanced down into the frigid lake. Nausea roiled inside her. "I—I think I killed him."

Riley angled his gaze into the water. "Not if I can help it."

"What—?"

Before she could form her question, he dived back under. A fist of fear closed around Ginny's heart, and she swallowed the knot tightening in her throat. Crying now would expend more energy than she could afford. She had to keep her wits until they could get out of the water and summon help for Annie.

When Riley surfaced seconds later, he dragged Walt Compton's still form with him. Blood seeped from the wound Ginny had inflicted at the back of Walt's head.

"Help me…get him to…shore," Riley panted.

"Is he—?"

"Hurry!" The blaze of determination in Riley's eyes galvanized Ginny.

She positioned herself under one of Walt's flaccid arms while Riley took the other. He set a swift pace, swimming toward the bank. Numb and tired though Ginny was, Riley was safe, and the end of her nightmare, Annie's nightmare, was in sight. That thought alone gave her the extra strength to paddle clumsily through the water, helping Riley tow Walt to land.

Teeth chattering, limbs trembling, she collapsed on the muddy ground while relief rushed through her like a warming balm.

But Riley didn't pause to rest. He rolled Walt onto his back and checked for a pulse. Quickly shifting into position, Riley started CPR. Arms shaking from the cold, he began chest compressions, then stopped long enough to puff a breath into Walt's mouth.

Ginny stared, too tired to move. "Riley, he tried to kill you."

He glanced up, his gaze as dark as the glassy lake. "I know."

A thousand questions darted through Ginny's brain, but the look in Riley's eyes silenced them all. His expression was set with determination. Lit with conviction. Alive with compassion and honor.

"My job is to save lives, Gin." He ducked his head and continued the chest compressions. "All lives."

Ginny's breath backed up in her lungs as a flood of emotion filled her. The answers that had begun forming after talking to her mother took shape as she watched Riley fighting for Walt's life. Despite everything Compton had done, Riley still valued life enough to save Walt's miserable hide.

Who I am is in everything I do and say and the way I live my life.

Everything she needed to know about Riley's heart and soul had been right in front of Ginny from the start. Her soul had recognized him for who he was the moment she woke at the fire, but her fears had shouted down the small voice in her heart and demanded proof.

Yet Riley had proved through every choice, every touch, every interaction with her that he was honest and faithful and true. He was a man of action, of conviction, of integrity. A man who lived his beliefs every day and showed his heart of hearts whenever he kissed her, defended her, laughed with her.

Any doubts she'd had about Riley's character or intentions fled. She'd truly found a man who was good to the core.

He was, quite simply, the man she wanted to spend her life with.

A man she could trust with her heart.

Tears pricked her eyes. As she watched Riley working to revive Walt, she was awed by the heroism of the man she loved.

"Daddy!" a tiny voice cried from down the shoreline.

Ginny looked up to find Haley running toward them, her eyes wide with grief. "Oh, no."

"Daddy!"

Ginny stumbled to her feet, ran to intercept Haley. She caught the child up in her arms and hugged her close. "It's okay, honey. You're safe."

"What's wr-wrong with Daddy? I want to see my daddy!"

Ginny could no longer hold back her own tears. Despite

all the pain and fear he had inflicted on his family, Walt Compton was the only father Haley had.

And she loved him with blind faith. Her little-girl heart clung to the parental bond, even though Walt had failed his daughter in the most elemental ways.

An ache dug into Ginny's heart, a hurt so sharp she thought her chest might split open. She squeezed Haley tighter, tried to breathe past the emotions clogging her throat.

Haley had enough childlike trust to overlook all her father's sins and love him, yet Ginny had denied Riley the faith and belief he had proved worthy of time and again. Her lack of trust had hurt him.

And still he'd come to her rescue when she'd needed him most.

A soul-deep love mingled with contrition as Ginny turned to watch Riley's progress reviving Walt. She cradled Haley's head to her shoulder so the girl couldn't see the frightening condition of her father. The child had witnessed enough trauma today.

Ginny saw Walt move, a twitch of his foot. Then he rolled to his side, with Riley's help, and spat up a mouthful of water.

Ginny sighed in relief.

The distant wail of sirens filtered through the foggy afternoon, and moments later an ambulance and two police cars bumped down the drive. Ginny walked to meet the arriving cavalry, shouting to them about Annie's injuries and the need to get her and Ben off the boat. Ginny motioned to Riley, still working on Walt, and filled the officers in on Walt's condition, his crimes, and Riley's position with the fire department.

With a nod, two policemen hurried toward the dock.

The EMTs grabbed a stretcher out of the ambulance and went to assist Riley.

Ginny handed Haley off to another policeman and accepted with gratitude the blanket and warm protection of the ambulance one of the EMTs offered.

Through the back door of the vehicle, she watched expectantly for Riley to join her. He needed warming as desperately as she did. By her calculations, he had spent longer in the water than she had, thanks to his struggle with Walt.

Instead, once Riley turned Walt's care over to the EMTs, he staggered out onto the dock, exchanged a few words with the police officers…and dived back into the lake.

Ginny gasped in shock and confusion. Clutching the blanket around her shoulders, she climbed out of the ambulance and ran back toward the lake. "Riley! What are you doing?"

One of the officers met her near the end of the dock, and she waved an arm toward Riley's swimming figure. "Why did you let him go back in the water? Couldn't you see he's hypothermic?"

"I…no, ma'am." The officer sent his partner a concerned look, then met Ginny's gaze again. "He just said since he was already wet, it didn't make sense for anyone else to go in the water. He said it was his family's boat, and he knew where the spare keys were kept. He volunteered to drive it back to the dock."

Ginny sighed and squeezed her eyes shut. Why couldn't Riley turn things over to the policemen now? What was he trying to prove?

Her answer came as a memory of Riley's pain-filled voice filtering through her mind.

It was my duty to protect my sister, and I failed! Jodi is dead because of me!

Riley was still punishing himself for his sister's death, risking his own life trying to make amends.

Ginny pulled the blanket tighter around her and shuddered. Blinking back tears, she turned to the policeman again. "He's going to need serious medical attention when he gets back. He's been in and out of the water a lot. His body temperature is bound to be dangerously low. Tell the EMTs to be ready to warm him up with blankets and a warm IV or whatever they use. Please!"

With a nod, the officer jogged to meet the medics wheeling a gurney toward the dock.

When the boat motor growled to life, Ginny turned to watch the *Arielle* approach the pier. The policemen caught the ropes to tie it up, then the EMTs jumped onto the deck to help Annie.

Ginny crowded closer, her heart in her throat. Finally, she saw Riley stagger out of the cockpit and climb stiffly to the dock, shivering and pale. She rushed forward and swung the ends of her own blanket around him, drawing him close to share the little body heat she had. "Riley! Oh Lord, you're freezing!"

He lifted a hand to her cheek, trembling violently from the cold, and whispered, "Love…you."

Then he collapsed at her feet.

"Help me! Someone help!"

A police officer and an EMT rushed over, and a second stretcher was brought down for Riley. As they strapped him down and began a preliminary check of his vital signs, Ginny brought his icy fingers to her lips. Tears leaked onto her cheeks, and her throat closed with grief. "Please, please, don't let him die!"

"We'll do everything we can, ma'am," the EMT replied. "Please step back."

Ginny bent and pressed a kiss to Riley's cheek as they prepared to roll him to the ambulance. With her lips close to his ear, she whispered, "I love you, too."

Chapter 16

After the EMTs thoroughly checked Ginny and treated her superficial wounds, her attention shifted to Annie's kids. She kept Haley and Ben Compton with her as she answered numerous questions for the local sheriff. Sitting in Maureen's living room, wearing dry clothes she'd borrowed from Maureen's wardrobe, she explained the entire history of Walt's abuse, the women's center fire and how he'd stalked her in recent weeks. The sheriff contacted Detective Rogers of the Lagniappe PD, and when the detective arrived on the scene, he assured Ginny guards would be placed in Walt's hospital room while he recovered from his injuries. When he was well enough to leave the hospital, he'd have a one-way ticket to jail.

Ginny made a mental note to contact Libby Walters and request she pull strings at the D.A.'s office to make sure Walt was denied bail before his trial. Although, with the list of charges and mountain of evidence the police had against Walt,

Ginny imagined Annie's husband would be spending the rest of his natural life behind bars.

Annie and her kids were finally safe to make a new start.

Ginny used Maureen's phone to call both her mother and Riley's. Hannah came out to the lake to stay with Haley and Ben, while Maureen headed to the hospital to be with Riley and Annie.

Ginny was antsy to get to the hospital herself. Not knowing Riley's condition was torture. Even as she repeated answers for the police time and again, her thoughts wandered to Riley, his deathly pale lips and icy hands after he'd returned to the dock with the *Arielle*.

Love…you.

Her heart ached as his whispered words replayed in her head. She longed to be with Riley, willing him to pull through.

But her first responsibility was to Annie's kids, and until the police released her to leave the scene, Ginny was stuck.

Though she had a thorough exam by one of the EMTs, and though her injuries seemed limited to bumps, bruises and mild hypothermia, she promised to get a complete recheck when she reached the hospital.

Two excruciating hours later, Detective Rogers gave the okay for Ginny to leave, and she accepted his offer to drive her to the hospital in her Cherokee. Distracted and upset as she was, she didn't need to be behind the wheel.

The detective dropped Ginny off at the door to the emergency room and told her he'd park her car in the side lot.

Ginny barely heard him, her mind already focused on getting to Riley once inside.

Hands shaking, and with a lump in her throat, Ginny rushed to the check-in desk. "I'm looking for Riley Sinclair," she told the nurse breathlessly. "Please, can you tell me how—"

"Ginny!"

She gasped, hearing the familiar baritone voice. Whirling around, she searched the long corridor behind her.

At the far end of the hall, her handsome firefighter struggled out of a wheelchair and staggered forward.

"Riley!" she whispered as tears blurred her vision. She ran to him, dodging orderlies and crash carts, and threw her arms around him.

"Oh, thank God!" she sobbed and buried her face in the blue hospital scrubs he wore. "I thought…I thought you were—"

"Naw." He kissed her head and squeezed her closer. "I'm all right."

"But you could have died," she said, her voice cracking.

"I knew the risks, knew what I was doing."

Ginny tipped her head back and met his piercing gray eyes. "And yet you went back in the water, knowing how dangerous it was for you, cold as you already were. You *did* almost die. You scared me half to death! When are you going to stop risking your life like that?"

He cupped her face in his palm and nuzzled her cheek. "Gin, risk is part of my job description."

She backed away from his touch and narrowed her eyes skeptically. "And the degree of risks you take has nothing to do with trying to make amends for Jodi's death?"

He was silent, his expression slightly guilty. He sighed and ducked his head. "Maybe so."

Ginny's chest tightened. "You've got to stop trying to rewrite history, Riley. Please. Before your mother loses another child."

His gaze snapped up to hers.

"Before *I* lose you." She swiped at her damp eyes and touched her forehead to his. "I—I thought I *had* lost you. I've been so stupid. So blind."

His expression shifted, grew more somber, and she knew he understood she was referring to the argument they'd had earlier in the day.

"No," he whispered. "I shouldn't have walked out. I'm sorry. I'll never—"

"Ginny!"

They both turned as Maureen rushed down the corridor toward them. Ginny saw the strain the day's events had taken on Riley's mom. Deep lines of worry creased her forehead and the skin beside her eyes.

"How is Annie?" Riley asked.

She dabbed at her cheeks with a soggy tissue. "I just spoke to her doctor. She's out of surgery and just waking up. The doctor thinks she'll have scars, but…she should make a full recovery."

"Surgery? For what?" Ginny asked.

Maureen sighed and twisted the rope of pearls at her throat with a trembling hand. "Broken jaw. Shattered cheekbone. Walt battered her face. The bastard."

Ginny curled her fingers into the scrubs Riley wore and, snuggling closer to him, savored the return of his body's natural heat. "He'll never hurt her again, though. Detective Rogers is seeing to that."

"Good." Maureen sighed. "The doctor said we could see Annie in a little while, but only for a few minutes. She'll need to rest."

Ginny nodded. "I need to let her know her kids are safe and with my mom. They can stay with her until Children's Services find a temporary foster home to keep them while Annie is in the hospital."

"I'm happy to help with them, too. Just let me know." Maureen glanced up at her son and frowned. "Are you supposed to be out of that wheelchair yet? I thought you were told to take it easy."

Riley lifted a corner of his mouth and grinned at Ginny. "See? It's all mothers. Not just yours."

Maureen arched an eyebrow and glanced from one face to the other. "Was that a slam?"

Ginny grinned. "Well—"

His mother held up her hand. "No. Don't tell me." She kissed

Riley's cheek, then Ginny's, and stepped back. "I'll go get some coffee in the cafeteria. Give you two time to talk." With a last maternal pat on his shoulder, she headed down the hospital corridor.

Ginny helped Riley back to the wheelchair, where he sank onto the seat with a weary sigh. "Geez, I'm sore. I feel like I was trampled by elephants, then had to run a marathon. I hate feeling so weak and tired."

"Yeah, well, someone told me once that everybody deserves a little TLC now and again."

Riley cut his gaze up to hers, obviously recognizing his words from the day she was released from the hospital after the fire.

She laughed. "It's my turn to take care of you now, so relax and enjoy it."

He returned a smile, but soon his grin faded to a troubled frown. "Gin, about this morning…"

She shook her head and placed her hand over his mouth. "No. Me first." She knelt beside the wheelchair so that she was eye-level with Riley. He held her gaze, a crease in his brow, and squeezed her hand.

Ginny fought down the knot of emotions that climbed her throat, making it difficult to speak. "This morning you said I didn't have faith in you, that I was expecting you to fail me, let me down. You were partly right. I was expecting the worst to happen. I was expecting to have my heart broken." Riley opened his mouth to argue, and she cut him off. "But not because of you. Because of *me*."

His eyebrows furrowed in confusion. "You?"

"I didn't trust myself. My judgment. What my heart was telling me. I let my previous failures with men color my expectations. I let the horror stories I heard on the job take root and grow into a paralyzing fear. I counsel women on how to overcome tragedy and move forward, yet I had become imprisoned by the fear that I could be hurt by someone I loved. I was the one who couldn't commit, the one who wasn't being honest about what I felt, the one who had built a wall."

He leaned forward, his eyes searching hers. "So how do I get past your wall, ease your fears? How can I prove to you that I'm in this for the long haul, that I'd die before I let you get hurt?"

The passion and sincerity in his expression brought the sting of fresh tears to her eyes. She smiled and stroked his stubbled cheek. "Just keep being you. You told me once that who you are was in everything you did, in the way you lived your life. I saw the heart and soul of who you are today when you came to help me, help Annie. When you saved the life of a man who'd just tried to kill you. But the answers and reassurance I'd needed were in front of me all along. My heart saw the real you even when my fears blinded my mind to the truth. That's why I fell for you."

She settled back on her heels. "But the more I cared about you, the more I feared losing you. I was scrambling to find something about you to fix, something I could blame if the worst happened. But you weren't the problem. I was. You were proving to me every day, with your gentleness and courage and integrity, exactly the kind of man you are. But it took nearly losing you for me to recognize the truth, to realize what really mattered."

He traced the line of her jaw with his finger. "And what matters to you, Ginny?"

She wrapped her hand around his and squeezed. "You do."

She felt him tense, saw the surprise that blanked his face for a moment before tenderness filled his eyes. His throat convulsed as he swallowed. "At the lake, before they took me to the ambulance, I thought I heard you say—"

She nodded. "I love you, Riley. Deeply."

A smile lifted a corner of his mouth, and he leaned in for a kiss. "Then I wasn't hallucinating?"

"No hallucination. I said it. And I mean it."

"I love you, too, Gin. And I want to spend my life showing you how much."

"That's all I need to hear. You know, even though I learned the truth about my parents' marriage, that it wasn't as perfect as I'd always believed, they are still my role models."

"Yeah?" Riley cocked his head.

She nodded. "They're living proof that if you love each other and are willing to work at a relationship rather than give up at the first sign of trouble, happily ever after is possible."

Riley slid his fingers through her hair and held her gaze with eyes full of conviction and promise. "I don't want to give up on us, Ginny. I want to love you and make you happy. For the rest of my life."

She tipped her head. "Is that a proposal?"

Riley grinned and looked down to where she knelt before him. "I believe it was. Except I'm supposed to be the one on my knees."

She laughed and shrugged. "Your knees, my knees. Whatever. I've never been big on convention."

"Is that a yes?" he asked, his handsome face filled with hope, with love.

Ginny brushed another kiss on his lips and smiled at the man of her dreams. "I believe it was."

* * * * *

*Watch for Annie Compton's story,
coming in early 2009
from Silhouette Romantic Suspense!*

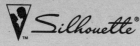

Romantic
SUSPENSE

**Sparked by Danger,
Fueled by Passion.**

Cindy Dees
Killer Affair

Seduction in the sand…and a killer on the beach.

Can-do girl Madeline Crummby is off to a remote
Fijian island to review an exclusive resort, and she hires
Tom Laruso, a burned-out bodyguard, to fly her there
in spite of an approaching hurricane. When their plane
crashes, they are trapped on an island with a serial killer
who stalks overaffectionate couples. When their false
attempts to lure out the killer turn all too real, Tom and
Madeline must risk their lives and their hearts….

**Look for the third installment
of this thrilling miniseries,
available August 2008
wherever books are sold.**

REQUEST YOUR FREE BOOKS!

2 FREE NOVELS PLUS 2 FREE GIFTS!

Silhouette® Romantic

SUSPENSE

Sparked by Danger, Fueled by Passion!

YES! Please send me 2 FREE Silhouette® Romantic Suspense novels and my 2 FREE gifts (gifts are worth about $10). After receiving them, if I don't wish to receive any more books, I can return the shipping statement marked "cancel." If I don't cancel, I will receive 4 brand-new novels every month and be billed just $4.24 per book in the U.S. or $4.99 per book in Canada, plus 25¢ shipping and handling per book plus applicable taxes, if any*. That's a savings of at least 15% off the cover price! I understand that accepting the 2 free books and gifts places me under no obligation to buy anything. I can always return a shipment and cancel at any time. Even if I never buy another book from Silhouette, the two free books and gifts are mine to keep forever.

240 SDN EEX6 340 SDN EEYJ

Name	(PLEASE PRINT)	
Address		Apt. #
City	State/Prov.	Zip/Postal Code

Signature (if under 18, a parent or guardian must sign)

Mail to the Silhouette Reader Service:
IN U.S.A.: P.O. Box 1867, Buffalo, NY 14240-1867
IN CANADA: P.O. Box 609, Fort Erie, Ontario L2A 5X3

Not valid to current subscribers of Silhouette Romantic Suspense books.

Want to try two free books from another line?
Call 1-800-873-8635 or visit www.morefreebooks.com.

* Terms and prices subject to change without notice. N.Y. residents add applicable sales tax. Canadian residents will be charged applicable provincial taxes and GST. Offer not valid in Quebec. This offer is limited to one order per household. All orders subject to approval. Credit or debit balances in a customer's account(s) may be offset by any other outstanding balance owed by or to the customer. Please allow 4 to 6 weeks for delivery. Offer available while quantities last.

Your Privacy: Silhouette is committed to protecting your privacy. Our Privacy Policy is available online at www.eHarlequin.com or upon request from the Reader Service. From time to time we make our lists of customers available to reputable third parties who may have a product or service of interest to you. If you would prefer we not share your name and address, please check here. ☐

SRS08R

NEW YORK TIMES BESTSELLING AUTHOR

KAT MARTIN

Neither sister can explain her "lost day." Julie worries that Laura's hypochondria is spreading to her, given the stress she's been under since the Donovan Real Estate takeover.

Patrick Donovan would be a catch if not for his playboy lifestyle. But when a cocaine-fueled heart attack nearly kills him, Patrick makes an astonishing recovery. Julie barely recognizes Patrick as the same man she once struggled to resist. Maybe it's her strange experience at the beach that has her feeling off-kilter….

As Julie's feelings for Patrick intensify, her sister's health declines. Now she's about to discover what the day on the beach really meant….

SEASON OF STRANGERS

"An edgy and intense example of romantic suspense with plenty of twists and turns."
—*Paranormal Romance Writers* on *The Summit*

*Available the first week of June 2008
wherever books are sold!*

MIRA®

MKM2554

Silhouette®
Romantic
SUSPENSE

COMING NEXT MONTH

#1523 DAREDEVIL'S RUN—Kathleen Creighton
The Taken
After Matt Pearson suffered a tragic rock-climbing accident that left him wheelchair-bound, he left his fiancée and business partner, Alex Penny. Years later, Matt's long-lost brother is determined to reunite Matt and Alex. But their planned trip back to the mountain reveals an enemy bent on destroying them.

#1524 KILLER AFFAIR—Cindy Dees
Seduction Summer
Can-do girl Madeline Crummby is off to a remote Fijian island to review an exclusive resort, and she hires Tom Laruso, a burned-out bodyguard, to fly her there in spite of an approaching hurricane. When their plane crashes, they are trapped on an island…with a serial killer.

#1525 HER BEST FRIEND'S HUSBAND—Justine Davis
Redstone, Incorporated
Gabriel Taggert's wife, Hope, disappeared eight years ago. Now her best friend, Cara Thorpe, has received a postcard from her, mailed on the day she vanished. Gabriel and Cara set off to find out what happened to Hope, and along the way they discover their true feelings for each other.

#1526 THE SECRET SOLDIER—Jennifer Morey
All McQueen's Men
When Sabine O'Clery is kidnapped in Afghanistan, Cullen McQueen is the perfect candidate to rescue her. Having reached a remote Greek island, vulnerable Sabine reaches out to Cullen, and their farewell kiss is captured by the press. With her kidnappers still after her, Cullen must save Sabine again, risking his life…and his heart.